Dear Reader,

I loved writing this story and seeing the whole town of Silver Peak get caught up in the filming of the science-fiction movie *Stranger from a Strange World*. From the moment Sadie and Edwin spot strange lights hovering over the mountainside to the final screening of the movie, this was downright fun.

The playful topic was tempered somewhat by Roz's depression. The sadness we feel when someone we love dies lessens over time, but it never really goes away. Like Roz, I have loved ones who have been gone for a long time, and I still miss them terribly. Knowing I will seem many of them again one day is a great comfort to me.

The close friendship between Roz and Sadie compels Sadie to find out what really happened when Roz's teenage brother, full of energy and promise, died tragically fifty years before. She also deals with Edwin's daughter, whose family is visiting from Atlanta, and temperamental "film people."

I hope you enjoy this story.

Susan Page Davis
writing as Carole Jefferson

Mysteries of Silver Peak

MYSTERIES
of SILVER PEAK

Lights and Shadows

CAROLE JEFFERSON

Guideposts

New York

Mysteries of Silver Peak is a trademark of Guideposts.

Published by Guideposts Books & Inspirational Media
110 William Street
New York, New York 10038
Guideposts.org

Acknowledgments

Every attempt has been made to credit the sources of copyrighted material used in this book. If any such acknowledgment has been inadvertently omitted or miscredited, receipt of such information would be appreciated.

Scripture quotations are taken from *The Holy Bible, New International Version*. Copyright © 1973, 1978, 1984, 2011 by Biblica, Inc. Used by permission of Zondervan. All rights reserved worldwide. www.zondervan.com

Cover and interior design by Müllerhaus
Cover art by Greg Copeland represented by Deborah Wolfe, Ltd.
Typeset by Aptara, Inc.

Printed and bound in the United States of America
10 9 8 7 6 5 4 3

Prologue

DEAR TY,

You were right. Things went better today. I still wish it all had gone differently and you were here doing the job, but this may turn out to be my big break. Best of luck in your new venture!

Mike

1

SADIE FIDDLED WITH THE CONDIMENTS AND WATCHED THE other customers flooding into Flap Jack's. She read the front and back of the stand-up card advertising dessert pancakes. She took a sip of her coffee and listened with amusement as Marge Ruxton, at the next table, described her recent shopping trip to Denver to the friend with whom she was having breakfast. Mostly she watched the door.

"Sure you don't want to order?" Diana, the red-haired waitress, reached out with the coffeepot and topped off Sadie's mug.

"Roz is supposed to join me, but she seems to be running late." Sadie glanced at her watch. "I'll give her a call and see if she's on her way."

"Sure. Just give me the high sign if you want to order." Diana smiled and moved on to the next table.

Sadie took out her phone and called her best friend's cell phone number.

"Hi, Sadie."

Roz's greeting sounded as though she had played it in slow motion.

"Roz? Are you coming? I'm at Flap Jack's."

Roz sighed. "I don't know."

"What's the matter?" Sadie sat up straighter, alert to Roz's listlessness and wishing she could see her. "Are you behind this morning?"

"Something like that. I'm not dressed yet."

"What?" That wasn't like Roz. Still, Sadie didn't want to tie up one of Diana's tables much longer during the rush hour. "You sound like you don't want to go out for breakfast. Why don't I come over to your house?"

"Sure," Roz said. "Thanks, Sadie."

Sadie signed off and took another mouthful of coffee. She put a few dollars on the table, stood, and waved to Diana. The waitress was in the middle of taking an order, but Sadie made sure she saw her before she strode out the door. Her Tahoe was parked out front, and she climbed in. It took her only a couple of minutes to reach the Putnams' house.

Roz opened the door, still in her fuzzy bathrobe and slippers. "Hi. I'm sorry."

"Don't be." Sadie gave her a hug and then moved into the entry. "Come on. I'll make us something to eat."

"You don't have to."

"Of course not," Sadie said with a chuckle, "but I'm starved."

Roz laughed and took her to the kitchen.

"What would you have ordered if we were at Flap Jack's?" Sadie asked.

"*Mmm.* Probably pancakes with raspberry sauce."

"Got any raspberries?"

"No," Roz said, "but there's a quart of strawberries in the fridge."

Sadie grabbed an apron off the towel rack and tied it around her waist.

"If you're going to be this way, I guess I'd better help." Roz opened a cupboard and took down a box of pancake mix.

Sadie knew her way around Roz's kitchen nearly as well as she did her own, and she soon had a skillet heating and batter ready to pour. Meanwhile, Roz had sat down at the table and was slicing fresh strawberries into a bowl. When Sadie had half a dozen near-perfect pancakes ready, she carried the serving plate over and untied the apron.

"Just let me get the coffee."

She poured for both of them, while Roz divvied the pancakes.

"You must be feeling better," Sadie observed as Roz smothered her own hotcakes with sweetened strawberries.

"Who can stay depressed with you around?"

Sadie sat down. Her mission was not complete, but she was making good progress. After asking a brief blessing, she took a bite.

"These are really good," Roz agreed after her first taste. "Thanks a lot, Sad."

Sadie gazed at her across the table. "You're welcome. Now, tell me. What had you so down this morning?"

Roz grimaced. "Have you read the *Chatterbox* lately?"

Sadie shook her head and cut another bite with her fork. "What does it say?"

Roz reached for her smartphone and tapped a few buttons on the screen. "Here's the latest." She handed it over to Sadie.

The Chatterbox was an online gossip blog. No one in Silver Peak knew who authored the stream of tidbits, or at least no one admitted knowing. But the *Chatterbox* seemed to get wind of every celebration, scandal, or feud in town.

Sadie frowned at the screen as she read: *A movie company is coming to Silver Peak! That old cult classic we all either love or hate,* Stranger from a Strange World, *is going to be remade in the same setting where it was done fifty years ago. Break out your bell-bottoms and your* My Favorite Martian *lunch box. It's coming, friends! Or are they among us already?*

She couldn't help a wry smile that tugged at her lips. "Cute. But I can see why that would give you pause. Edwin told me a while back that the studio was thinking of doing a remake."

Roz said nothing but lifted her mug, took a sip of coffee, and set it down carefully on the table.

Sadie hadn't wanted to admit it, but the mention of the old film had filled her mind with recollections too. Obviously, it had hit Roz with more force, and she shouldn't be surprised. She laid down the phone. "I'm sorry, Roz. It must be hard for you, with all the memories this brings up."

"You could say that." She looked up at Sadie, her eyes filled with pain.

"I didn't mean to make light of it."

"I know. The worst part for me is, hardly anyone even remembers Mike."

"That's not true," Sadie said. "Honey, lots of people in town remember your brother."

"Nobody ever mentions him. And if the topic does come up, everyone clams up or changes the subject."

Sadie reached over and grasped her hand. "Mike Tabor was one of the nicest boys I ever knew. People may be uncomfortable with thinking about how he died, but that does not mean they've forgotten him."

Roz blinked back tears. "Do you think about him much?"

"Sometimes. But I admit, it's not as often as I used to." Sadie sat back with a sigh. She had realized recently that days went by when she didn't even think much about T.R., her dear husband who had been gone several years, let alone Mike Tabor. "Time does that. I think it's a blessing, really, or we'd be constantly in despair. God eases our sorrow and lets us look beyond it to the future."

"I suppose you're right." Roz picked up her fork and toyed with a piece of pancake on her plate. "But to me, it seems impossible that anyone could forget something like that."

"They haven't. But after all, we were twelve. We were very impressionable. Remember how excited we were when we first heard that a movie was going to be filmed in Silver Peak?"

Roz smiled grudgingly. "I thought it would be the most wonderful summer ever."

Sadie nodded. "We used to go and watch the movie people every chance we got, and get as close to the set as they would let us."

"I'm afraid I didn't get much else done that summer. And when Mike came home to supper one night and told us he'd gotten on as an extra—well, that was the icing on the cake."

"Yeah, that was so fun." Sadie smiled, thinking about how jealous she and her friends had been when they had learned that a few local people had chances to be in the film.

"I know it may sound flaky," Roz said, "but I've wondered all these years if Mike's death was really an accident."

Sadie shifted uneasily in her chair. She had heard this suggestion from Roz before, but it had been years since they had spoken of it.

"Do you really think that?"

Roz shrugged. "I don't know."

"Your dad was a police officer," Sadie said gently. "They investigated it thoroughly."

"Did they?" Roz's chin came up a stubborn fraction of an inch. "He never would tell me what they found."

"Honey, you were so young. He probably didn't want to trouble you any worse with the details. He and your mom probably figured it was bad enough that you lost your only brother. And besides, things were different back then. Grown-ups didn't discuss things like that with kids."

"It's not like we were babies."

"I know. But twelve is still pretty young." Sadie sighed. "Your father did see the police reports, I'm sure. He must have been satisfied."

"He never told me anything." Roz gulped. "I asked him about it lots of times, but he would just brush it aside and say something like, 'You don't need to get all worked up about it, Rosalind.' I hated that. I wanted to know every detail."

"Of course you did." Sadie's heart ached as she gazed at her friend's anguished features.

"I'm not saying Mike was murdered. But I'm not saying he wasn't either. Maybe it was criminal negligence—but if so, why wasn't anyone charged? If it was something besides a freak accident, why can't I know that? I just want to be sure of what really happened. Is that too much to ask?"

"No, it's not. But we'll probably never know for certain what happened." Sadie considered things for a moment. "Of course, this is very important to you. Why don't I see if I can find out anything you didn't already know?"

Roz's shoulders drooped. "You don't have to. It would probably lead nowhere anyway."

"I don't mind asking a few questions."

"I know I'm being crazy right now," Roz said. "You're a busy lady, and I wouldn't ask you to spend your time on this. Although, you are pretty good at finding out things. But this is something that happened fifty years ago."

Sadie lifted her coffee cup and took a sip. This had bothered Roz for so long, she knew deep down that her friend would not be at peace unless she learned more about her brother and why he died when he did. She smiled at Roz.

"That's what I'm best at—historical events."

"If you're sure, it would mean a lot to me." Roz leaned across the table. "You know some odd things happened right around the time Mike died. It was only two days after he replaced that actor who'd been fired, Sadie. Two days. I've never been able to shake off the feeling that the guy who was fired might have had something to do with it."

"Really? I never thought of that."

"Why not?"

Sadie shook her head helplessly. "I guess because I assumed the police thoroughly questioned him."

"Maybe. But how do we know? Maybe there was someone else in the cast who had hoped to get that part, but Mike got it instead. And there was another kid at school who had it in for Mike. Do you remember the cheating scandal?"

"Vaguely."

"Well, there you go. That's a lot of bad feeling against my brother. It's called motive."

"Now, Roz…"

"I'm not saying anyone meant to kill Mike. But what if someone wanted to give him a little shove so he'd mess up the scene, just to make him look bad? Something like that, maybe. Or a prank gone wrong."

Sadie let out a deep breath. "I'll make a few inquiries, but there might not be anything there to learn."

Roz's mouth twitched, but she nodded. "I understand."

"Okay. Now, finish your breakfast and go hit the shower. I'll clean up the kitchen while you get dressed."

"You don't need to do that."

"Well, I'm doing it. And I will think about everything you've said and see if I can find out anything. Maybe Mac can help me, although he wasn't around when it happened."

Roz brightened. "That's a great idea. The sheriff would come at it without prejudice, since he wasn't part of the investigation."

Sadie held up one hand. "Remember, I'm not promising anything."

"Okay." Roz picked up her fork. "And thank you. I really appreciate it."

Twenty minutes later, Roz came back to the kitchen dressed in designer jeans and a plaid blouse.

"Feel better?" Sadie asked, giving her a little hug. "You look great."

"Thanks. I do feel better now."

"Want to come over to the store for a while?"

Roz shook her head. "Not just now. Maybe later."

"Okay. I'd better get going, but call me if you want to talk again." Sadie picked up her purse and headed out the door.

Once she arrived at the Antique Mine on Main Street, she went into high gear. She had a lot to do today—new stock to log and display, online ads to prepare, and upcoming sale flyers and auction catalogs to browse, so she could plan her next buying sprees. That was in addition to the usual summer flow of tourists at the shop.

Her assistant, Julie, breezed in a few minutes after Sadie arrived. "Morning!"

"Hi, Julie. Could you help me get these new things out before we open? I'm running a little late this morning."

"Oh, and tonight's the big night, isn't it? The dinner theater, I mean?"

"Yes. Are you and Chad going?"

"Planning on it," Julie said. "I hear the play's really funny."

Sadie was looking forward to the evening out with Edwin Marshall. The refurbished opera house was the perfect venue for dinner theater productions. Sadie was on the Preservation Committee that had overseen the restoration, and she sometimes helped write scripts for the local players, but tonight she would be watching someone else's work for fun.

"Great. We'll see you there."

"These are cool." Julie's eyes danced as she removed a set of carved jade bookends from a box.

"They're not that old, but I thought they'd catch someone's eye." The sight of the stone lions made Sadie smile. For some reason, she'd found it hard to pass up the garage sale owner's souvenir of Hong Kong, even though she knew the bookends were crafted for the tourist trade. "And the price was right," she added.

"Speaking of cool, did you hear about the movie?" Julie asked. "They're going to film right here in Silver Peak."

"Yeah, I did." Julie was too young to remember the original frenzy of filming the science-fiction classic. Sadie wasn't surprised that Julie was excited about it. "It should bring in some extra business. Maybe we'll get some aliens in here to buy souvenirs before they head home to Mars."

Julie laughed. "Maybe we should stock postcards that say, 'Greetings from Earth.'"

"That's a good one." Sadie reached into another box. "Now, where do you think these pewter plates should go? With the china or with the Americana?"

———

That evening, Sadie dressed with care. An evening at the opera house always felt special, and she put on one of her best dresses, blue with shimmery silver threads in the bodice. She wasn't much for wearing makeup, but she applied a little lipstick and blow-dried her short hair just enough to give it some body.

Edwin's car crunched gravel in the driveway, and Hank heard it too. He barked once, and Sadie heard him leave his bed in the kitchen and pad to the front door. The faithful golden retriever was waiting in the entry when she went downstairs. The bell rang just before she reached the door.

Edwin's eyes lit up when she swung the door open. "Hi. You look terrific."

"Thanks," Sadie said with a smile. "Let me grab my purse."

The night's entertainment was the first dinner theater production of the summer, and Sadie knew that tickets for the play had sold out. The room quickly filled with local residents, all of whom seemed upbeat and eager for a fun evening. Sadie enjoyed talking to friends and seeing people she usually saw in jeans and flannel shirts turned out in regal style. She and Edwin took small portions of goodies from the appetizer bar and mingled with the others.

The first act of the play was announced, and they found their seats. Julie and Chad joined them at their table for eight, along with Martin and Paula Deering and Jane and Jerry Remington. Martin was the song leader at Campfire Chapel, and Paula was the church pianist. Jerry and Jane owned the Silver Peak Bed-and-Breakfast. The Remingtons had also been instrumental in the restoration of the opera house.

"Everything looks wonderful in here," Sadie said to Jane.

"Doesn't it?" Jane grinned. "The committee put in hundreds of hours getting everything just right for this season."

"Well, the Preservation Committee certainly brought the opera house back to its old glory," Edwin said.

The lights dimmed for a moment, and everyone stopped talking. Luz Vidal, who was chairman of the opera house board's program committee for the season, stood at the end of the hall near the stage. "Welcome to the new season at the Silver Peak Opera House. We hope you're pleased with tonight's show."

Sadie enjoyed the first act of the play and found herself laughing along with the others as the zany plot unfolded. Tonight's production was a light comedy, and she was almost glad it wasn't something that would require her to think, though she loved the interactive mysteries that were sometimes presented.

At the intermission, their main course of chicken Kiev was served. The diners talked about the play for a few minutes, and then began to catch up on each other's family news.

Edwin leaned closer to Sadie. "I don't think I told you that Noelle and Carl have bought their plane tickets. They'll arrive on Friday."

"How nice," Sadie said. Edwin had not seen his daughter for several months, and she knew he looked forward to showing Noelle what he had done with the old family home. "I'll be happy to see them again. Will they be here long enough for us to spend some time together?"

"She said they're planning on a couple of weeks."

"Great." Already Sadie was mentally planning a family dinner at her house and a fun afternoon showing Noelle around the Antique Mine.

"How are you doing, Edwin?" Paula asked from across the table. "Are your mayoral duties keeping you busy?"

"Not too bad," Edwin replied. "I was just telling Sadie that my daughter and her family are coming to visit soon."

"That's great," Paula said.

"Will they be staying with you?" Jane asked.

"Oh yes," Edwin said, smiling broadly. "I wouldn't let them go anywhere else."

"That's a good thing," Jerry told him. "The B and B is filled to capacity next week. I guess you've heard about the movie crew that's coming."

"So soon?" Sadie asked.

Jerry nodded. "Yes, they've got everything planned, and the director's ready to start."

Edwin said, "I attended a meeting with the opera house board recently to talk about what we can do to welcome them. They're quite excited about it, and they're going to see if the film studio will actually hold the premiere here next spring, when the film releases."

"Wouldn't that be something?" Paula said.

The others agreed with her. Sadie didn't chime in, but kept her thoughts to herself. The more hoopla surrounding the movie, the more memories would be stirred up. She hoped she could find out something that would ease Roz's misgivings. She let the others chatter on about the film, the actors, and the flurry of business the enterprise would bring to Silver Peak.

A comment from Jerry caught her attention. "Hey, wouldn't it be great if they showed the old movie—the one they're doing the remake from?"

"*Ooh*, I like that idea," Jane said. "We could have a showing here at the opera house. Everyone in town could see the classic now."

Paula nodded. "I've never seen it, but now I want to."

"Then it would be fresh in everyone's minds when the new one comes out," Jerry said.

Sadie kept her eyes on her plate to avoid giving away her dismay. She knew at least one person who would not love this idea—Roz Putnam. At least she could forewarn her friend, so she would have time to get used to the idea.

The dishes were cleared, and the lights flickered, signaling that the second act of the play was about to begin. Sadie wasn't sorry. She turned her chair slightly so that she had a better view of the stage.

When the play had finished, they all applauded enthusiastically.

"Not too cerebral, but good, fun entertainment," Martin Deering said.

Sadie and Edwin said good-bye to their friends and went out to the car. Edwin pulled out of the parking lot and turned toward her home.

"Are you tired?" he asked. "You seemed awfully quiet this evening."

"Mostly thinking," Sadie said.

"Care to tell me what about?"

"Roz mostly, and how the flap over the filmmaking will make her feel." Briefly, she told Edwin about her conversation with Roz that morning.

Edwin sighed. "She's right, in a way. I remember when the accident happened, but I confess I hardly thought about it this week, even when people were talking about the movie. Of course, it was fifty years ago, and I suppose no one much younger than us remembers very much about it. Most of the people connected to the opera house are younger, and they're very enthusiastic about tying local events in with the film crew's presence and the premiere next spring."

Sadie chuckled. "Makes me feel old. Was 1965 really that long ago?"

"I'm afraid it was. And a lot of people might not put it together that the young man who died was Roz's brother."

She nodded. "Especially people who've moved to Silver Peak since then."

"I don't think it would do much good to go around and clue everyone in," Edwin said.

"Heavens, no. I can just see Troy Haggarty doing a feature story on the old film, though. What if he dredged up the whole thing, accident and all, and put it on the front page of the *Sentinel*, without ever realizing who Mike was?"

"I can see how that might upset Roz," Edwin said.

"She'd be devastated." Sadie was silent for a moment, thinking about it. "I suppose we could tell Troy, to make sure he avoided that very thing. Or would that backfire? I mean, why call his attention to it if he's blissfully unaware?"

Edwin frowned and shook his head as he turned onto Sadie's road. "Troy's a journalist, and a good one. He'll work this movie company story for all it's worth, and it wouldn't be fair to ask him not to."

"Maybe we should just tell him right up front how damaging it could be to sensationalize the accident."

"I'll have a word with him if you'd like. I could caution him to be sensitive about that angle." Edwin looked over at her, his eyebrows raised in question.

"That might be best. Don't give the impression that you're trying to censor him, but call on him to treat the family with respect."

"Troy's a good fellow," Edwin said. "I think he'll understand. And as you said, if no one tips him off, he could unintentionally cause a lot of pain." After a moment's silence, he said with more confidence. "Yes, I'll talk to him. Tomorrow if I can."

"Do you remember Mike?" Sadie asked.

"Sure. Wasn't he a senior that year?"

"Yes, he'd just graduated. He was quite a bit older than Roz."

Edwin nodded. "I know everyone from school was very upset by it. But I still think this new film project could be good for the town if no one lets it become a dark, gloomy cloud hanging over Silver Peak."

"Yeah, I agree. But Roz…I'll be there for her if she needs me." Sadie had given her promise that morning under pressure from her friend, but now her determination grew. She would put the unanswered questions about Mike's death to rest for Roz.

As Edwin drove higher up the mountain toward Sadie's house, she noticed a glow in the sky that seemed to originate at some point beyond her house.

"What's that?" She pointed.

Edwin peered ahead. "I don't know. It's the wrong direction for the moonrise."

"Could it be a fire?"

He said nothing, but drove up her driveway and parked in front of the house. Both of them got out of the car and hurried to the side lawn.

"It's some kind of aircraft," Sadie said uncertainly. "I saw a blinking light."

"It's steadier now," Edwin said. "But it's not moving the way a plane would."

"A helicopter?" Sadie hazarded.

"Can't be. It's not that far away, and there's hardly any wind. We'd hear a chopper for sure."

"I think it's over Milo's pasture." Sadie couldn't look away from the eerie illumination. The light reflected off the clouds, but the object from which it seemed to emanate sank slowly toward the horizon.

"Is it landing?" Edwin asked, his eyes still fixed on the blinking lights. The flying object lowered out of sight and then rose again to where they could see at least two distinct lights on it blinking. Edwin and Sadie turned and stared at each other.

"Okay, what is that thing?" she asked.

He shook his head slowly. "I haven't the faintest idea."

2

"Wow." Edwin looked back toward Milo's property and shook his head. The mysterious object had lowered again, as though sinking below the mountainside, and all they could see was the glow Sadie had first noticed.

"I wonder if anyone else can see it," Sadie said.

"Let's call Milo."

"Good idea." Sadie pulled her cell phone out and quickly keyed in Milo Henderson's number. He owned the large ranch abutting her property and a good chunk of the mountainside.

"Hello?" He sounded a little sleepy when he answered.

"Milo, it's Sadie. Do you see anything odd in the sky?"

"What?"

"There's something weird in the sky over your pasture."

"Hold on."

She heard his footsteps and his breathing. A moment later he said, "What on earth? What is that thing?"

"We don't know, but it was up in the sky before. Now all we see is a glow."

"I see light on the clouds," Milo said.

"Do you hear anything?"

"No."

Suddenly, the sky was dark.

"It's gone," Edwin said.

Sadie followed his gaze, but even the ghostly glow on the clouds had vanished.

Milo echoed with, "It just quit."

"Could you tell what it was?" Sadie asked.

"Nope. It looked like…"

"What?"

"I don't know," Milo said slowly. "Could it be a beacon or something on the clouds? You know, like an airport beacon?"

"There's no airport close enough for that," Sadie said. "Besides, Edwin and I saw an actual *thing* in the sky. Not an airplane. It was too quiet, and it didn't move right for a plane."

"I can't see anything now," Milo said.

"Neither can we."

"I'll go out in the morning and look around, but I'll tell you, that was really strange."

"Let us know if you find out anything about it," Sadie said. "Good night, Milo." She closed her phone and looked at Edwin. "You heard what he said?"

"I sure did. At least no one can say we're crazy," Edwin said with a low chuckle. "We can vouch for each other."

"Come on in," Sadie said. "I won't be able to sleep for a while after this."

Edwin followed her onto the porch. Hank met them at the door with a glad *woof.* Sadie patted him and then let him out for a short run. She closed the door and faced Edwin.

"Okay, what was that thing?"

Edwin eyed her coyly. "You first. Best guess."

Sadie frowned. "Some newfangled kind of helicopter. Electric-powered, maybe?"

"The batteries would have to be huge."

"Nuclear-powered, then?"

"I don't know," Edwin said slowly. "It just didn't seem right for a helicopter."

"Well, we can't identify it, and it was flying, so I guess it's a UFO." Sadie smiled at him.

"That's exactly what it was," Edwin said.

Sadie chuckled. "We must be special to have been allowed to see it. Maybe we qualify for one of those 'I've seen an alien spacecraft' clubs now. Coffee?"

"No, thanks. Come sit down." Edwin walked into the living room and sat on the sofa. He patted the cushion beside him.

Sadie went over and sank onto the sofa, placing her purse on the coffee table.

"Do you really think it could be military?" she asked.

"It's possible. I suppose the air force could be testing a new piece of hardware. Although I'd like to think that, as mayor, I'd know about it."

"Good point. Maybe it's a secret surveillance drone," Sadie suggested.

"Now, that's a thought." Edwin reached for her hand. "I was thinking more in another direction. Remember all the talk at the theater?"

"What? You mean about the movie?"

He nodded. "What if this was some sort of publicity stunt? I mean, the movie *is* about aliens."

"Could be, but it seems odd. I mean, they haven't even set up for filming yet. Wouldn't they wait until the film was about to release for something like that?"

"I don't know. The marketing world is all over the place these days. I can imagine the studio wanting to start some buzz about the project. What better way than to make sure a UFO sighting was reported near the site of the filming of *Stranger from a Strange World* fifty years ago?"

Sadie eyed him thoughtfully. "I guess it could be something like that. But wouldn't it have been in a more populated place, like right in the middle of town?"

"I'm just saying, let's keep our objectivity."

"Our skepticism, you mean."

Edwin smiled. "If you want to put it that way. I certainly don't think it was a spaceship from Mars."

"Well, no," Sadie said.

"I'm just saying…The film crew is expected to arrive next Thursday, and they plan to start filming a few days later. Let's just keep our eyes and ears open."

"Then you don't think we should tell anyone?"

"Tell anyone you like. If you want to discuss it with Mac, go ahead, but I doubt the sheriff will take it seriously."

"Yeah," Sadie said. "Knowing Mac, he'll probably tell me I'm spaced out."

"He might at that." Edwin stood, his eyes twinkling at the pun. "Well, I'd better be going."

Sadie jumped up and walked with him to the door. "Thanks, Edwin. It was a very interesting evening."

"Wasn't it?" He laughed and stooped to kiss her cheek. "I enjoyed it, even if it was a little—out of this world."

———————

Sunday dinner with her daughter, Alice, and her two grand-children was always a highlight of the weekend for Sadie. After church, she followed Alice's Jeep home and helped Alice and four-teen-year-old Sara put the food on the table.

"Grandma," Sara said after the blessing, "all the kids are talking about a movie being made here. Did you hear about it?"

"Yes, there was a lot of discussion about it at the opera house last night. Some folks are very excited about it."

"Mia wants to be in the movie," Sara said.

"They won't let just anyone be in it," Theo told her with the knowledgeable air of a big brother.

"Mia says they might need extras. Sometimes they do that when they're filming on location—hire local people, instead of bringing tons of actors in."

Sadie's momentary dismay when she thought of Mike prompted her to speak, but she resisted. There seemed no point in bringing up the past.

"It's possible," Alice said, "but I wouldn't get my hopes up if I were you."

"It's a space opera." Theo held his plate out for his mother to serve him from the casserole dish. "What would you play? An alien extra?"

"Not me." Sara scowled at him. "Mia's the one who's crazy about being in the movie. She said maybe she can be one of the shocked people in the crowd when the spaceship lands."

"Oh, right." Theo set his plate down and shook his head disdainfully.

"Stranger things have happened," Sadie said gently.

Sara turned to her eagerly. "Speaking of strange things, I heard people at church talking about odd lights they saw last night. Did you see anything?"

"As a matter of fact, I did." Sadie helped herself to a generous spoonful of green beans and passed the serving dish to Theo. "Edwin and I were coming home from the play, and just as we arrived back at my house, we saw it."

"What was it?" Theo asked.

"We're not sure. But we saw blinking lights, and then a glow against the low clouds. It looked like it was over Milo's property. I called him, but by the time he got outside, the show was pretty much over."

"Was it an airplane?" Alice asked.

"We didn't think so. It didn't move like a plane. And it was quiet. At least, we didn't hear anything. We figured it was close enough that we'd have heard a helicopter engine or something like that."

Theo frowned as he listened carefully to her words. "Maybe it was farther away than you realized."

"*Hmm.* In that case, it would have had to be really big."

"Or maybe it was closer and smaller than you thought," Alice suggested. "You know, a remote control toy of some sort."

Sadie tilted her head to one side and considered that. "I don't know. Of course, it was dark, but it didn't seem that way. And Milo did see the glow from his yard. It wasn't really like anything I've seen before."

Sara, wide-eyed, said, "Do you think it could have been angels, Grandma?"

"Oh, I don't think so, honey. But then, I guess we wouldn't know for sure if it was, would we?"

"I think they have fun surprising people," Sara said.

"Yeah, that would be shocking." Sadie smiled at her. "I hadn't really thought that it might be a heavenly event."

"Well, if you don't think so, Sara should quit *harping* on it," Theo said with a laugh.

Sadie and Alice chuckled, but Sara only rolled her eyes.

"Maybe they just came down to say 'halo' to your grandma," Sadie retorted.

"Good one. Gram, you didn't hear any singing, did you?" Theo asked.

Sadie passed her plate to Alice for a serving of ziti. "No, we didn't. That's an interesting thought, though, Sara. No singing, no motors, nothing. It was very odd."

"I'll bet it was kids," Alice said. "The teenagers I teach have all sorts of gadgets these days."

"Maybe. I admit, it was unsettling," Sadie said. "And Edwin was standing right beside me. He's the most practical man I know, but he couldn't explain it either."

"I guess you'll never know what it was," Theo said.

Sadie nodded thoughtfully and picked up her fork. "Well, something's going on for sure."

Everyone who came into the Antique Mine on Monday seemed to be talking about the expected arrival of the film crew. Sadie didn't pay much attention at first, but residents who were her age or older sought her out to reminisce. When Harry Polmiller, the oldest member of Campfire Chapel, came in, she went to meet him with a ready smile and a big hug.

"How are you doing, Harry?"

"Just great. Been out working in the garden this morning."

"You put me to shame," Sadie said. "How can I help you today?"

"Just wanted to get out of the house. I'm going to eat lunch at the Depot, but I thought I'd pop in and see what's new in the antiques biz."

Sadie laughed. "I've got something you might enjoy looking at." She led him behind the counter and set up a stool for him. "I got a very nice stereoscope at an auction last week. Some of the pictures are really something."

"That sounds like fun," Harry said.

Sadie brought it to him, and while she puttered around the counter and checked out a couple of customers, he went through the stack of double photographs, holding them up on the stereoscope and exclaiming over the striking 3-D images.

"Oh, the ones inside Mammoth Cave are something, aren't they?"

"I like those too," Sadie said.

"I never get tired of looking at old pictures, even though photography has come such a long way." Harry set down the stereoscope. "Speaking of which, I saw on the *Chatterbox* that they're going to remake that old movie they did here in the sixties."

"That's right," Sadie said. "The film crew is supposed to arrive on Thursday, or so Edwin tells me. The actors and the director will be here early next week."

"Big doings for Silver Peak."

"Yes." Sadie frowned.

"You're thinking about what happened the last time," Harry said.

"You read my mind."

He gave a sage nod. "For some folks, the memories aren't very pleasant."

"Yes. I was thinking of Roz."

"Too bad, what happened to her brother."

"It was terrible for the family at the time, and Roz is feeling it now, with all the talk about the new movie," Sadie said.

"I can imagine. How old were you girls?"

"About twelve. We were going into eighth grade that fall."

Harry shook his head. "Hard time for a girl to lose her brother."

"She thinks nobody remembers," Sadie said.

"Oh, we remember. Some folks might feel awkward if the subject comes up nowadays, but we remember."

"It's a difficult time for her. And so many of the young folks don't know about it. I can imagine things might be said that would be painful for Roz. But you can't undo the past. I say, look for the best in a situation, and you might find it."

Harry nodded. "It's fun to see everyone getting so keyed up about the movie and the famous people who will be here. We'll just have to be extranice to Roz." The bell on the door jingled, and Harry stood. "Well, it looks like you've got a bus full of customers arriving, and it's time for me to get on over to the Depot."

"Yeah, you'll want to beat the crowd. Have a good lunch." Sadie waved to him and turned to greet the customers streaming in.

"Is this the place where they're going to make the space movie?" one of the first women in asked.

"It sure is," Sadie replied with a grin. "Welcome to Silver Peak, the UFO capital of Colorado—and maybe the world."

The customers were soon laughing about their favorite science-fiction films and TV shows, and browsing Sadie's merchandise for treasures.

She took a late lunch hour, leaving Julie with several patrons still in the store, though most had gone in search of food themselves. The Depot, Flap Jack's, and Los Pollitos all seemed to be overflowing with customers, so she headed for the Market, where she could get a sandwich at the café. Before going inside, she gave Roz a call.

"Hey, how you doing?"

"I'm better, thanks," Roz replied.

"I'm grabbing a sandwich for lunch. Want to join me?"

"Actually, Roscoe came home for lunch. It's time for him to get back to work, though. You're eating late, aren't you?"

"Yeah, we had a run this morning. A bus of seniors came up from Breckenridge."

"Great. And thanks, but I'll pass this time."

Sadie had no sooner put her phone in her pocket when it rang. She dredged it out and saw Milo's name on the screen.

"Hi, Milo. What's up?"

"You wanted me to tell you whether I found anything on the mountain that might tell us something about those lights. I did some looking around this morning, but I didn't see anything."

"Where did you go?" Sadie asked.

"I rode around the two pastures nearest the house, and I went along the trail that goes up to the bluff."

"Where they filmed some of the scenes from the sci-fi movie?"

"Yeah. That was before my time, but that's the place. My mom's told me about it a hundred times at least. Nothing up there this morning."

"They're remaking that movie, you know," Sadie said.

"Yeah, I know. They're paying me some cold cash to use the same piece of real estate."

"You're kidding! They're going to film it in the exact same place?"

"That's the plan. I wasn't crazy about the idea at first, but when they made me an offer, it was pretty attractive. Not much money in ranching these days. It'll be a nice bonus."

"That's terrific, Milo. But it really makes me wonder if those lights we saw had something to do with the movie."

"I dunno. Nobody's come by the house or driven up there yet. I understood they'd be arriving on Thursday. Asked me to stand by and be ready to show them the exact boundaries of the land they're leasing for the project. They say they'll be real careful and make sure nobody messes things up or goes poking around my place where they shouldn't."

"Good." Sadie frowned as she thought about Saturday night's spectacle. "Did you look at the bottom of the cliff?"

"What, down below the bluff?"

"Yeah."

After a slight pause, Milo said, "No, I didn't go down there. You think maybe there's something there?"

"I don't know. I sort of got the impression that whatever we saw sank below the horizon, but the glow was still there. I thought maybe if it was some kind of aircraft or—I don't know, machine—that it might have disappeared down over the edge of that bluff."

"*Hmm*. Well, I can't go out there today," Milo said. "I've got to take some young stock into Breckenridge. And one of the fellows from the movie crew wants to use some space in my barn, so I've got to clean out the haymow for him."

"What about tomorrow?" Sadie said. "I'll ask my grandchildren if they want to ride with me tomorrow afternoon."

"What?" Milo said, "You're not afraid of the big, bad aliens?"

Sadie chuckled. "I don't scare easy. Want to go with us, or are you the one who's scared?"

"Sure, I'll go. What time? I'll have the horses ready."

Sadie settled the details with Milo and then hurried into the Market for her sandwich. When she came out a few minutes later, Edwin was just leaving his office at the town hall. He waved, and Sadie walked toward him.

"Hi! Out and about today?" he asked.

"Just grabbing a quick lunch," Sadie replied. "We were pretty busy this morning."

"Have you seen the *Chatterbox*?" Edwin asked.

"No. What now?"

"Apparently we weren't the only ones who saw the strange lights Saturday night. People are asking if it's a UFO."

"I was just talking to Milo. He checked the top of the bluff and didn't find anything, but we're going to ride out around the mountain tomorrow afternoon, to the base of the cliff. Want to join us?"

"Thanks, but I'm meeting with the road commissioner at three tomorrow, and I'm trying to take care of some loose ends before Noelle gets here."

"Okay. I doubt we'll find anything, but it hasn't rained, and I want to take a look. I figure once the filming starts, any traces that might have been there will be gone."

"What sort of traces would you find of a flying object on the ground?" Edwin asked.

Sadie sighed. "Probably none, but I'll feel better if I look."

"All right. Keep your eyes peeled for extraterrestrials. And keep me in the loop." He gave her hand a squeeze.

"No worries there." Sadie headed back to the store with a spring in her step. Edwin knew this was important to her, but he wasn't taking it too seriously, which was as it should be. Chances were slim that she would find anything out near the cliff, she knew, but if she didn't go out and check before the movie crew arrived and started trampling over the ground, she would regret it.

3

Julie was waiting on a customer in the tools section when Sadie returned to the store. She spotted Anita Slattery, the sheriff's wife, browsing the shelves of Depression glass and went to greet her.

"Hi, Anita! Good to see you."

"Hello, Sadie. I'm just looking around today, but I'm drooling over this lemon-colored glass. It's just beautiful."

"Thanks. I like it too. I picked up quite a few of those pieces at an auction in Colorado Springs last month."

"So," Anita said, facing her with a smile, "we're getting a movie crew this week. Mac is going to step up patrols while they're in town."

"Does he expect trouble?" Sadie asked.

"Not really, but he says you never know with Hollywood people. He wants to make sure they see we have a law enforcement presence."

"Probably a good idea," Sadie said.

Seeing Anita reminded her that she had intended to call Mac about the strange lights she and Edwin had seen. As soon as Anita had left the store, she called the sheriff's office and left a message for Mac. She was soon immersed in helping more customers. The lovely June day had beckoned people out to drive in the mountains, and Sadie would be the first to say that Silver Peak had some of the most beautiful vistas in Colorado.

Around four o'clock the traffic slowed, and she called Alice and invited her and the kids to go riding the following day. She smiled as she heard her daughter telling Sara and Theo, "Grandma wants us to ride out to the base of the cliff in Milo's west pasture and look for alien footprints."

Sara came on the line. "Grandma! Are you really going out looking for Martians?"

Sadie laughed. "No, but the horses need exercise, and I thought we might as well take a look out there on the other side of the cliff, where that glowing, flying whatever-it-was seemed to hover."

"Cool. We'll be there."

Sadie hung up a moment later, still smiling. The door opened, and she turned to find Mac Slattery walking in, wearing his uniform.

"Hi, Sadie. You wanted to talk to me?"

"Well, hello. I didn't expect a personal visit, Mac."

"Things are a little slow, so I thought I'd walk Main Street and touch base with the business owners. Everyone's het up about this movie thing."

"A lot of people who've come in here are talking about it too. But I called you about something that happened Saturday night. Did anyone tell you they saw some odd lights over the mountain, maybe out toward Milo Henderson's place?"

"You're the second one who's mentioned it to me. Ben Armstrong was out late on a veterinary call, and he says he saw something as he was driving back into town. Around nine forty-five, he said."

Sadie's pulse quickened. "Edwin and I saw it around the same time. We'd been to the show at the opera house, and we were just going home. We stood in my yard and watched it. Some other people who had been to the play may have seen it too."

"Not a meteor?"

"Definitely not. It didn't move at all like that, and it seemed close. At least, that's the impression I got. The light reflected off the clouds, so the source had to be underneath them, right?"

"Makes sense. So what did you see?"

"At first it was like a glow on the horizon, and reflecting off the clouds."

Mac nodded. "Ben said he knew it wasn't the northern lights or anything like that because of the cloud cover. He said they seemed to catch the glow from underneath."

"Exactly. I thought at first it could be a fire," Sadie said. "Then it sort of rose up, and we could see some blinking lights."

"That so?" Mac cocked his head to one side. "Definite blinking lights?"

"Yes. It hovered like a helicopter, but we couldn't make out its shape, and it was quiet. Very quiet. Milo was in his house, and he didn't hear it."

"So . . . are you saying you don't think it was a chopper?"

"Right."

"How about a hovercraft?"

Sadie frowned. "My guess would be that it was too high, but I don't really know much about them to say so with any confidence."

"Well, I suppose if it was one, you would have heard that too."

"And after a while it seemed to sink again, and we saw that eerie glow for a little while. Then it was gone."

"What did you make of it, if it wasn't an aircraft?" Mac asked.

"I don't know. You can ask Edwin about it. We thought maybe some sort of remote control device, although it seemed big. Bigger than a toy. Could it possibly have been a military project?"

"Now, just how big are we talking?" Mac asked.

"I don't know. It was dark, and we're not sure how far away it was or how big. But if it was good-size—say, as big as a helicopter—then I'd say my impression was that after a short while it lowered behind the mountainside."

"Uh-huh." Mac shrugged. "Well, I don't know any more than you do, Sadie. If I get more calls and find out anything, I can let you know, but it doesn't seem like something to worry about."

"Oh, I'm not worried," Sadie said. "Just curious."

"Well, there's got to be a logical explanation."

Sadie eyed him cautiously. "I wondered if you might possibly contact the military?"

"What for?"

"Just to ask them if they were doing any tests or anything like that out here Saturday night."

"Aw, Sadie," Mac said. "What makes you think they'd tell me if they were?"

"Well, they certainly would be more likely to talk to you in your official capacity than they would be to talk to me."

"You want me to tell them the citizens of Silver Peak are panicking and we need to know what's going on?"

"Oh, quit teasing. You know I don't mean that. You've got three very sane, down-to-earth people who saw it. And Milo saw the glow too. It's not like we're a bunch of kooks."

"Well, I dunno . . ." Mac eyed her significantly.

"Very funny."

Mac sighed. "I guess I could give the liaison at the air force base a call, but I'll feel kind of silly."

Sadie touched his sleeve. "Thank you. We'd all appreciate it."

"I'll let you kooks know if I hear anything."

Sadie smiled gratefully. "That's all I'm asking."

———

Milo had Sadie's horse, as well as Alice's and the children's and one of his own trail horses, Opie, saddled and lined up at the pasture fence when the family arrived to ride. The cool, dry weather had held for several days, and the horses were in high spirits.

"Thought we'd go up top first, if you want," he said.

"Great. I haven't been up there in a long time." Sadie swung up onto Scout's back.

Theo's black gelding, Bronco, snorted and pranced when Theo mounted.

"We need to ride more often." Theo reined the horse in small circles until he calmed down.

The five of them rode along a Jeep trail for the first half hour. Summer was just coming into its full glory, and Sadie drank in the beauty of it. The views from Milo's land were unbeatable, as far as she was concerned. With mountain peaks towering around them, they rode up the hillside and around the side of Silver Peak to a gate. They went through it, and Milo shut it behind them.

"Is this still your land?" Theo asked.

"Yeah, but I don't let the horses up here," Milo said. "I didn't want to put my fence too close to the edge of the bluff."

They rode along in silence for several minutes. Because of the fences and the steep side of the mountain falling away on one side, this was a route they rarely took on their trail rides. They came out in a flat area at the top of a bluff. Milo reined his horse in about twenty yards from the edge and sat for a moment looking out at the panorama before them.

"Wow, this is so beautiful," Alice said softly.

Milo nodded. "This is where they filmed part of the old movie."

"You mean *Stranger from a Strange World*?" Sara asked.

"Yeah," Theo said, riding up close to them. "I've heard people talking about it. Now I want to see that movie."

"You can probably stream it on your laptop," Alice said. "Maybe we can all watch it some Sunday afternoon."

Milo glanced at Sadie and then back at the drop-off before them. "This is where Roz Putnam's brother fell, isn't it?"

"Yes." Sadie's heart clenched, thinking about it. She was glad she hadn't been there the day Mike died.

"I didn't know that!" Sara rode up beside Alice, distress written on her face. "Mom, is it really?"

"I'm afraid so, honey."

"It's too bad." Milo shook his head. "I know it bothered the folks who owned this ranch before Mom and Dad bought it. But Dad always told me the owner had warned the movie folks about the edge and even asked if they wanted a fence or something put up. They said no, because they didn't want it to show in the film, but ... well, they just got too close, I guess." He shook his head, his face mirroring dark thoughts.

"It wasn't their fault," Sadie said.

"I know. But I do worry about something similar happening again. Fox Monahan promised he'd keep all the actors and crew at least fifteen feet from the rim. I refused to sign the agreement until they put that in writing. And it also says I'm not to blame if anyone gets hurt, but I'll be glad when the whole thing's over with."

"How does your mother feel about it?" Alice asked.

"She didn't think I should do it, but she understands that the money will be a big help to me. Let's just say she's not going to come around to watch the filming when the crew is up here."

"Was she there the first time?" Sadie asked.

"No, she was just a kid. She always said she was glad she wasn't around to see it." Milo's sudden smile transformed his face. "But, hey, this is one of the most beautiful places in the world. I'll always be thankful my folks let me buy it from them."

Sadie leaned over and patted his arm. "It's been a real blessing for you."

"Right. I wouldn't want to live anywhere else. We can take a look around, but I told you I came up here Monday. It didn't look like anyone had been up here for a while." He swung down from the saddle and dropped Opie's reins.

As he walked along, surveying the grass between the riders and the cliff edge, Sara sidled Daisy closer to Alice's horse.

"Can we go back now, Mom?" she asked.

"Chicken," Theo said. "It's safe here, or Milo wouldn't have brought us."

Milo walked along parallel to the edge, but keeping back several feet from the drop-off, watching the ground. He made several passes and then ambled back to where they waited.

"Nothing here. Let's go." He gathered Opie's reins and mounted. "You wanted to check the Jeep trail that runs below the cliff, right?"

"Probably a good idea," Sadie said.

Sara smiled. "Maybe the UFO is down there."

Theo's face scrunched up. "Yeah, right."

Sara grinned at Milo, seeming to have forgotten her earlier gloom. "From what Grandma said about Saturday night, I'm almost surprised you didn't get grabbed by some spacemen."

"Not me," Milo said, his face sober. "I'm too ugly."

Theo smiled sweetly at his sister. "If they don't like ugly, then I guess you don't have to worry, Sara."

"Okay, let's be nice," Alice said with a frown at Theo. "Maybe it's time to move on, Milo."

They rode back through the gate into the upper pasture and down toward the ranch. Once in the barnyard, they headed along one of Milo's gravel trails that skirted his main pasture, where a couple dozen horses grazed.

They came to a gate leading into his west pasture, a long strip of grassland along the hillside, more remote from his ranch house.

"You don't have any livestock out here, do you?" Sadie asked.

"No," Milo said, riding over close to the gatepost. "I don't like to put horses this far from the house. If I have extra animals and need more grass, I'll run them out here. But usually I just let it grow, and then I cut the hay for winter."

"It's gorgeous," Alice said, tipping her head back to survey the peaks. "I haven't been on this trail for ages."

In the distance they could see the rock face rising sixty feet above the field. At the top was the bluff they had ridden to earlier.

"Will the movie crew be down here at all when they're shooting?" Sara asked.

"No, they're using the top of the bluff, and also my front section. And they asked to be able to use the barn for exterior shots if they want to. They weren't real sure about that when I talked to them."

"You said they'll have a workshop in the barn, I believe," Sadie said.

"Yeah, but that's not going to be on film. It will give them a place to work on props and sets out of the weather." Milo swung the gate open without dismounting and held it while the other horses passed through. Then he signaled Opie to sidestep while he closed the gate.

"You've got to teach me to do that," Sara said.

"It's more a matter of your teaching Daisy to do it." Milo's smile faded as he studied the ground. He leaned down for a closer look.

"What is it?" Sadie asked.

"Looks like someone's driven through here since the last rain." He looked toward the gate, then back at the ground.

"It's been over a week since it rained," Theo said.

"You haven't been out here?" Sadie asked, but she knew Milo hadn't, or he would have said so.

He shook his head. "I haven't driven here since the end of May. I've been really busy the last few weeks." He urged Opie along slowly, still looking at the trail.

"Those tire tracks look kind of wide," Theo said.

"Yeah. It's some kind of truck." Milo stopped his horse. "Or even a truck pulling a trailer." He swung to the ground and stooped over the tracks for a moment, then straightened and looked ahead to the base of the bluff.

"You said you weren't here when they made the old movie, right?" Sara asked.

Milo laughed. "I wasn't even born yet. Come on."

He mounted, and they trotted their horses toward the rock face. When they reached it, Milo halted and dismounted. Sadie got down too and let the reins trail to ground-tie Scout. The chestnut gelding immediately began to graze on the lush grass. Sadie went to stand beside Milo, who was frowning at the grass recently bent down by tires.

"So they drove off the road, and right up here near the cliff," she said softly.

"Yeah. Looks like they turned around here too. Made some ruts."

"A heavy load?" Sadie asked.

"Maybe. They backed off the trail. I'm thinking now it was a pickup pulling a trailer."

Alice came to Sadie's side. "What are we looking at?"

"The place where the trespasser turned around," Milo said.

"If the thing Edwin and I saw descended behind the bluff, it could have landed here," Sadie added. "I mean, it had to touch down somewhere."

"I don't see any burn marks on the ground," Alice said with a chuckle as Sara and Theo joined them.

"No, but there was quite a bit of activity here," Milo replied. "Remember, that was three days ago. The grass is all trampled, and there are ruts over here."

"Wow. Maybe it was a stock trailer," Alice said. "It might not hurt to count your horses."

Milo frowned. "They were all there when I fed them this morning. I don't like to think there might be horse thieves in the area. But that's partly why I don't let them graze out here—too far from the house."

"And that wouldn't explain the reason we're here," Sadie said.

"Yeah, horse thieves and rustlers don't do their work in spaceships," Theo put in.

"That we know of," Sara added, and her brother scowled at her.

Something in the matted grass caught Sadie's eye, and she stooped to see it better. "This can't have been here long." She picked up a shiny bolt.

Milo whistled. "Looks new."

"Too new for you to have dropped it," Sadie added.

Milo took it and examined it closely. "Nothing I would have been using lately." He handed it back to Sadie. She and Alice and the kids watched as Milo walked around slowly, fanning the grass with his boot. Finally he came back to where they stood. "I don't see anything else. We might as well go back."

"If you don't mind," Sadie said, "I'll take this bolt and see what I can find out about it."

"Maybe you should show it to Sheriff Slattery," Theo said.

Sadie wrinkled her face and shook her head slightly. "I talked to him yesterday about the lights we saw. He didn't seem to take it seriously, but he finally agreed to call the air force liaison and ask whether they'd done any testing in these parts."

Milo nodded. "I doubt he'd do anything about these trespassers unless I could tell him who it was or show that they stole something. He'd probably just tell me to put locks on my gates." He shook his head. "What a pain that would be."

Sadie pocketed the bolt. "At least we've got proof that someone was out here with a fairly large vehicle. That's a start."

Sara grinned at her. "Yeah, but knowing you, Grandma, it's not the finish."

4

SADIE SLID INTO A CHAIR ON THE PATIO AT LOS POLLITOS, BESIDE
her longtime friend and occasional verbal sparring partner, Janet
Parks, who was Mac Slattery's receptionist. Across from them
sat Rita Dodd, who manned the desk at Doc Conroy's office.
Both were old classmates of Sadie's, and once in a while they got
together for lunch.

Rita looked up from her menu and pushed the frames of her
purple eyeglasses up on her nose. "Hey, Sadie! Glad you could
make it."

"Thanks. Julie assured me she'd be fine for an hour on her
own, although we've been pretty busy this week." Sadie settled
into her chair and picked up her menu.

"Just wait until all the movie people get here," Janet said. "Mac
says the town will be overrun with hangers-on and wannabe
actors."

Sadie laughed. "That sounds like Mac. So optimistic. As long as
these visitors have money to spend in Silver Peak, I say bring it on."

"Isn't it wild how they're remaking that movie?" Rita said,
rolling her eyes skyward. "I can hardly believe it. It makes me feel
like a kid again."

Janet smiled. "Yeah, remember when the cast had a special day when the local folks could go and talk to them and get autographs? They wore their costumes and everything."

Sadie nodded. "It was their thank-you to Silver Peak for being such good hosts for the production."

"Think the new cast will do that?" Rita asked.

Sadie shrugged and opened the menu, though she knew it almost by heart. "You never know. Of course, a lot of the new stars are people we've never heard of."

"That's true," Janet said. "But really, some of them might go on to be megabox-office draws. I think I'll get autographs again. Maybe even dig out my old autograph book from junior high and have them sign in the same book the stars of the first movie did."

"That might be worth a fortune someday," Sadie said.

"It can be part of your legacy for your kids." Rita pulled off her glasses and laid them on the table. "So, Sadie, are you ready to order? Here comes Gloria."

"I sure am." Sadie smiled at the woman who came to their table with her order pad in hand. Gloria Garza was truly beautiful, and her warm, generous spirit always made the customers at Los Pollitos feel special. "Hi, Gloria. How's it going?"

"Very well, thank you." A breeze tugged at Gloria's wavy brown hair, and she tucked a strand behind her ear. "What can I get you ladies today?"

They all gave their orders, and Sadie chose a chicken quesadilla.

"Gloria, you should be in the movie they're making," Janet suggested.

Gloria's lips skewed. "No thank you. I heard it's about monsters from outer space."

Janet laughed. "Not monsters. Extraterrestrials for sure, though."

"I loved the old version," Rita said. "I must have seen it six or eight times when it first came out."

Janet grinned at her. "Me too. In fact, I think we went together a couple of times. I just loved the star—Blaze Foster."

"Oh, he was so handsome." Rita put the back of her wrist to her forehead, as if she were about to swoon. "I'd have gone to see anything he was in back then."

Gloria laughed. "Well, let's hope the new star is as handsome, eh?" She went inside to put in their orders.

Janet turned to Sadie. "What about you? Were you a fan?"

"I was as nutty over the stars as you two," Sadie said.

"So how many times did you go to see the picture?"

"Actually, I've never seen it."

Janet and Rita stared at her.

"Why ever not?" Rita asked.

Reluctant to put a damper on the conversation, Sadie sighed. "Because of Roz. She was so upset at the time."

"Oh yeah," Janet said soberly.

Rita shook her head. "That was so awful, what happened to Mike."

"I hadn't thought about that for a long time," Janet admitted. "What does Roz think of this new movie they're doing?"

"It's got her a little down," Sadie said.

Gloria brought their beverages, and assured them their entrées would be right out. A pair of women had sat down at another table on the patio, and she went to take their order.

Rita leaned in closer to her companions. "I was pretty depressed when it happened too. I'd had the most painful crush on Mike, but he didn't know I existed."

"His death must have been really difficult for you," Sadie said, eyeing Rita with new insight.

"It was. I cried buckets."

"But you still went to see the film," Janet pointed out.

"Well, yes. But it didn't release for months and months after Mike died. By then I guess I was able to get past it. It was all kind of bittersweet, seeing the final product. I'd gotten to watch them film a couple of scenes, but when I saw it on the screen, it was totally unexpected. I remember getting all caught up in the story."

"I watched the sky for weeks," Janet said. "Every time I saw a shooting star, I'd wonder if it was a spaceship burning up when it entered the earth's atmosphere."

Sadie chuckled. "Funny the impression things leave on kids."

"They're talking about showing the old movie again in town," Rita said. "Are you going to see it?"

"I don't know. My grandchildren mentioned wanting to watch it. Maybe it's time I did. But I think I'll sound Roz out first. I wouldn't want her to feel betrayed."

"That's silly," Janet said. "Watching a film her brother would have had a small part in if he'd lived is not betrayal."

Sadie shrugged and picked up her mug. "It's complicated."

Gloria brought their food, and the three began to eat.

"Didn't Mike just have an extra's spot in that movie?" Janet asked a few minutes later. "No lines or anything, right?"

"I think he got a bigger part," Sadie said, trying to remember the details.

Rita swallowed a bite and said, "Yeah, there was another actor who got fired."

"Oh, that's right," Sadie said. "He was the sheriff's deputy in the movie, wasn't he? What was his name?"

"Ty Zinfeld," Rita said readily.

"I don't remember him at all." Janet sighed and took a bite of her chimichanga.

"I thought he was absolutely dreamy, but I don't think I've seen him in anything since," Rita said.

"Maybe he didn't stay in show business." Sadie thought about it while she ate.

"It's possible. The director got angry and fired him, remember? And Ty wasn't very nice to Mike after that. I guess when he heard they were giving Mike his part, it upset him."

"That made it final, so he couldn't undo it," Sadie suggested.

"Probably so. I know he said something unkind to Mike. Something like, you're a loser, or you'll never make it, or something like that. Mike was pretty upset about it."

"I didn't know that," Sadie said. She wondered if Roz knew.

———

Roz came by the Antique Mine that afternoon, fifteen minutes before closing time. She browsed the merchandise while Sadie totaled the day's sales and filled out her deposit slip.

"Wow, you've put out a lot of new stuff since I was in here last," Roz said.

"I've been stocking up for the tourist season." Sadie put the cash and checks in her bank bag with the deposit slip and closed the cash register.

"And now it's upon us." Roz walked toward the counter smiling.

"It sure is. Today was a good day. There were quite a few out-of-towners through here, and I'm happy with the sales. But I'm sorry to tell you I sold that cranberry glass pitcher you liked."

"Ha. You're not really sorry."

"Neither are you," Sadie said. "If you couldn't live without it, you'd have bought it."

"True." Roz leaned on the counter.

"You seem to be feeling better," Sadie said.

"I'm coming to terms with it. The movie, I mean. Yes, they're making a new version, but it will be all new people, right? And I won't have any loved ones involved in the production. I need to just relax and let things take their course."

Sadie nodded, eyeing her sidelong as she zipped the bank bag.

"So you haven't found out anything yet, have you?" Roz asked.

Sadie smiled. She had known Roz wouldn't let it go that easily. "Not really. I had an interesting conversation with Rita and Janet today, though. The topic of the movie came up."

Roz sighed. "Rita had the biggest crush on Mike."

Sadie cocked her head to one side. "She mentioned that. I'd completely forgotten. Do you remember Ty Zinfeld?"

"Sure. He was the guy who got fired. Mike was going to replace him in the movie."

"Right. Rita said he and Mike weren't on the best of terms when Ty left."

Roz frowned. "Really? I thought they got along all right. And it wasn't Mike's fault that Ty was fired. Mr. Monahan got angry about something Ty had done."

"J. B. Monahan," Sadie mused.

"Yeah. He went on to make some blockbuster films. Not like the one they made here."

"Well, *Stranger from a Strange World* wasn't exactly a flop, was it?"

"To be honest, I didn't keep track. They say it has a huge cult following among teenagers now."

"Yeah, like it's the campy old sci-fi movie they all think is so quaint-chic."

"Something like that," Roz said. "I guess that's why they're remaking it."

"Walk to the bank with me?" Sadie asked.

"Sure. Then I'll go meet Roscoe. He should be closing up too."

They went out, and Sadie locked the door. Traffic seemed a little heavier than usual on Main Street, and the parking lots at the eateries were full. They crossed the street, and Sadie dropped the bank bag into the deposit slot on the wall of the Silver Peak Bank.

"Man, I've seen license plates from four different states just in the last minute," Roz said as they hurried across to the hardware store.

Roscoe hadn't locked the door yet, and they went in. He stood behind the counter, cashing up a late customer's order.

"Hello. Be right with you," he called with a smile.

Roz elbowed Sadie. "He's in a good mood. He must have had a good day too."

Roz had stopped at the end of an aisle that contained a row of bins. Each bin held a different size of nails, screws, nuts, or bolts.

"Oh, that reminds me." Sadie dug her hand into the pocket of her jeans. "I wanted to ask Roscoe about this." She held up the bolt she had picked up during their ride.

Roscoe walked his customer to the door, chatting all the way.

"'Bye, Jim."

"See you soon," the customer said as he went out.

Roscoe shut the door and turned the lock. As he flipped the open sign to closed, he called over his shoulder, "Was your place as busy as mine today, Sadie?"

"We had quite a rush this afternoon."

He walked back toward them. "I got two big orders for building materials, and the movie producer called to see if I could provide some basic stuff for the sets they'll be building."

"That's great," Roz said.

"Yeah. They're bringing some specialty items, like signs for fictional businesses, but they wanted to make sure they could get studs and plywood and things like that here. Good thing I got that big shipment last week." He went behind the counter and opened the cash drawer.

"Can I ask you about something, before you start cashing up?" Sadie said.

"Sure."

She laid the bolt on the counter. "What can you tell me about that?"

Roscoe picked it up and held it about eight inches from his face. "Standard-size bolt—quarter inch. We stock them. People use them a lot."

"So it's very common."

"Sure. I've got a whole bin full over there." He pointed toward the row Sadie had noticed earlier.

"Has it been used?" she asked.

He held it up again and squinted at it. "I can't tell. If it has, it's not scratched up or anything like that. What's it from?"

"I found it on the ground," Sadie said.

"Somebody dropped it."

"Probably."

Roscoe shrugged. "I can toss it back in the bin and resell it. If anyone comes in and says they're one short, I'll give them one."

"Thanks, but it might not have come from here."

"True enough," Roscoe said.

"I'm going to hang on to it for now." Sadie took it from him and put it in her pocket.

Roz eyed her closely. "What's this about, Sadie? You don't usually run around carrying hardware in your pocket."

"I found it on Milo's land. Remember I told you how Edwin and I saw some strange lights out there Saturday night?"

"Yeah," Roz said. "Do you think that bolt has something to do with it?"

"I don't know, but as Roscoe said, it's fairly new, and Milo says he didn't put it there."

"So your UFO wasn't a figment of your imagination," Roz said. "That's concrete evidence for you that something was really out there."

"Only if I can find out how it got there, but yeah."

Roscoe chuckled. "Good luck with that. I heard someone else say they saw odd lights that night. Nobody could say what it was, though."

"Who was that?" Sadie asked.

Roscoe gritted his teeth for a moment. "I can't remember. A lot of people have come through here in the last couple of days."

"It's okay," Sadie said. "Mac told me that Ben Armstrong saw it, and I plan to compare notes with him. I'm wondering if anyone else saw something Edwin and I didn't."

"If it really was on Milo's land, you were probably the closest ones to see it," Roz said.

"Could be." Sadie smiled at them. "Well, I'll get on home. I think I'll do a little research on hardware and Saturday night's weather."

"Maybe you should do a little digging on Ty Zinfeld too," Roz said.

"Who's Ty Zinfeld?" Roscoe asked.

Roz squared her shoulders. "He was the young man who was fired from the movie. My brother was going to have his part after Ty was fired."

"Oh." Roscoe gazed at her for a moment, and Sadie wondered how he was taking all this—the impending arrival of the film crew and its effect on Roz. Roscoe had been nowhere near Silver Peak when Mike Tabor died, and he hadn't seen the frenzy that had descended on the town with the filmmakers. "Do you think he had something to do with Mike's death?" he asked.

Roz huffed out a breath. "Not really. Oh, I don't know. I just want to know more. I want to know what really happened."

Sadie patted her shoulder. "If there's anything out there to find, sweetie, we'll find it."

5

SADIE SPENT THE EVENING AT HER COMPUTER. AS SHE HAD
promised Roz, she tried first to find some information about Ty
Zinfeld, but the lack of hits on her searches discouraged her. Surely
if this man had continued his acting career, something would pop
up. It occurred to her that Ty Zinfeld might not be his real name.
It could be his screen name, or he could have changed it to something else after J. B. Monahan fired him, hoping that disassociat-
ing from the incident would help his career.

She gave up her search after a while and turned instead to
data she could verify. She checked the weather from the previous
weekend on a historical weather site. As she had expected, the site
confirmed that Saturday evening had been cloudy in the area, but
with no measurable precipitation.

Out of curiosity, she looked up the weather for the summer of
1965. As closely as she could, she pinpointed the week of Mike's death.
Vaguely, she remembered the film crew losing a few days of outdoor
shooting because of rain. Sure enough, within the week leading up
to the accident, rain had fallen on four days, two of them heavy rain.

Satellite photos of the bluff and the area below the cliff face surprised her. They showed every stark detail of the terrain, leaving

her with the feeling that there was no such thing as privacy left. But nothing in the images put up any red flags for her. It looked peaceful. Rugged but beautiful. The photos were a couple of years old, she noted. Had the landscape changed at all in the past fifty years?

She wondered whether any of the scenes had been filmed at night. What phase had the moon been in? That was easy to find out, but was it important? She wished she had paid more attention to the film and at least viewed it. Maybe she ought to take Alice's advice to Theo, and watch it on her computer. She connected to a site where she could stream vintage movies. Sure enough, it was listed.

After fixing herself a bowl of popcorn and a cup of tea, she settled down to watch *Stranger from a Strange World*. On the small screen, Sadie couldn't pick out a lot of detail, but the opera house and the courthouse jumped out at her in panoramic shots of Main Street. Some of the other buildings had been renovated since the filming. A few had signs for businesses that she didn't think had ever existed in Silver Peak. An interior restaurant scene was definitely filmed in what was now Flap Jack's, but it bore a sign that said "Annie's." What was now Putnam's Hardware appeared to be a clothing store in the film. She instantly recognized the outside of a house portrayed as a main character's home as one of the proud Victorians on Jefferson Avenue, near Edwin's home.

As to people, a few of the major players were actors she had seen in other films, but a lot of the faces were unknown to her. In a street scene, she was startled to see a brief close-up of a woman she was certain was a young Judith Marley, who would have been about twenty-seven at the time. Judith must have gotten a spot as an extra. Sadie made a note of that. Judith might be a good one to talk to about the old film.

Sadie was mildly surprised that the story, though it seemed a little corny, kept her interest. She wasn't big on science-fiction films. Maybe it was the familiar setting, and the excitement of recognizing people and vistas, or the puzzle of trying to work out exactly where each scene was filmed, that kept her riveted to the screen.

She paid special attention to a scene that showed a spaceship hovering over the bluff, with distant mountain peaks in the background. It was a daytime shot, but very effective. Sadie noted that a couple of the actors seemed to move quite close to the cliff as they tried to get a better view of the spacecraft, while most people shrank and ran from it. The spot was definitely the one where Milo had taken them on their ride.

Of course, the locations were all mixed up in the film. The main character got in his car to drive to the courthouse, when in real life it was only a block and a half and easily walked. Milo's property, where the spaceship scene was shot, was really a couple of miles out of town. The bluff lay half a mile up the mountain from Milo's house, but in the movie it seemed just yards from the center of town.

She noted the actor playing the sheriff—no one she recognized. That must be the young man who finally replaced Mike in the role.

At the end of the story, the credits rolled, and she jotted down a few of the names. Most of the people had probably passed away, but a few might still be living. She looked up the actor who had played the sheriff and found he had also had bit roles in several other films, but he never became a big star. She was growing tired, so after a quick perusal of the long list of impressive films

J. B. Monahan had directed after *Stranger from a Strange World*, she decided to turn in.

The movie tech crew was scheduled to arrive in Silver Peak tomorrow, and she had a feeling Main Street would be swarming with people who hoped to get a peek at anyone connected to the production. Edwin had invited her to lunch, and Sadie had jokingly said they might need a reservation in order to get a table.

Her prediction proved not far from the truth. The Depot was crowded when they arrived, and several of the diners were out-of-towners. Sadie spotted Edwin drinking coffee at a table in the far corner and hurried to join him.

"Wow! Imagine what it will be like when the actors get here." She sat down next to him, so they wouldn't have to shout across the table to be heard. The buzz of conversation was louder than usual in the old railroad station–turned–restaurant.

"I guess it will be worth it, if all the businesses in town have a bumper year," Edwin said with a smile. "I love it when Main Street is buzzing."

"I know what you mean. So how're things?" Sadie asked.

"Great. Noelle and Carl are coming into Denver tomorrow. I'll be driving over to get them at the airport. Can't wait to see Sam too."

Sadie smiled. Edwin seldom got to visit with his little grandson. "I'm blessed to have Sara and Theo so close. I know you and Sam will have a great time together."

A waitress arrived at the table, and Sadie smiled up at her. "Hi. Have you got plenty of spaghetti today?"

"Always," the young woman replied.

"That's what I'll have, and water," Sadie said.

"The same for me," Edwin added.

"Coming right up."

From the next table, Wade Marley called, "Hey, mayor, big doings in town."

"Yes," Edwin replied. "This must be a good week for you, Wade."

He nodded. "Every one of my vacation rentals is booked for the film crew and actors, and I hear the B and B is full too."

"That's the way we like it," Edwin said. He turned back to Sadie. "By the way, I spoke to Troy Haggarty this morning. He seemed to appreciate the sensitivity of the situation. He agreed not to print anything about Mike Tabor's death unless it came up from another source."

"Well, that's something, I suppose," Sadie said.

Edwin nodded. "I'm sure he won't sensationalize it. He's a reasonable young man, and he doesn't want to cause anyone distress."

The waitress came back with their water and a basket of breadsticks.

Edwin turned back to Sadie and reached for the basket. "Breadstick?"

"Thanks." Sadie loved the garlicky flavor. "I'll have to douse myself with mouthwash before I go back to waiting on customers, but I can never resist these."

"I guess the crew will be busy setting up the scenes for filming," Edwin said. "The director and the actors are supposed to arrive this weekend and start filming on Monday."

Sadie swallowed and said, "What exactly will they be doing in town? Roscoe said something about fake signs for stores, things like that."

"Yeah, I understand they want to film at Flap Jack's, but they'll call it something else, and the bank and outside City Hall. I'm not sure where else."

"Surely the opera house will be in it."

"Oh yes, of course," Edwin assured her.

"Should be interesting. I was sure I saw the interior of Flap Jack's in the old movie."

"You've seen it, then?"

"Yeah, I finally buckled down and watched it last night," Sadie said. "It was kind of fun, seeing all the spots around town, and a few familiar faces. Odd that it's all going to happen again this summer."

"It could get to be a pain, I suppose, with all the Hollywood people in town," Edwin said, breaking his breadstick in half, "but we can put up with it for a few weeks. When they're filming downtown, we'll have to ask most people to park on side streets, so that Main is clear for whatever they want to do."

"I hope people don't complain too much," Sadie said.

Edwin shrugged. "Most of them are glad we have this opportunity."

Milo Henderson came in just as their food arrived, and Sadie waved to him. He wove between the tables to theirs.

"Hi, Milo," Edwin said with a glance around the crowded dining area. "Would you like to join us? Tables seem to be at a premium today."

"Thanks." Milo sat down. "I'm meeting some of the movie people at one and taking them out to my place so they can mark off the areas where they'll be filming."

"That's exciting," Sadie said with a smile.

Milo, deadpan as usual, said, "I suppose, if you like extraterrestrials and Hollywood types."

"Personally, I love them," Edwin said, winking at Sadie.

"Now, Milo, don't pretend this isn't a bonus for you." Sadie laid a cajoling hand on his sleeve. "Just think how many sacks of oats their fee will pay for."

"That's true. And I'm charging them plenty, in case they tear up the ground or knock down fences or something." He frowned at Sadie. "Did you find out any more about those lights?"

"Not really," she said. "Edwin and I agree that whatever it was had to be too large for a remote-control toy."

Edwin nodded. "Sadie told me about the tire tracks you found. Do you think something was hauled out to your back field on a trailer and launched from there?"

"Could be," Milo said. "But what it was or why, we can't seem to find out."

Edwin's thick eyebrows drew down over his twinkly blue eyes. "I've heard that some real estate agents use drones to take aerial photos of property they plan to sell."

"Real estate agents?" Milo scowled at him. "They'd better not be doing that on my property. My land is not for sale."

———

Tourists flooded the Antique Mine on Friday afternoon. Julie and Sadie bustled about helping one customer after another. Edwin's call at quarter to five slowed Sadie down for a minute.

"Did the travelers get in safely?" she asked.

"They're here," Edwin said. "We just got home. Noelle and Carl are getting settled, and I'm going to light the grill. Come join us for supper?"

"Oh, are you sure you want that?" Sadie asked.

"Of course. Come any time. They're on Eastern Time, so they're getting hungry."

"Well…" Sadie looked around the shop, which was still crowded. "I don't know if I can get away for a bit. We're pretty busy. How about if I have dessert with you?"

"You sure?"

She smiled at a woman who had come to the counter with several items she wanted to pay for. "Yeah, go ahead and eat," Sadie said. "I'll get there by seven. I promise."

She was glad she had made that decision when five o'clock passed and a dozen shoppers still lingered. She and Julie patiently waited on the buyers, and they saw the last one out the door at half past five.

"Wow, what a day," Julie said, turning the dead bolt on the door.

"You go on home," Sadie told her. "I'll cash up and drop off the deposit."

"Let me at least do a little straightening up." Julie picked up a basket of items that shoppers had changed their minds about and left at the counter.

"Would you rather come in early tomorrow?" Sadie asked.

Julie hesitated. "I can if you want. You did say you were supposed to go over to Edwin's tonight, didn't you?"

"Yes, and I'd like to run home and get a shower and change first." Sadie pushed back an annoying strand of her salt-and-pepper hair.

"You talked me into it." Julie set down the basket. "I'll see you here at eight thirty in the morning. Deal?"

"Deal." Her assistant usually arrived half an hour or so before Sadie opened at ten, but this arrangement would give them plenty of time to prepare for another onslaught of customers.

Sadie finished her accounting and dropped off her bank deposit, then drove home. Hank greeted her at the door, and she could tell he was eager for some playtime.

"Sorry, boy. I've got to run out on you tonight."

Hank barked and gazed at her so hopefully that Sadie laughed.

"All right, we'll play ball for ten minutes."

After their short session of fetch, she let Hank run loose in the yard while she made herself a cold-cut sandwich. She called him in and gave him fresh water and food, then went upstairs to get rid of the day's grime.

She rang Edwin's doorbell at ten to seven, and he flung it open.

"Hi! Come on in." He kissed her cheek. "We're out back. It's such a nice evening, I thought I'd serve the cake out there."

Edwin looked well-groomed and handsome, but casual in Dockers, a polo shirt, and loafers. Sadie followed him through the stately Victorian house's entrance hall, into the gleaming kitchen. He had modernized it when he moved back to Silver Peak, and Sadie was sure Noelle must have been impressed when she saw what her father had done with the lovely old home.

On the kitchen counter was a plastic cake container from a bakery, and she recognized the confection right away.

"Oh, you got one of Maggie's coconut cakes."

"Yes, they're always well-received."

"And how." Sadie held out a plastic container. "I brought you some soft oatmeal cookies, from my freezer. I figured with a boy in the house, you can't have too many cookies on hand."

Edwin laughed. "Thanks. I'm sure Sam will appreciate those, and I can vouch for how good they are."

They went out the back door onto the rear part of the wrap-around porch. Noelle, a slender woman with a dark bob, and her husband, Carl, both in their midthirties, sat in wicker chairs, while their little boy played on the deck with some plastic action figures. The adults stood as Sadie and Edwin came from the house.

"Hello," Noelle said, stepping forward.

"Hi, Noelle. So good to see you again." Sadie smiled and hugged her. Noelle had striking features. She was tall like her father, but more willowy in build. Her large brown eyes and high cheekbones must have been inherited from her mother, but Sadie saw a hint of Edwin's strong jaw.

"And Carl." Sadie hugged the sandy-haired young man. "I know Edwin is delighted to have you all here."

"We're glad we could come," Carl said.

"Sam," Edwin called to the boy.

He got up and came to his grandfather's side with a toy in his hand.

"Sam, do you remember Mrs. Speers? She's my good friend."

Sam looked up at her doubtfully.

Sadie bent down and smiled at Sam. "It's been a while, and you've gotten so big since the last time I saw you. You can call me Sadie, if your mom and dad don't mind."

Sam looked to his father, and Carl nodded.

Sam turned back to Sadie. "I'm five. Do you like astronauts?"

"Uh, well, I don't know any personally, but yes, I think space travel and the stars and planets are interesting subjects."

Edwin chuckled. "He's a future rocket scientist."

"Sam's crazy about astronomy and space travel," Noelle said, almost apologetically. "I'm told young boys often fixate on one area of interest for a while."

"For me, it was dinosaurs," Carl said with a laugh.

"I like what Dad's done with the house," Noelle said.

"Yeah, my friend Julie helped him a little. I love what he's done with it too."

"Some of the new things he's got are great," Noelle said. "The framed prints in our bedroom are fantastic—and the wallpaper in the kitchen."

"I like that too," Sadie said.

"How's everything going at the antique store?" Noelle asked.

"It's going very well, thank you." Sadie did not volunteer that several of Edwin's decorative pieces came from the Antique Mine. "The place suits me—I've always been interested in the past."

"You might remember that Sadie's a former history teacher, and she's very well-versed in local history," Edwin said, and Noelle nodded. "Noelle, would you mind cutting the cake? I'll get coffee for everyone."

"Sure."

"Let me help," Sadie offered Edwin.

As they entered the house, Edwin drew her aside.

"Noelle has been after me already to move back East, closer to them. She isn't too keen on my staying here in what she thinks of as 'the sticks.' I listed you as one of the attractions for me here, and I'm afraid she wasn't too pleased. I'm starting to wonder if her mission in coming out here was to talk me into moving closer to them. Please don't take it personally."

"I'll try not to. Thanks for the heads-up."

When Sadie went back out on the porch, she walked over to where Noelle was removing the lid from the cake plate. "Shall I get the forks and napkins?"

"That would be fine, thank you," Noelle said.

The three of them soon had the dessert served, and they all settled at the glass-topped table on the back porch to enjoy it. Noelle allowed Sam to put his plate and glass of milk down on the floor so that he could continue to play while he ate.

"You've got a beautiful view off the back porch here," Carl said, looking out toward the mountains. "It must have been great, growing up here."

"It was," Edwin replied, "though I'm afraid I took it for granted as a youngster. I didn't realize how much I missed the mountains and the open spaces until I came home again."

Noelle eyed him soberly. "It is lovely, Dad, but you're so far away from everything."

Edwin laughed. "What's 'everything'? There's a lot going on here in Silver Peak."

"Oh, sure, you've got the movie people coming. That's exciting, but after it's over this will be like a ghost town again."

"Oh no," Edwin said. "We may be a ways from the city, but we're a popular spot in the summertime, aren't we, Sadie?"

"We do get a lot of tourists up here," Sadie said. "The opera house events draw in a lot."

"As do the antiques," Edwin put in, nodding at her meaningfully.

Sadie smiled at him. "Well, yes, we do get a lot of people looking for antiques, but the beautiful setting itself is a big attraction."

Noelle gave a little chuckle. "I must say that for overall quaint-
ness, the town gets high marks. As for antiques, nothing in the
West is more than two hundred years old."

"That's not quite fair, honey," Carl said. "People did bring
older furniture with them when they came West."

"I suppose." Noelle turned eagerly to Sadie. "When we visited
New York last fall, I found a four-hundred-year-old French break-
front for our dining room. You don't have many great shopping
opportunities here, or much of a night life either."

"Personally speaking, I have all the night life I can stand."
Edwin stood. "I'm going to top off my coffee. Anyone else want
more?"

"I'd take a little," Sadie said.

"I'll bring the pot out." Edwin headed inside.

Noelle eyed Sadie soberly across the table. "I'm not sure Dad
ought to bury himself in a place like this."

"What do you mean?" Sadie asked. "He loves it here."

"I know, but he has so much to offer. He could have gone into
politics, you know."

Sadie almost choked. She was glad Carl jumped in before she
had a chance to frame an answer.

"He *is* in politics, dear. Your father is the mayor of this town
now."

"Yes, and he's doing a marvelous job." Sadie beamed at Carl.

Noelle gave what sounded like a quiet snort. "It was bad
enough when he told me he was moving back to Colorado, but
then he had to run for mayor."

"What's wrong with that?" Carl said mildly.

Noelle shrugged. "It means he'll stay here a while. I could see him settling in Denver, maybe, but Silver Peak? He's got to be outside every loop anyone's ever heard of."

"I don't know about that," Sadie said. "He keeps up with a lot of his old colleagues. And he does seem happy." As Edwin came through the doorway, holding up the coffee carafe, she decided it was time for a new topic. "By the way, Noelle, your necklace is absolutely lovely. Isn't that an art deco piece? It looks like René Boivin's style."

Noelle put a hand to her throat and blinked at her. "Why, yes. I found it in a shop in Atlanta, and Carl bought it for me as an anniversary present."

Sadie nodded. "I don't keep a very large stock of jewelry at the Antique Mine, but once in a while I get something special. I had one of Boivin's brooches last year, but it didn't stay in my display case long."

"Perhaps I'll have to stop by your shop." Noelle held up her cup so Edwin could refill it.

"Would love to have you," Sadie said. *Wouldn't she just!*

Sam came over to the table and held up one of his action figures. "This is Neko. He's really smart. He speaks seven alien languages."

Sadie took the plastic figure and examined it. Red and black from head to toe, Neko looked like a perfectly normal human figure, except that he had three eyes.

"Does the extra eye help him with his reading?" she asked.

Sam nodded. "He reads extrafast because of it."

"I see. And does he speak any earth languages?"

Sam frowned for a moment and then grinned up at her. "I think so, because he talks to me."

"Ah, so he can at least communicate in English."

Sam nodded and held the little figure close to his chest.

"Did you finish your cake, Sam?" Carl asked.

"Uh-huh. Can I watch a video?"

Edwin darted a glance at Noelle. "I can set up a DVD for him if you want."

"He can watch it on my tablet." She pushed her chair back and stood. "Come on, Sam. I saw you yawning a minute ago. One short cartoon, and then it's off to bed."

"In Atlanta time, it's already way past your bedtime," Carl added as Noelle shepherded Sam inside the house. He bent down to retrieve Sam's dishes and set them on the table. "I'd just as soon we weaned him off the cartoons, but it may be too late for that. I'm afraid the sitter lets him watch far too many while we're at work."

"We have lots of things he'd enjoy doing here," Sadie said. "Maybe he'd like to meet my golden retriever, Hank, and my granddaughter's pets."

"I'm sure he would," Carl said. "He doesn't get to be around animals much, although we did take him to the zoo last month."

"We could take him over to Milo's to see the horses one day," Edwin said, brightening.

"Oh yes. He could even have a ride on one of the gentle horses, I'm sure." Sadie turned to Carl. "This is a perfect opportunity to introduce Sam to small-town life."

Carl glanced toward the door and lowered his voice. "I just wish Noelle was more open to it."

"Not thinking of leaving Atlanta, are you?" Edwin asked.

"No, our jobs are there, and Noelle will always want to live in the city, I'm afraid. But I think we all could use a dose of the slow lane."

Edwin chuckled. "You've come to the right place. The longer I'm here, the more I love it."

Later that evening, Sadie arrived home worn-out. She took Hank out for a quick run and then headed upstairs. Her phone rang, and she was surprised to see Edwin's name on the screen.

"Hey, what's up?" she asked.

"Not much. The guests have retired, and I thought I'd check in with you. What did you think?"

"I had a nice time. Noelle has obviously missed you. Carl was his usual charming self. Sam is just adorable."

"Okay, yeah. What did you *really* think?"

Sadie hesitated. "Edwin, I wouldn't be dishonest with you. I did sense that Noelle was a little uncomfortable with your move here, and I also think she may be a bit uneasy about our relationship, if that's what you're getting at."

"It was." He sighed. "I'm sorry, Sadie. I'm sure she'll come around."

"Sure," Sadie said. "We'll give it some time."

"Noelle isn't really a snob," he insisted.

"I get that. She just isn't sure this is what's best for her dad. And like I said, she misses you. I think you're right that she hoped you'd consider moving closer to them."

"Well, she wasn't happy when I moved back here. I know that, and I get it. She's never lived in a rural area, and that's my fault. She's always been opinionated too. I admit I encouraged her to form her own thoughts and stand by them. But this time our opinions differ."

"I'm sure you can give her a glimpse of what you love here," Sadie said. "It's too bad they missed the play at the opera house. Maybe there'll be something in Breckenridge next weekend."

"I'll check. I wouldn't be opposed to driving all the way to Denver for something special, but that would sort of defeat the purpose. I mean, I want her to see that we do have plenty going on here to keep me busy without continually running into the city."

"Well, it would show her you're not so far from the hubbub that you can't get to it if you want to. But I think you're right. She needs to see that you don't need all that."

"She seemed a little dazzled when I told her Fox Monahan is coming here soon."

"Who's that?" Sadie asked.

"The movie director. His father, J. B. Monahan, directed the original picture, and Fox is doing the new version."

"Oh, sure," Sadie said. "I didn't realize J.B.'s son was directing the new film."

"Yes, apparently *People* magazine did a feature on it, and Noelle saw it."

"Maybe she'll get to meet them," Sadie suggested. "After all, she is staying at the mayor's home."

"I wouldn't be at all surprised." Edwin chuckled. "She's trying to act blasé about the whole movie thing, but Carl told me confidentially that she loves the leading man, Jason Singer, and she'll watch any picture with him in it."

"*Hmm*, that's a bit of information that might work in your favor, Mr. Mayor."

"You never know. Thanks for cheering me up, Sadie."

"Anytime."

"Well, I don't just want to impress her with the town, you know. I'd like her to see how wonderful you are too."

Sadie laughed. "Clue me in when you figure out how to do that, will you?"

6

TRUE TO HER WORD, JULIE ARRIVED AT THE STORE EARLY ON
Saturday. She and Sadie took extra care to make sure the displays
were spotless, and they rearranged a few areas to highlight some
of the rarer pieces.

"Think those Hollywood people will buy much?" Julie asked.

"I don't know," Sadie replied, struggling to straighten a framed
Yul Brynner poster. "I admit, Edwin's daughter has me a little on
edge. Noelle can be very nice, but she's trying to convince her dad
that small-town life isn't for him."

"Oh?"

Sadie nodded. "Afraid so. And if she comes in here, I don't
want her to find anything she can criticize. Is this straight now?"

"No, it's a hair lower on the right."

Sadie sighed. "This thing just wants to hang crooked."

"Want me to get the level?" Julie asked.

They managed to fix it, and Sadie stepped back to survey the
wall. "There. We don't have much movie memorabilia, so let's
think about what else they'd like. Oh, I want to take a look at the
jewelry too. We still have some retro pieces, and I might spotlight
them."

"Because of when the movie was made?"

Sadie shook her head. "Actually, it's Noelle Carson I was thinking of. She was wearing a gorgeous art deco necklace last night. If we have anything that might appeal to her, it might be something from the same era."

"Well, people's tastes are so individual," Julie said. "But you do have that nice bracelet with the square-cut links. Isn't that from the 1920s?"

"Yes. That's a good one to feature. I'll move it to the middle of the display."

Shortly after they opened, a young woman with shoulder-length blonde hair came in with a much older woman whose gray locks were cut short.

"Oh, look," the blonde cried. "Don't you love this old teapot? My nana had one almost like it."

"It's cute," the older woman said, stepping toward a cluster of kitchen tools. "I like this old chopper myself. I collect utensils with the old green paint on the handles."

"That's part of the fun of going on location," the blonde replied. "We get to see little shops we wouldn't find otherwise."

"Are you with the movie crew?" Sadie asked, stepping forward.

"Yes, we are," the gray-haired woman said with a smile. "We don't actually start work until Monday, but Mr. Monahan said we could come up here anytime this weekend and get settled."

"Great. And welcome. I'm Sadie Speers."

Julie came to her side. "Sadie has lived here all her life, and she remembers when the first version of the film was made."

"Really? I'm Glee Rossignol, and I was with the crew in 1965." The woman held out her hand. "I'm pleased to meet you, Sadie."

"Were you really here then?" Sadie felt an unexpected warmth, as though she had reconnected with an old friend, although she didn't remember Glee. "Were you in the cast?"

"No, I'm just the script girl. Same job I held fifty years ago. Crazy, isn't it? I was twenty-two then. Oops." She smiled. "Guess I gave away my age, but who's counting?"

Sadie chuckled. "I won't tell anyone."

"Thanks, honey." Glee looked around and sighed. "Getting to come back here is a real nostalgic journey for me."

"You must be good at your job," Julie said.

She laughed. "I was pretty good at it. J. B. Monahan asked his son to hire me for this production just for old times' sake. I retired several years ago, but J.B. and I go way back. He's looked out for me over the years and made sure plenty of work came my way. We were talking a couple of months ago, and he mentioned this project. Asked if I'd like to be in on it, and I jumped at the chance. Besides"—she winked at Julie—"I wasn't going to turn down a well-paying job and a couple of weeks in the mountains. This has to be the prettiest town in the world."

"Well, thank you," Sadie said. "I happen to agree."

A trio of women entered the store, and Julie went to help them. Sadie said to Glee, "May I ask you about someone who was connected to the picture fifty years ago?"

"Sure."

"Do you remember the boy who fell from the cliff during the filming—Mike Tabor?"

Glee's face darkened. "Oh my, yes. That was such an awful thing. I expect the people here were very upset by it. We all were, but we didn't know the boy personally, of course."

"My best friend is his sister," Sadie said. "I didn't ask to make you sad, but I'm trying to learn what I can about what happened that day."

"So far as I know, he tripped and fell, and he was too close to the edge," Glee said. "I didn't actually see it happen."

Sadie nodded. "What about Ty Zinfeld, the actor Mike had replaced?"

"*Hmm*, let's see." Glee frowned. "Mr. Monahan let him go, didn't he?"

"Yes, I'm told the director was angry about something and fired Ty."

"I don't recall the details," Glee said. "I'm sorry."

"It's all right," Sadie assured her. "I just thought I'd ask, since you were there." She picked up the vegetable chopper Glee had admired. "Let me give you this as a welcome present."

"Oh no, I couldn't let you do that," Glee said. "You need to meet your costs on what you sell."

"Really," Sadie insisted. "I'd like to give it to you. It's such a pleasure connecting with somebody from the old days. Please."

A smile teased at Glee's lips. "In that case, I want this potato masher too. They go together perfectly. But I'm paying for that."

Sadie laughed. "All right. I'll hold these for you at the counter. Please take your time browsing with your friend."

A few more members of the film crew ambled in during the day, and Sadie chatted with them all, revealing that she remembered the original production. They were all much too young to have been part of that project, but all had seen the old movie several times and were excited to be part of the new one. Sadie didn't see any point in bringing up Mike's accident, since none of them were there at the time.

Midway through the afternoon, Sadie came out of the back room, where she had snatched a few minutes to order some replacement hardware for a customer's antique dresser. Julie was helping a customer, and Sadie went to the counter.

A sheet of paper lay beside the old brass cash register. Sadie glanced at it and then leaned over to look more closely.

Stop investigating. Just say it was an accident.

The words were hand-printed in block letters, on a plain sheet of white memo paper. As Julie and her customer approached, Sadie slid it onto a shelf under the counter and greeted the woman with a smile.

When the door had closed behind the contented buyer, Sadie called Julie over and took out the note she had found.

"Julie, do you know where this came from?" She laid it on top of the glass case of jewelry and other small items.

Julie's eyes widened as she surveyed the note. "Good grief, no!"

"It was sitting right here next to the cash register," Sadie said.

"When?"

"Just a few minutes ago."

Julie shook her head slowly. "Several people came in while you were in the back." She looked around the store. "In fact, there are still a couple of people looking at dishes and books. I guess anybody could have put it there."

"This is from someone who knows me, though." Sadie frowned. *How many people knew she was looking into Mike's death for her friend?* "Did anyone from town come in within the last hour or so?"

"Not that I saw, but I'll admit, I wasn't always watching the door. I'm sorry, Sadie."

"It's okay."

"It's kind of creepy," Julie said.

"A little."

"Do you think you should show it to Mac?"

Sadie considered the words and the tone of the note. "It's not exactly threatening. I'll think about it. But let me know if anything else odd turns up."

"You can count on it."

———

That evening, Sadie phoned Rita.

"I won't keep you long," she said, "but I've been thinking about something you told me the other day. Remember, we were talking about the fellow Mike Tabor replaced in the movie?"

"Yeah."

"Well, you said Ty Zinfeld was mean to Mike after he was fired. Did he stay in Silver Peak after that?"

"Oh no. He left right away," Rita said.

"So he wouldn't have been here when Mike fell?"

"He was gone long before the accident. I'm sure he left immediately after Mr. Monahan fired him."

"So when you said he was mean to Mike…"

"I just meant he said something nasty. He didn't hang around long at all. I would have remembered."

Rita sounded so positive that Sadie decided she could take her word for it. When they had finished talking, she again turned to her computer for information about Ty Zinfeld. Her first efforts had failed, but perhaps she hadn't tried hard enough.

"Maybe Ty is short for something else," she said to herself. She typed in "Tyler Zinfeld," and a couple of hits came up, but after scanning them, she decided they didn't have to do with the actor, who would now be in his early seventies.

At Campfire Chapel the next morning, Edwin and his family were nowhere to be found during the Sunday school hour. Before the worship service, however, Edwin came in leading Sam by the hand. They stopped at the end of the pew where Sadie sat with Alice and her grandchildren.

"May we sit with you?"

"Of course." Sadie moved over, and Edwin sat down on the aisle, with Sam between them.

"Good morning, Sam," Sadie said.

The little boy, clutching a plastic astronaut in his silver space suit and helmet, grinned up at her. "Hello, Miss Sadie."

Edwin leaned over Sam's head and whispered, "I couldn't pry Noelle out of bed this morning. She says she's still jet-lagged and has a headache."

"Well, they say it takes a full day for each time zone you cross," Sadie replied. "And maybe it's the elevation here. Altitude sickness."

Edwin's eyebrows arched. "Maybe. She does get headaches, I know. Carl offered to stay with her, though I thought she'd be fine on her own for an hour."

Sadie reached over and patted his hand. "Don't fret about it."

Sara, who sat on Sadie's other side, leaned forward and spoke to Sam. "Hey there, Sam. Are you having fun at your grandpa's?"

Edwin's characteristic smile blossomed. "Sam, do you remember Miss Sadie's granddaughter, Sara?"

"Hi," Sam said, eyeing Sara cautiously. "Sara has her own horse," Edwin added, putting great importance into the words.

Sam's eyes gleamed. "Really? Is he big?"

"Pretty big," Sara said. "And it's a she."

"Is she wild?"

"No, not at all. Maybe you'll get to see her if you stick around a few days."

Sam nodded.

The music leader rose for the first worship song, and Sara sat back. "He's adorable," she whispered to Sadie.

Sam sat quietly through most of the service. If his antics with the spaceman got too vigorous, Edwin reached over and laid a gentle hand on his sleeve. When the service ended, they all gathered their things and stood.

"I'd ask you to dinner," Edwin said apologetically, "but for all I know, Noelle is still in bed."

"Don't worry about it," Sadie said. "I'm heading over to Alice's today. I hope Noelle feels better and can enjoy the rest of this gorgeous day." She stooped so she could look Sam in the eye. "Great seeing you again, Sam."

He smiled and ducked his head.

"I'm sure we'll see you again soon," Edwin told her.

———

Julie arrived at the store Monday morning just as Sadie was unlocking the door.

"Whew! What a rush at Arbuckle's," she said, nodding toward the coffee shop next door.

"Well, those Hollywood types must have their coffee, you know," Sadie said. "Of course, a lot of us natives do too."

"They'll find the brew at Arbuckle's as good as anything they can get in LA, I'm sure." Julie followed her inside and shut the door.

Sadie laid her purse and laptop case on the counter. "If this flurry of activity means the actors have arrived, we'd better look sharp."

"They'll be busy all day, won't they?" Julie asked.

"Maybe. I'll bet they're just getting settled today, though. I don't think the director was going to arrive until this morning, so I doubt they'll begin actual shooting today."

"You may be right. He might want to look over the locations. So what shall we do first?"

The sound of a large vehicle braking outside drew Sadie's attention to the front window. "There's the parcel man. I hope he's delivering some things I ordered online. Let's take care of that first. We may want to change some of the displays."

"I love it when we have new stock," Julie said with a smile. Her decorator's instincts were a big help in making each part of the store attractive. Sadie firmly believed that the way they presented their merchandise gave the customers ideas of how to use the pieces in their own homes. To her delight, the deliveryman brought several boxes in, and she signed for them.

"Now the fun begins," Julie said. "There's enough here to keep us busy all morning."

She was right. Even after they opened, one of them was kept busy unpacking and logging the new items while the other waited on customers, and between patrons they decided where each new piece should go. Sadie was especially happy with a collection of embroidered linens. She had several regular patrons who watched for fancywork textiles.

When Julie returned from her late lunch, she came over to Sadie with an air of suppressed excitement.

"The directors are here. I heard Fox Monahan and his father, J.B., are sharing one of Wade's vacation rentals."

"His father is actually here? Edwin told me he was expected, but I'm a little surprised that he came back. He's so famous now and everything."

"He sure is. Troy Haggarty is going to interview them both for the *Sentinel*. Just think of it. When he was here fifty years ago, J. B. Monahan was a young director hoping to have a hit. Now he's a multi-Oscar winner. He's a legend, like Steven Spielberg and... and Peter Jackson."

"I see," Sadie said judiciously. She would probably have said Frank Capra and Francis Ford Coppola, but she got the idea.

"Oh, and the producer has set up an arrangement with Lou and Maggie Price to provide light lunches on the set every day for the crew and actors."

"My goodness, you're a font of information. How did you learn all this?"

"I stopped by the Market," Julie said. "Maggie is all excited about it. She showed me a copy of the menu list she gave the producer. Those actors are going to eat well while they're here!"

"If Maggie's cooking, of course they are. Now, would you rather take the checkout or go help that lost-looking woman in the linens section?"

"Linens," Julie said decisively. "I'll bet I can sell her some of those things we just got in."

All afternoon, bits of information filtered into the Antique Mine. Friends and loyal customers came by to browse and share their news. The camera crew would set up on Main Street in the morning for some background shots and a scene with the fictional police chief and some of the prominent "citizens" of the movie's fictional town.

Marge Ruxton bustled in with an eager look in her eye.

"Sadie! Did you hear?"

"Hear what, Marge?" Sadie asked.

"The movie people are using Simon Riley's house on Jefferson Avenue for some of the interior scenes. They're actually paying him to move out for three days and give them full run of the house."

"That's interesting," Sadie said. She wasn't sure she would want to let strangers make themselves at home in her house. "Are they moving all their personal belongings out?"

"I don't think so. Mr. Fox Monahan looked at the house this morning and said he loved the interior decorations and the architectural details." Marge nodded as though pleased with herself for remembering the facts.

"Well, it's a beautiful house," Sadie admitted. "I hope the aliens like it."

Marge laughed. "But not too much. We wouldn't want Martians moving here permanently, now, would we?"

"Oh, I don't know. It might drive a lot more tourists here. Intergalactic ones, even."

When Marge left a few minutes later, Julie came over. "Did I hear Marge actually making a joke with you?"

"She seemed in high spirits today," Sadie said with a smile. "She also took a liking to that lap desk that the deliveryman brought this morning. I wouldn't be surprised if she came back for it."

Sara and Theo came to the shop a few minutes before closing. Sara's hazel eyes glittered with excitement.

"Grandma! We saw the movie people setting up at the ranch."

"Oh, really?" Sadie looked from Sara to Theo and back. "What were you doing out there?"

"Mom let us go riding. She said it was okay if Milo agreed. He just told us to stay back from where the movie people are working. They're setting things up for the scenes they're going to shoot on the mountain."

"We didn't try to get real close," Theo said, "but it was kind of neat."

"And we saw Fox Monahan!" Sara's grin was infectious, and Sadie found herself smiling too. "He's done some awesome movies."

"His father was the big cheese when I was your age," Sadie said.

"I guess he did a lot of classics." Sara seemed a little doubtful.

Theo eyed his sister critically and said to Sadie, "She's an infant."

"I see."

"Hey, Grandma, I've got a riddle for you. It's sort of related to the movie."

"Let's hear it." Sadie loved to banter with the kids, and they seldom disappointed her.

"Okay," Sara said. "What do you do if you see a spaceman?"

"*Hmm.*" Sadie rolled her eyes toward the pressed tin ceiling, trying to think of a snappy comeback. "Call the space patrol?"

"Nope." Sara grinned. "If you see a space, man, you park, man!"

Sadie laughed, but Theo let out a groan.

"That is *so* corny."

"The cornier the better," Sadie said.

"Oh, and guess what?" Sara said. "Fox Monahan ran over his father's luggage."

"What?" Sadie caught sight of a late shopper approaching the counter. "Excuse me for a minute while I help this woman, but I'm going to have to hear the rest of that story when I'm finished."

She went behind the cash register and greeted the woman. "I see you found the old mining tools."

The customer laid two gold pans, a bitters bottle, and a delicate glass basket on the counter. "My husband is going to be thrilled with these things. Well, the basket is for me."

Sadie laughed. "I'm glad you're treating yourself too."

As soon as the customer had left, she locked the door and went back to the counter.

"Okay, you two, spill it. What happened to Mr. Monahan's luggage?"

Theo laughed. "It was the craziest thing!"

"Let me tell it," Sara said.

"Why? You told about our ride up the mountain."

"So. I brought it up."

Theo sighed. "Go ahead."

Julie came over with the Dustbuster in her hand. "What's up?"

"Only the funniest thing you ever heard," Sara said. "Milo told us that when the movie people got out to the ranch, Mr. Fox Monahan went to get something out of the trunk of their rental car, and he set his dad's suitcase out on the ground and forgot to put it back in. So when he backed up to drive up the trail to the location site, he ran right over it."

Julie laughed.

"I'm guessing his father wasn't pleased," Sadie said.

"I'd say not," Theo put in. "He broke a bottle of aftershave in the suitcase, so now all of J.B.'s clothes smell."

Sara glared at him. "You stole my punch line."

Theo shrugged. "Wish I'd seen it happen."

Sara's lower lip pouted out. "Well, I'm just glad I didn't smell it."

7

THE PHONE AT THE STORE RANG SHORTLY AFTER LUNCH ON Tuesday.

"Sadie, it's Edwin." Julie handed her the receiver and took her place at the cash register.

"Hi," Sadie said. "What's up?"

"I wondered if you could drop by my office for a minute, or are you too busy?"

Sadie glanced around the shop. Julie was totaling one customer's order, and four others were browsing. "I guess I could come for a few minutes." She arched her eyebrows at Julie, who gave her a quick thumbs-up.

When she had ended the call, Sadie waited until Julie had finished with her customer and then said, "I think I'll call Alice and see if she can lend you a hand."

"No need," Julie said, but as she spoke, two women came through the door. "Well, maybe..."

Sadie smiled and hit Alice's speed-dial number. Her daughter was more than happy to put in some time at the store. Sadie left for the town hall confident that reinforcements for Julie would arrive within minutes.

Curious, she strode down the sidewalk wondering if Edwin was going to suggest an outing with Noelle and her family. But if that was his reason for calling, why hadn't he just asked her over the phone? Workers were placing sawhorses in the traffic lanes on Main Street, with signs directing them to detour for two blocks. The camera crew was setting up their dollies.

Sadie hurried up the steps and into the lobby of the town offices. The receptionist, Kaitlyn, smiled at Sadie. "Go right in. Mr. Marshall's expecting you."

Sadie tapped on the door to the mayor's office and opened it. To her surprise, two other men were inside, talking with Edwin. They all stood when she entered.

"There you are," Edwin said, smiling broadly. "I wanted to introduce you to J. B. Monahan and his son, Fox."

"How nice to meet you." Sadie stepped forward and took the older man's hand first. His eyes twinkled behind his bifocals, and his silver hair was still thick and lush.

"Mrs. Speers. Delighted to meet you."

"Thank you." Sadie almost laughed when she detected a whiff of his aftershave, but it wasn't overpowering, and she managed to control herself. "I think I got your autograph when you were in town fifty years ago."

"Oh heavens, really? Surely you're not that old."

"That's very kind of you," Sadie said. "I was in eighth grade, and my friends and I were autograph-crazy that summer."

His son stepped forward and extended his hand.

"Mr. Monahan," she said as she shook it.

"Glad to meet you, but please call me Fox. Otherwise, the confusion could get hilarious over the next couple of weeks."

"That's right," his father said. "I'm J.B. We're not junior and senior, though some folks like to try that out on us, and he may be 'Young Monahan,' but I don't like to be called 'Old Monahan.'"

Sadie chuckled. "All right then, and I'm Sadie."

"Edwin's told us about your store," Fox said. "If we need any period pieces for props, can we call on you?"

"Of course," Sadie said, "but I thought the new film was going to be set in the present."

"It is," Fox said. "We're going to have a couple of flashback scenes, though."

"I see. I'd be glad to give any help that I can."

J.B. said, "It's a lot of fun coming back up here after all these years. Of course, there are some bittersweet memories, but I think we'll make a good job of this."

Sadie wondered if he was thinking of Mike Tabor.

Fox chuckled. "I had to ask Dad to consult, to make sure we didn't ruin his story."

"Surely not," Sadie said.

"Well, a lot of people have practically memorized the original. If we mess up the details, I'm sure the critics will point it out in their reviews."

"Actually, I mostly came to keep my son in line," J.B. said, his eyes twinkling.

"Right, Dad," Fox said. He looked at Edwin. "Some of the cast and crew have been asking what they can do for nightlife around here."

"We like to look at the stars," Edwin deadpanned, and they all laughed. "No, seriously, we have a few nice restaurants, and I believe the opera house is hosting a concert Friday evening. We try to have something going there every week in the summer for the tourists. Do you know when the next play will be, Sadie?"

"Not for another couple of weeks, I'm afraid," Sadie said. "They're doing a light mystery, and it's in rehearsal now."

Edwin nodded. "There's more entertainment in Breckenridge. I can call over there for some suggestions, if you'd like."

"Oh, those kids can figure it out," Fox said.

"Well, don't forget that you're both invited to dinner at my house on Saturday. Sadie, I'm hoping you can make it."

"I'd like that," Sadie said. "Thanks."

Edwin nodded. "Of course, my daughter and her family will be there too. It will be a real treat for us."

"We wouldn't miss it," J.B. said.

"We'd better get to work, right, Dad?" Fox clapped his father on the shoulder. "We've asked them to barricade Main Street this afternoon, and we don't want to inconvenience your citizenry any longer than we have to."

Sara's silly joke about the parking space popped into Sadie's mind, and it was all she could do to keep a straight face.

"Thanks for coming by," Edwin said. "If there's anything I can do to make your stay in Silver Peak more pleasant, let me know."

"I'll look forward to seeing you on Saturday," Sadie said.

Back at the store, Julie and Alice were eager to hear every detail of their meeting.

"Wait until I tell the kids," Alice said. "They'll be so jealous!"

"I know," Julie added. "I'm a big fan of Fox Monahan's films myself."

"Maybe you'll have a chance to meet them," Sadie said. "They're really quite approachable."

Traffic through the store had slowed enough by three that she sent Alice home and looked over her computerized inventory for 1960s items. She almost hoped Fox Monahan did call on her for some props. It would be fun to point them out later when they got to see the movie.

Roz breezed into the shop while Julie was cashing up a customer's purchases.

"Hi!" Sadie took her arm and steered her into the back room. Roz smiled indulgently. "Feeling better?" Sadie asked.

"Yes, I am, thanks." Roz eyed her keenly. "That doesn't mean you'll quit looking into...you know...does it?"

"No. I'll find out anything I can. I'm just pleased to see you getting out and taking an interest in things."

Roz sat down on the corner of Sadie's worktable. "I've decided to do the hall bathroom over, and I want more than a new shower curtain and bath mat."

"Oh?"

"Yes. And I'd like some primitives. Do you have a nice print, and maybe a few old household items I can hang?"

"Of course. How about a watercolor of Anasazi petroglyphs, and maybe a beaded basket or two? Or is that too primitive?"

"Wow. Hadn't even thought about going in that direction."

"What did you have in mind?" Sadie asked.

"I don't know. Folk art. Old tools, maybe."

"That sounds like what Roscoe would like."

"True," Roz said. "Okay, let's go a little more feminine."

"You know what?" Sadie picked up the coffee carafe. "Julie could show you a few things and help you focus on what you like."

"She's really good at decorating, isn't she?"

"Better than I am. How about I make some coffee?"

"You're not busy? I could grab a couple of cups from next door."

"Okay." Sadie opened a drawer and took out a few dollars. "Get Julie a latte too. When you come back, I'll make sure she has some time to consult with you."

"Sounds so official and glamorous."

"She'll love doing it. Oh, Roz?"

"Yeah?"

"How much do you know about drones?"

Roz laughed. "Now, that's changing the subject."

"True. I'm asking because of what Edwin and I saw last week. I haven't been able to come up with a good explanation, and I keep coming back to drones. I thought maybe one of your sons had one."

"Not that I know of."

"Okay. But aren't most of them really small? I've seen videos, of course, of the camera ones and those little ones they say they can deliver parcels with."

"You think it was bigger than that?"

"Much. Edwin does too. And when he mentioned that real estate agents use them to take pictures for advertising, Milo got really upset. Is that common around here?"

Roz shook her head. "I really don't know anything about it, but you could ask my son the Realtor."

"Thanks. Could you give me Randy's phone number?"

"Sure." Roz bent over Sadie's worktable and wrote the number on a piece of scrap paper. "Just tell him his mom sent you."

An hour later, Roz left the Antique Mine with a lumpy package and a contented smile. Sadie grinned at Julie.

"Brilliant idea about the collage of doilies and crocheted gloves."

"I think it will be really sweet," Julie said. "And putting it all together with the framed classic ads and the old tins will keep Roz occupied for a while."

"I can't wait to see it when she's done," Sadie said.

"I offered to stop by her house tomorrow morning in case she needs any help."

"Good. Just give me a call if you're going to come in late."

The bell on the door jingled, and Sadie looked toward it. Instead of another customer, Mac walked in.

"Hello, ladies."

"Hi, Mac." Sadie came from behind the counter. A visit from Mac in full uniform always had some purpose behind it. "How can we help you?"

"I made a couple of calls about your UFO."

"Thank you. Did you learn anything interesting?" Sadie asked.

Mac shrugged. "The spokesperson for the air force says there haven't been any military flights or tests in this area within the last month. Sorry."

"I'm glad you ruled it out. Thanks a lot."

"I wish I could tell you what it was, but at least you know it wasn't government stuff."

"Well, that's something," Julie said.

Sadie hesitated, then said, "Mac, could I speak to you in the back for a minute?" She turned to Julie. "I want to show him that note I found."

"Good," Julie said.

Mac followed Sadie into the room they used for extra stock, repairing pieces, and coffee breaks.

Sadie took the note from her tote bag. "I found this on the counter yesterday. No envelope. The store was busy, and Julie and I have no idea who left it there."

Mac held the paper by one edge and frowned at the message. "What do you think it means?"

"I think it has to do with my looking into Roz's brother's death."

"How's that?"

Sadie sighed. "I was going to tell you about it, but I didn't think you could help, since it happened fifty years ago."

"Oh, another one of your forays into town history?"

"Sort of. He was hired to work on the movie they're remaking now, when J. B. Monahan filmed the original version in 1965. Mike was only eighteen. He fell off a cliff while they were filming. It was very sad."

"I'm sure it was. So what are you investigating?"

"Roz's dad was the first responder, which was extremely traumatic for him, of course, and he would never talk about it with Roz. With all the to-do about the new movie, Roz is a little on edge. It's brought up old memories for her. She was young when it happened, and she's always wondered if there was more to it— something her dad didn't tell her."

Mac frowned at the note. "Maybe she's changed her mind and decided to have you quit poking into it."

"No, she didn't write that. She was just in here, and she asked me if I'd learned anything yet."

"So tell me what you're thinking about this," Mac said.

"I'm not sure it's anything to worry about," Sadie said slowly. "It seems as if it must have been left by someone who knows me and who knew about Mike's death. Maybe someone who lives in town and is my age or older. It crossed my mind that somebody cares enough to not want the past brought up."

"You think there was a cover-up?"

"I don't know. If you'd asked me this morning, I'd have said no."

"It's not exactly threatening. There's no 'or else.' What do you want me to do?"

"Just be aware, I guess. If anything else like this comes up, I'll come straight to you."

"Good. I think that's best." Mac handed her the note. "I don't think you're in danger, but be careful, Sadie. And you know how to reach me."

"Thanks."

Mac headed out again as two middle-aged couples came into the store.

"Hi," Sadie said with a smile.

The shoppers returned her greeting and strolled down a row of displays.

Julie sidled up to Sadie. "Are you going to quit trying to find out what that thing in the sky was?"

"No way," Sadie said. "It was real, so there's an explanation somewhere, and I'm going to find it. In fact, I'd like to make a phone call about it right now." She returned to the room, leaving Julie at the checkout, and dialed Randy Putnam's number. She explained why she was calling and asked him about drones.

"I haven't actually used one," Randy said. "I've seen some training videos about drones, but to be honest, they're pretty expensive, and you have to get permission."

"I wondered about that," Sadie said.

"A lot of people don't like the idea of having them around. Privacy, you know. So the government is starting to come up with regulations about when and where you can use them."

"Yes," Sadie said, thinking hard. Privacy was important. Why *would* anyone want to view Milo's mountain property, anyway? The filmmakers had already signed the lease agreement when she and Edwin saw the lights of the UFO, so it couldn't have been for the purpose of deciding whether or not the location would be good for the movie. Besides, they had seen it at night.

"Yeah, I don't see much point in it personally. But my brother Raleigh probably knows more about drones than I do," Randy added. "He works for a tech company. He might be able to answer some questions for you."

"Thanks, but I probably won't bother him," Sadie said. "I'm pretty sure that whatever I saw was bigger than one of those little camera drones."

"Well, if you wanted to be sure, you could ask your local Realtors' association," Randy suggested. "They could probably tell you if any agents in your area use them."

"That's not a bad idea," Sadie said. "I'm trying to rule out possibilities. Thanks, Randy."

Traffic through the store slowed down during the last part of the afternoon. Between customers, Sadie sneaked a moment to look up a Realtors' association in Breckenridge and note their hours. She jotted down the address.

"Would you mind if I left now?" she asked Julie at four.

"Go ahead," Julie said. "I can close up and make the bank drop."

"Thanks. I'm going to make a quick run to Breckenridge. Call me if you need anything."

Sadie cruised into the picturesque town twenty minutes later. Her GPS unit helped her find the Realtors' association easily, located at the office of one of the larger local real estate agencies. Inside, she met one of the partners, Samantha Nelson.

"Have a seat," Samantha said, leading the way to her cubicle. She looked very professional in her royal blue skirt suit, high heels, and a layered gold necklace with matching earrings, but her smile seemed genuine. Sadie, in her khaki pants, plaid blouse, and sneakers, felt a bit underdressed.

"I'm really only here to ask you about drones," she said as she took a seat in a padded chair facing Samantha's desk.

"Drones?" Samantha's eyebrows shot up.

"Yes. It's not really that random." Sadie gave her a sheepish smile. "I asked a friend, and he suggested I contact the association. I wondered whether any of the agents here use drones in their business."

Samantha leaned back in her chair. "Interesting that you should ask. Several of us have been talking about going in on one together. I think it's a great idea. They're quite expensive, but if we all contributed, members of our group could take turns using it."

Sadie nodded. "So nobody around here has one yet?"

"No. We're having someone come in next week and give us a presentation on them. We're leaning toward doing it—overhead pictures can be quite attractive in our advertising. Would you like some coffee?"

"No, thanks," Sadie said. "I won't take up that much of your time."

"Did you have some property you want photographed?" Samantha asked.

"Actually, a friend and I saw something in Silver Peak that we thought might be a drone. Our sheriff has made inquiries, and it wasn't a military aircraft of any sort, so I guess it had to be for either business or pleasure."

"A toy?"

"Maybe. Several people saw it, but we're still puzzling over it." Sadie rose. "Well, thank you, Samantha."

"Sorry I couldn't help you. And if you're ever looking for property…"

Sadie smiled. "I'll remember you."

That evening, in the quiet of her living room, she did more reading about drones on her laptop. Hank snuggled on the rug at her feet as she searched. She found a lot of rants against government use of drones to monitor civilians, but there seemed to be an equal number of people complaining about restrictions on their use. She also found several companies that manufactured the items.

"Wouldn't you hate having one of those things buzzing around?" she asked Hank, leaning down to scratch behind his ears. Hank sighed in contentment. Sadie noted the prices. Samantha hadn't been kidding about the cost. She turned to something that interested her more—searching her favorite auction sites. A lot of small antiques and a couple of pieces of furniture had made their way out the door of the Antique Mine this week. With the tourist season in full swing, she needed to constantly replenish her stock at the store.

She had made a list of auctions to watch online or attend by the time Edwin called at half past eight.

"So hobnobbing with celebrities?" she teased.

"Yeah, isn't it wild?" Edwin laughed. "I love some of the movies J. B. Monahan made. But you know, I had to bone up on his son's work before they came in. I couldn't name a single one of his films until I looked him up online."

"Well, several thousand people at least are going to be jealous when they hear he's having dinner at your house on Saturday."

"Did I tell you they're seriously considering holding the new movie's official premiere here?"

"No! I knew people were pushing for it, but I didn't expect the studio to do it. When?"

"Not until next spring. Apparently the editing and advertising process takes months. They're looking at March. Fox wanted to know if people would be able to drive up here then."

"He's got a point," Sadie said. "The roads can be pretty dicey that time of year."

"He said they haven't set a definite date yet, and it could be into April. That would be better. Anyway, I'm going to talk to the opera house board about it. That would be quite a coup, and it would bring some interest—and money—to Silver Peak well before the usual tourist season."

"Maybe you can talk Fox into slowing production down until May," Sadie said. "You could be pretty sure the roads would be clear then. We wouldn't want any movie stars hitting ice on their way here and having an accident."

"It might be easier to talk to the road commissioner and have him lay in extra salt and sand for the event, just in case the weather's bad."

"Good luck with that," Sadie said. "You'd have to run it by the budget committee too."

Edwin chuckled. "I got together with most of the town council members this afternoon, and they're very excited about it. And they want to go ahead with showing the old movie again soon at the opera house. They figure the more we do to keep the buzz going, the more the town will benefit."

"I suppose so." Sadie sighed. "Most people don't remember the tragedy from last time, and it's probably better that they don't."

"That's right," Edwin said firmly. "We want good publicity, not bad memories."

8

JULIE CAME INTO THE ANTIQUE MINE THE NEXT MORNING AS Sadie was setting up the cash register for the day.

"Come on in," Sadie said. "I doubt we'll get many shoppers today, with half the length of the street blocked off. But that's okay—I want to hear all about Roz's decorating adventure."

"It's going to be so cute," Julie said. "Give her a couple more days, and then go see it."

"I will," Sadie promised.

Ten minutes later, while Sadie was at the other end of the store assessing their stock needs, the door opened, setting the bell jingling. Perhaps they'd do a little business today after all.

"Well," she heard Julie say, "to what do we owe the honor?" Without waiting for an answer, she called to Sadie, "The mayor's here. It must be important."

Edwin laughed as Sadie left her task and walked toward them with her clipboard under her arm.

"Hi," she said. "What's up in the gristmill of town government?"

"Can't a man stop by to say hello without everyone assuming it's an official visit?" Edwin's eyes twinkled, and Sadie knew he wasn't really put out with them.

"Of course you can." She stood on tiptoe and kissed his cheek.

"I guess you already know that the movie crew will be using Main Street again today, but this should be the last day for a while, unless they need to retake some scenes. Probably next week they'll use it again. But after lunch today, they'll be moving over to Jefferson Avenue to film at the house they're leasing."

"Okay." Sadie frowned at Julie. "We aren't expecting any tour buses today, are we?"

"Not that I know of. We don't get many on Wednesdays."

"Good," Sadie said. "I think it does put people off when they drive into town and see the barricades."

"Business will be slow today, I imagine," Julie said.

Sadie nodded. "Do you want the day off? I'm sure I'll be able to handle things here."

"Or you could take some time if you want. I know you've got a couple of things you've been researching."

"That's true." Sadie looked at Edwin. "What are you up to today?"

"Not much. If you'd like to visit the movie set, I'd be happy to go with you. J. B. Monahan told me their makeup people are doing some 'aliens' this morning, and he invited me to come and watch if I wanted to. Might be interesting."

"Sure. Julie, I'll take an hour or two, I guess, if you're sure you don't mind. Then we can swap off and you can have the afternoon if you want it."

"Oh, I also meant to tell you that Noelle thought she might come in this afternoon," Edwin said. "She does want to see the shop."

"How's the headache?" Sadie asked.

"All gone. Yesterday she and Carl took Sam to the park, and then they had ice cream at the Depot. She said our town is charming."

"Well, that's progress." Sadie turned to Julie. "I'll be back no later than one."

"Great," Julie said.

Edwin smiled. "Sounds like we'll have time to grab lunch together."

"Sure." Sadie smiled wryly. "If we can get through the crowds and get a table."

"There are always sandwiches and salads from the Market." Edwin took her hand and drew her out the door.

As they walked toward the opera house, she could see that the crew was in place and Fox Monahan strode about the open space before the entrance.

"Okay, when Sandra comes out the door, I want you right here, Jason." He turned and called over his shoulder to one of the assistants, "Phil, put a marker right here for Jason."

"Every step is choreographed before they start shooting," Edwin said.

Sadie looked up at the beautiful redbrick façade with its arched windows and decorative cornices. "There's a scene in the original that happens in this very spot. I watched it the other night, and Mr. Monahan did a really good job of using our historic buildings."

"Let's hope this one comes out as well, or even better." Edwin squeezed her hand and drew her toward a motor home that had been parked just inside the barricades—the type wealthy people used when they went on vacation. "This is the makeup team's headquarters."

The makeup director and two assistants were hard at work on the actors who would be filmed in the morning's scenes. The lead actors had finished their stints, but the characters now being enhanced by the team were interesting creatures.

"Sam would love this," Sadie whispered as she watched a makeup artist slather an actor's face with blue-tinged foundation.

"If he didn't find it too scary." Edwin nodded toward one alien with a bulging forehead. "That fellow looks like he's been in a few fights."

"Quiet on the set," they heard from the direction of the opera house's main entrance.

Edwin leaned in close. "Come on. They're starting to film over there."

They walked across the deserted street and stood in silence behind the cameras and the crew's folding chairs as Fox directed the scene, with the actor Jason rushing to tell his girlfriend that something terrible was happening in town. They met at the bottom of the steps in front of the opera house, which in the old film had been designated as the town hall. Sadie wondered if they would use computer effects on this version to change the words *Silver Peak Opera House* on the front to something else containing the name of the film's fictional town.

The actors did well, she thought, but Fox yelled, "Cut!" and jumped from his chair.

"Let's do it again, but Sandra, slow it down a little. I don't want you looking panicked until after you talk to Jason. Worried, but not in a hurry."

Sadie and Edwin watched in fascination until Fox declared it was a "wrap" and gave the actors a ten-minute break.

"That's Glee Rossignol," Sadie said, nodding toward her new friend, the script girl. She had told Edwin about her meeting with Glee.

"She's the one who was here fifty years ago?" Edwin said.

"Yes, but I couldn't remember her. I must have been too star-struck by the actors."

"Of course. We had Gina Tarino."

"I was thinking more of Blaze Foster," Sadie said.

They both laughed.

"After you called last night, I did a little digging on the old film. It was much more popular than I'd realized. I'd heard people say it was a 'cult classic,' but I wasn't sure what that meant."

"Did you find out?" Edwin asked.

"Yeah, it seems that what's called a cult movie is one that has a really passionate fan base. They watch the film over and over. Sometimes they get together to watch it or reenact it. Costumes, props. And the film doesn't have to be a smash hit when it releases. In fact, some of them were considered flops, or were obscure, almost-forgotten movies for a while, and then younger people discovered them and loved them."

"I guess *Stranger from a Strange World* would qualify," Edwin mused.

"It's odd how young people especially get so caught up in a thing like that."

"I agree. It goes beyond what we thought of as fans when we were young."

"Or maybe we simply weren't among those in the extreme sector of the viewers. Maybe that's why they're called fans—they're *fana*tical."

J. B. Monahan crossed the area they were using as a set, and Sadie watched with interest as he approached Glee.

"Glee, can you phone that woman who's supplying the coffee and tell her what we have is cold? See if you can get us some hot coffee!"

"Of course, J.B.," Glee said.

Sadie was glad it wasn't her responsibility. Maggie would be happy to sell a lot of refreshments to the crew, but she wouldn't like hearing that J.B. had complained.

"And send one of the kids to the cleaners and see if my jacket's ready," J.B. added. "This mountain air is chilly. I don't care if it is the end of June."

"I'll send Javi," Glee said.

"Who's that?"

"He's one of the grips."

"No, don't send him. Fox will need all of the tech crew to set up for the next bit over at the other location."

Glee shrugged. "Maybe one of the wardrobe girls can go. If not, I'll do it myself."

"Good," J.B. said, smiling at last. "I knew I could count on you."

"Looks like your friend is kept busy," Edwin whispered.

Sadie nodded. "It also looks like J.B. isn't easy to please."

"I've heard he gets a little peevish if things aren't exactly the way he wants them. I wonder how hard it is for him to keep quiet when his son does something a little differently than he would do it himself."

Sadie chuckled. "So far they seem to get along all right."

"Yes, but they're both opinionated people. We'll see how it goes when things go wrong and time is short and they're over budget," Edwin said sagely.

Sadie said nothing, but she knew working with family members could be a trial. She wondered if Edwin and Noelle had had any run-ins. She did notice that crew members and bit players seemed to try to avoid drawing J.B.'s attention.

Fox, meanwhile, was deep in conversation with his assistant director and the head cameraman. The assistant left the huddle and shouted to the cast and crew at large, "Okay, we'll shoot the street scene with the aliens, and then we're done here. We'll reassemble at the house on Jefferson Avenue in a half hour. If you're in scenes two-A or two-C, be there. The rest of you are free until noon."

Much of the cast scrambled down the sidewalk. A couple of them ducked into Arbuckle's, and the rest hurried on down the street in the direction of Jefferson Avenue. Those staying at the Remingtons' B and B would have time to make a quick run to their rooms.

The strangely made-up actors portraying the aliens startled Sadie, though she had just seen one of them being transformed from an ordinary young man to an extraterrestrial.

"I wouldn't want to meet them in a dark alley," Edwin said, studying their ridged foreheads and bald pates.

They observed as Fox told the actors how he wanted them to progress stealthily down the street, taking in the architecture. "Stay alert for humanoids. Remember, these guys have done this before. They know there are intelligent beings on this planet, and that some of them are probably inside these buildings watching them."

"Humanoids." Sadie shook her head, smiling.

The creepy-looking actors apparently did the job well, because Fox was happy after three takes and dismissed them.

"I guess the show's over for now," Sadie said. She and Edwin turned away. "I've been making a list of each scene in the old movie and where it was filmed, and I copied off a list of the cast members and crew."

"Isn't this a little out of character for you?" Edwin asked. "I never knew you to get wrapped up in old movies before."

"I can't help thinking those lights we saw over the mountain-side are connected to all of this somehow," she explained. "It may turn out to be nothing, but... "

"You told me you went to see a Realtor about their drones."

"Yeah, I did. I think those are way smaller than whatever we saw. Besides, she said none of the real estate agents around here has been using one."

"Hello, Sadie!"

She looked up to see Glee approaching them with her script in her hand.

"Hi," Sadie said with a smile. "Glee, I'd like you to meet Edwin Marshall. He was here in 1965 too."

"Mr. Marshall?" Glee looked Edwin up and down. "Aren't you the mayor?"

He chuckled. "I am. Glad to meet you." He shook Glee's hand.

"It looks like they're keeping you busy," Sadie said.

"Yes, but I love it. I'm just waiting for the coffee lady, to tell her we need to move the refreshments over to Jefferson Avenue. As soon as she gets here and I place a fresh cup of java in J.B.'s hand, I'll get over there myself. When Fox is ready to roll, he wants everyone else to be ready too."

"He seems to be jumping right into the plot," Edwin said.

Glee smiled broadly. "Just wait until we get out on the mountain. That will be the fun part. We've still got a few days to get ready for that, and it's a good thing. We'll need to run electric lines out there, and have portable toilets delivered, and..." As she listed all the things the crew would need on the mountainside, Glee ticked them off on her fingers, with the pages of the script flapping as she did it. Suddenly she stopped. "Oh, here's the coffee lady."

Sadie turned to see Maggie Price pull her red hatchback in at the curb and jump out.

"That's Maggie. And she makes wonderful food."

"I agree," Glee said. "Sampled some this morning." She hurried over to meet Maggie on the sidewalk and explain that the production crew was moving to Jefferson Avenue.

"Do you want to walk over there?" Edwin asked. "It's only a couple of blocks."

Sadie looked back toward the intersection beyond the hardware store. That part of Main Street was nearly deserted, and two of the property assistants were removing the barricades.

"Sure. We've got plenty of time."

When they reached Jefferson Avenue, they turned right, in the opposite direction from Edwin's house, and walked past the sheriff's office and another block along the sidewalk.

Simon Riley's magnificent house rose against a backdrop of sparkling blue sky and wooded mountains. The white house boasted a turret at one front corner, rising up beside the pitched roof of the attic. The siding consisted of three different decorative shingle patterns, and carved brackets graced the soffits beneath the eaves. A wraparound porch was studded with wicker furniture, bright cushions, and a double chair swing.

"I've always loved this house," Sadie said with a sigh. "Almost as much as yours."

"They picked a good one for the movie," Edwin said.

She looked over at him. "What if they'd asked for yours? Would you have leased it to them?"

He smiled, leaned down close to her ear, and said, "They did."

Sadie pulled back to stare at him. "You didn't tell me."

"It didn't seem important." He shrugged. "You know I'm set in my ways. Besides, I didn't want a film crew in there while Noelle was visiting."

"Does Noelle know they offered?"

"Yes. She was horrified that I'd turned them down. Carl thought it was funny."

Sadie chuckled. "It is, in a way."

The exterior scenes at the house consisted mainly of the lead actor walking into his house and shutting the door, then running up the walk, dashing inside, and slamming the door. Then Fox had him come out and walk slowly toward the street, craning his neck to look at the sky.

"Cut," he yelled. "That's it out here, except for the special effects." He turned and sought out one of the crew members. "Derek, we'll do that tomorrow morning. Make sure you've got the model ready. You can fix the CGI stuff later."

"Got it, Fox," said the middle-aged man with wire-rimmed glasses.

"Okay, everybody, we'll be doing the interior scenes now. Cameras are ready inside. Let's do it!" Fox and most of the others went into the house.

"I wonder where Simon is staying while this is going on," Sadie said.

Edwin shrugged. "I think he's visiting his daughter in California."

"Good choice."

While they talked, Maggie and one of her employees from the Market arrived and began setting up a refreshment table in Simon Riley's side yard, under the direction of the properties manager. The special effects man strolled toward it, coming close to where Sadie and Edwin stood.

"Hello, folks. We're enjoying your town."

"Thank you," Edwin said.

The man stopped as though willing to talk, so Edwin introduced himself and Sadie.

"I'm Derek Todd, in charge of the special effects."

Sadie shook his hand. "Nice to meet you, Derek. The altitude's not getting to you, is it?"

"Not so far. But everyone's been warned to take it easy and stay hydrated. I can see why Fox wanted to do this film here, and why his father chose the location fifty years ago. A few inconveniences are certainly outweighed by the beauty of the place."

Sadie was curious about the special effects. "So how do you make the spacecraft look authentic?"

"I've wondered that myself," Edwin said. "Is it all computer graphics now?"

Derek's eyes took on a serious cast. "We do use some computer-generated images—what we call CGI. In fact, if Fox Monahan has his way, that's all we'll use, other than the mock-up set for the scenes that actually take place inside the spacecraft."

"But you still use models?" Edwin asked.

"Oh, sure, for the shots of it at a distance, roving through space, and when the ship appears in the sky above the earth. Did you see the first *Stranger from a Strange World*?"

"I just watched it a few days ago," Sadie said. "It was impressive, although I'm sure it's even more so on the big screen."

"Oh yeah, you people need to have a screening. In that film, sure, the technology was primitive compared to what we have today, but the people *believed* it. You know what I'm saying?" Derek eyed them expectantly.

"I think I do," Sadie said.

Edwin nodded. "Like the radio broadcast of *War of the Worlds*. It seemed real, like it could actually be happening, right outside your window."

"Exactly. I studied the original movie meticulously when I learned they were doing a remake. I learned a lot from it, and I'm sure that helped me get the job."

Sadie frowned. "So those scenes in the 1965 movie, where the aliens dragged Blaze Foster inside the spaceship—that was a real set, wasn't it? I mean, it was a little clunky-looking, but it sure looked real."

"Oh yes. It was built by a very adept construction chief, on a sound stage in Hollywood."

"So that scene wasn't actually shot here?" Edwin asked.

"I think the interior spacecraft scenes were made at the studio, and the mountain backdrop was morphed in behind it."

"Wow. I thought it was all filmed here," Sadie said.

"Well, it's hard to shoot some things in very remote locations, especially scenes with complicated sets that require lots of electricity and things like that. It could be done, but it would be expensive. I mean, running all the electric lines we need up the mountain for those scenes out at the ranch…" Derek shook his head. "It does come with a price."

"Are you using the set back in Hollywood this time too?" Sadie asked.

"I think Fox is going to try to shoot everything here. That might mean building an indoor set in the school gym, or some other large building."

"We were discussing that at the town council meeting," Edwin said.

Derek's eyes widened. "Oh, are you on the council?"

"He's the mayor." Sadie held back a laugh at Derek's obvious surprise.

"Oh, wow. Well, anyway, what I hope we can do with this one is to improve on the special effects of the original. They were great, and I wouldn't want to scrap them all and go completely with CGI effects. Sometimes the old ways are better. For this project, I think we should keep the mock-ups and make everything as tactile as we can."

"The final product will be better that way?" Sadie asked, not exactly sure what he meant.

"I think so. It will be more tangible and seem more real to the viewers. Sort of like when you use real antiques in a historical film."

"*Hmm*," Edwin said. "Well, if anyone knows about antiques, it's Sadie here. She owns the Antique Mine shop on Main Street."

Derek nodded. "The new technology can be amazing, but it can also be rather sterile. I wasn't born when the original film was made. I was about twelve the first time I saw it, and I loved the old spaceship. I'd really like to re-create that, if I can bring Fox around to agreeing."

"Fox prefers the CGI effects?"

Derek shrugged. "It's certainly cheaper, and he also feels it's safer and less hassle." He looked at his watch. "I'd better get going. Nice talking to you folks."

Fox and the head cameraman came out of the house. Fox paused on the porch.

"Derek, get in here! We've got a glitch."

"Coming." Derek smiled apologetically and hurried up the walk.

Fox scowled at him. "I need you where the filming is. Do you understand?"

"I sure do."

"I don't think that special weapon you built is going to do it. If it's not going to work, we need to do something different."

"I can make it work," Derek assured him.

Not mollified, Fox raised his chin. "Well, if you can't, we'll film it as is and fix it later in editing. We're on a deadline here, in case you didn't know it."

As he spoke, J. B. Monahan came outside.

"Take it easy, Fox. Give him a chance."

Fox frowned at his father. "We've got to keep rolling, Dad. If there's a rough spot, we can splice something in later to cover it, but we can't spend more than two days doing the scenes in this house."

"Relax. It's barely noon. Come on in, Derek." J.B. moved aside to let Derek pass, and the special effects man ducked through the door. The cameraman followed him.

Fox eyed his father in exasperation. "Dad, I wish you wouldn't butt in when I'm talking to the crew."

"There are ways to talk to them that will get the results you want," J.B. said.

"Oh yeah? How about when you talk to the director? How do you get the results you want out of him?"

9

SADIE HELD HER BREATH AND HOPED NEITHER OF THE MONAHANS looked her way.

"Sorry, son," J.B. said, "but I think you'll find things go more smoothly if you give them space to do their jobs. Derek's good at what he does. So there was a little speed bump. He'll work it out."

Fox shook his head. "All this ray gun stuff and vaporizing weapons. I'd rather freeze it at the moment of impact and add CGI later."

"It worked the first time, and the viewers loved it. Give it a chance."

Fox sighed. "Okay, I will, but can you do me a favor?"

"Sure, name it."

"Can you just stay off the set while we get this one scene done?"

J.B. frowned. "Sure, if that's the way you want it." He started down the steps without another word.

"Oh, come on, Dad." Fox hurried after him. "I'm not angry, I just need to be able to think clearly for about twenty minutes, and when you're here I keep second-guessing myself and wondering if I'm doing it the way you would, or if there's a better way and I should just go with my gut."

J.B. turned to face him. "Look, this is your project. I'm sorry I made you feel otherwise. I'm only here to advise, Fox, at your pleasure."

"And I want you here, Dad," Fox said quickly. "I just need to get through this one scene on my own."

"Okay." J.B. threw his hands up. "I'll take an early lunch. Go to it."

"I'll see you later." Fox swatted him on the shoulder, then turned, jogged up the steps, and went inside, closing the door behind him.

"Well." Sadie looked up at Edwin.

"Families," Edwin said.

J.B. came slowly toward the sidewalk. "Oh, hello, Sadie. Edwin. I guess you heard."

"Yes, but please don't be embarrassed," Sadie said. She glanced at Edwin. "We were just going to lunch ourselves."

Edwin smiled. "Why don't you join us, J.B.? We'd love to have you."

He eyed them keenly. "Are you sure?"

"We're sure," Sadie said. "I need to eat and get back to the store."

They ambled back toward Main Street. "Los Pollitos?" Edwin asked.

Sadie checked her watch. "Sounds good. But won't Noelle and Carl be ready for some lunch too, not to mention Sam?"

"I told Carl I might be out most of the day and left some groceries there for them. They can fend for themselves."

"Then let's go to Los Pollitos—if you like Mexican, J.B." Sadie glanced at him.

"I love it, as long as it's not too spicy," the older man replied.

"We'll tip Luz off," Sadie said.

"She makes the most delicious food," Edwin said. "I'm sure she can steer you to something mild."

They walked toward the corner. Before they crossed the street, Edwin pointed out his house to J.B.

"It's lovely. Such beautiful old homes here," J.B. said. "I hope you two don't mind, I'm a slow walker these days."

"We're not in a hurry," Sadie assured him. "And it's just down there, past the Market."

"I'm really getting too old for this," J.B. confessed. "I only came because Fox begged me to."

"I'm sure he's glad you're here," Edwin said. "Do you want me to get a car?"

"No, no, I can make it. It's probably good for me, all this walking."

They reached the restaurant and went inside. Since the movie crew was still working, it wasn't too crowded. They took a table near the window, and J.B. sank into his chair with a sigh. Marisol Vidal, the owners' daughter, was home from college for the summer. She came to take their orders right away with a big smile.

"Welcome, Mr. Monahan. We're honored that you chose our restaurant today."

"You're welcome, sweetheart."

Sadie wondered how Marisol felt about that designation, but the young woman kept her smile in place.

"May I bring you a drink, or do you want to order right away? I know some of the movie folks want to be served quickly."

The three of them asked for iced tea, and soon placed their entrée orders.

"Nice place," J.B. said after Marisol had left them with the assurance that his food would not be too spicy. "It wasn't here fifty years ago."

"No, that's true," Sadie said. "The building was here, but I'm not sure what it was back then."

Marisol brought their cold drinks and nachos to eat while they waited for their entrées.

"Mr. Monahan," Sadie began, but at his look of reproof she started over. "J.B., I wonder if you remember a young man who was in the original movie. That is, he started out in the movie, but then he was let go."

J.B. frowned. "What was his name?"

"Ty Zinfeld."

"Oh yes, I do recall that young man. Nice-looking, and he wasn't half bad as an actor. But he showed up late on the set two days in a row, if I remember right. He was holding up the production. I couldn't put up with that." He smiled in chagrin. "I guess I must sound about the way my son did a few minutes ago. Peeved at everything. Impatient."

"Sometimes you have to be, when you're the boss," Edwin said mildly.

"I suppose. But there was something else about that young man. He had some sort of clash with Blaze. Hard to work with a star who gets snippy with other cast members."

"Ah, now we get the real scoop." Edwin smiled at Sadie.

J.B. shook his head. "Blaze was all right. He was a fine actor, but now and then he took a dislike to someone, and it was just impossible for them to work on the same set. Did you know that young fellow you mentioned?"

"Not really." Sadie hesitated. She didn't especially want to bring up Mike's death. "I just wondered if you knew what became of him."

"I don't think I've worked with him since. Zinfeld, was it?"

"Yes."

"You could ask Glee. Do you know her? Our script girl."

"Yes," Sadie said. "She came into my store the other day."

"Nice lady," J.B. said. "She could contact SAG for you and ask if he's still a member."

"The Screen Actors Guild?" Edwin asked.

"That's right. If he hasn't kept up his membership in that, he's probably not still active in the business."

"That's a great idea. Thank you," Sadie said. They chatted while they ate their meal, and then she prepared to leave. "I guess I'd better get back to my store now."

"Shall I walk you over?" Edwin asked.

"You don't have to. Why don't you stay here with J.B.? He looks to me as though he might like another cup of coffee and some of Luz's chocolate cake."

Edwin and J.B. rose as Sadie stood and picked up her purse.

"I hope Noelle follows through and visits the store later," she said to Edwin.

Out on the sidewalk, she breathed in the crisp mountain air deeply. Summer in Silver Peak never got truly hot, but it was glorious. She noticed several of the actors and film crew members coming from the direction of Jefferson Avenue.

One of the men stopped beside her. "Hi. Aren't you the antique lady?"

Sadie laughed. "Well, if you mean I'm getting old, how dare you? But if you mean do I own the antique store over there, yes, that's me."

He smiled. "Sorry. I'm Bob Willis. I'm one of the cameramen for the film."

She nodded. "I think I saw you at the house on Jefferson Avenue a while ago, when Edwin Marshall and I were talking to Derek about the special effects."

"That's right. Derek's a good guy. Knows his stuff. He and Fox don't agree on everything, but that's just—you know—artistic differences."

Sadie nodded. "Like whether to use CGI or actual props and mock-ups."

"Yeah, stuff like that. Derek's only forty or so, but he's a bit old school on that score."

"He seemed like a nice man." Sadie fell into step with Bob.

"He is. And he really wants to use a spaceship in the mountain scenes, like J.B. did in the old days."

"I remember that in the movie," Sadie said. "It hovered over the cliff."

"Yeah."

"Does Fox just think it's too much trouble?"

"Partly." Bob ran a hand through his hair and looked away for a moment. "Did you live here back then?"

"Yes, I remember that summer well," Sadie said.

"Well, a kid was killed during the filming."

She nodded. "Mike Tabor."

"So . . . you knew him?"

"Yes." They both stopped walking. "Does the whole crew know about it?"

"Oh yeah," Bob said. "We all watched the old film about fifty times, and we heard all the stories. But nobody talks about it around J.B. And Fox doesn't want to remind the people here too strongly of what happened before—not anyone, for that matter, not just the residents of Silver Peak. But especially not his father."

"It must have been traumatic for everyone involved," Sadie said.

"Oh, it was. J.B. almost didn't finish making the movie."

"I didn't know that."

Bob nodded. "They say it's always bothered him, and he felt partly responsible when that kid fell."

"Why?"

"I guess because he was the boss. You know. He was in charge, and he must have thought he'd done something wrong if somebody died on his set."

"I see."

Bob shrugged. "Anyway, Fox doesn't want to remind him of it. I think he even feels that using more CGI will ensure there's not a repeat of the accident, and people won't be as nervous when they're working up on the mountain. He doesn't want anyone to associate that scene with death."

"I hadn't thought of that," Sadie said. "So there's not going to be a spaceship in the sky when they do that scene?"

"Nope. They'll add it later. All computer generated." Bob pulled out his cell phone and glanced at the screen. "Well, I'd better get some lunch and get back over there. Fox hates it when people are late."

"Thanks, Bob. Drop by the Antique Mine anytime."

He waved and strode off toward Sophia's Italian restaurant. Sadie crossed the street to her store, thinking about everything Bob had said.

———

Sadie lifted the lid of a nineteenth-century music box, and the melody of "Lara's Theme" wafted through the store.

"It's beautiful," the customer, a fiftyish woman from Kansas, said.

"I love the inlay on the cover," her friend said. "It would make a nice addition to your collection."

"Yes," the woman agreed. "And the price is very reasonable. I'll take it. Could you wrap it up, please?"

"I'd be happy to," Sadie said.

"And then I want to see if we can get a glimpse of the movie stars," the buyer said to her companion.

Sadie headed for the cash register smiling. This week was turning out to be a very good one for the Antique Mine.

As the two women left the store with the music box wrapped and tucked safely in a shopping bag, the Carsons arrived at the store. Sadie quickly cleared off the counter and went to greet Noelle and Carl.

"Hi! So glad you could come in. But where's Sam this afternoon?"

"We left him with his grandpa," Carl said.

"Yes, we weren't sure, but I thought you might have a lot of fragile things on display," Noelle added.

"That was thoughtful of you, but if Sam wants to visit, I'd be delighted to show him around." Sadie smiled. "I know he'd like to see the old toys and books."

"You're probably right," Carl said. "He was a little pouty when we told him he couldn't come, but then Edwin said he would take him around to see his neighbor's kittens."

"Anything that purrs is better than antique toys," Sadie admitted. "I do hope Sam will come out to my place and meet my dog, Hank too. He's very good with children."

Noelle had been gazing about as they spoke, and she caught her breath.

"What is it?" Sadie asked.

Noelle took half a dozen quick steps toward where a Colonial-era mirror in a gilded and carved frame hung over an oak sideboard.

"Oh, look out," Carl said. "She's been looking for the perfect mirror for the front hall."

Sadie smiled and followed Noelle. "Isn't that marvelous? It came out of one of the wealthy mine owners' homes. It's in the Adam style."

Noelle studied the old glass and the rectangular, hand-painted panel above it. "This would go well with those candle sconces we saw in Atlanta," she said.

"What's Adam style?" Carl asked.

"It's named for Robert Adam," Sadie told him. "He was a Scottish architect in the 1700s, and he had a lot of influence on furniture style and interior design."

"Well, I like it," Carl said.

Noelle discreetly turned the price tag, and Sadie looked away.

"Yes, I like it too. Very much." Noelle turned to Sadie. "Do you have any more provenance on it?"

"Let me look it up." Sadie went to the counter and quickly pulled up her computerized inventory. "I bought it at an estate sale, and it had been in the house at least since 1920. But I'm sure it's much older than that."

Noelle conferred in low tones with Carl, and a woman approached the counter with a folded quilt in her arms.

"Did you find something you like?" Sadie asked.

"Something I love!" The woman laid down the quilt and opened her purse.

By the time Sadie had rung up the purchase, Noelle had made up her mind, and Carl had removed the mirror from the wall.

"Looks like this is going to Atlanta." He brought it over to the counter. "Can you help us with shipping it? We're flying, so..."

"Of course," Sadie said.

While she processed Carl's credit card and wrapped the mirror to transport it safely to the shipping center, Noelle continued to browse. Sadie waited on a couple of other customers. When Julie returned from her lunch hour, Sadie let her take over the checkout and found Noelle gazing into the jewelry case.

"Are you looking at the silver and onyx bracelet?" she asked with a smile.

Noelle looked up in surprise. "Why, yes, I am. I was thinking how perfectly it would go with a black wrap top I have."

Sadie opened the case and took out the bracelet. "I thought of you too, when Julie and I rearranged the display a couple of days ago. Try it on."

Noelle did and held out her hand to admire the piece. "I have to admit, your shop has surprised me."

Sadie chuckled. "It's a little like me. Full of nice, comfortable old stuff and a few surprises."

Noelle nodded thoughtfully and then seemed to come to a decision. She slid the bracelet off over her hand and held it out to Sadie. "I'll take this too. Are you shipping the mirror?"

"Yes. I'll drive it to the shipping center before I open tomorrow morning."

"Great. I'll take this with me today."

Carl materialized at Sadie's elbow. "Let me take care of that."

"Thanks." Sadie walked with him to the checkout and handed the bracelet to Julie. "For Mr. Carson."

"Oh, hi," Julie said with a smile for Carl. "You must be Edwin's son-in-law."

"That's right."

Sadie left them together and headed back to Noelle, who gave the jewelry case a final scrutiny and turned away from it.

"Is there anything else I can help you with, Noelle?"

"I don't think so, though I do look for mixed metal vases."

"I don't get a lot of Asian stuff, but I do see them once in a while. Right now I don't have any in stock."

"It's all right." Noelle smiled. "This was fun. Thanks. Dad said something about horseback riding. Is that an option?"

"Well, I'm here all day, of course, but my daughter, Alice, is a teacher, and she's off for the summer. She and her teenagers might be available to take you out if you're interested."

"Is it something Sam could join us for?" Noelle asked.

"Very much so. Milo Henderson, the man who owns the stable, has a very gentle mare named Sunflower. I'm sure Sam would get along great with her. And she could carry him and his father together, if Carl wanted to take Sam on the saddle with him."

"Sounds like a plan," Noelle said.

"Why don't you give me your cell number?" Sadie said. "I can ask Alice to call you. If she can't go, I'm sure either Sara or Theo could. Their horses need exercise, and you can use my gelding, Scout, or one of Milo's other horses."

"Dad said he goes out riding with you once in a while. Any chance we can convince him to go along?"

Sadie gave her a conspiratorial wink. "I wouldn't be at all surprised. He's an excellent rider. He knows most of Milo's trails too."

By the time Noelle and Carl were out the door, Sadie felt that she and Noelle had made a lot of progress. Although the younger woman still seemed a bit stiff and sophisticated, Sadie admired the way she wanted to include Sam and her father in her vacation activities.

"Roz called while you were busy," Julie told her.

"Should I call her back?" Sadie asked.

"No, but she'd like you to stop by after closing if you can and see what's she done with her bathroom."

"I sure can." Sadie went about humming as she straightened the merchandise.

Late in the afternoon, Glee came into the shop.

"Well, hi," Sadie said, grinning at her. "You must have wrapped for the day."

"Mostly. They're doing some retakes, and Fox told me I could leave. I wanted to see you because J.B. said you were interested in that young man who was fired from the original filming."

Sadie had almost forgotten J.B.'s recommendation that she ask Glee about it. "He did say you might be able to help out with that."

"Well, I gave the secretary at SAG a call, and I can tell you that Ty Zinfeld is no longer a member."

"So he's not acting anymore."

"I'd say not. He's getting older, as we all are, but she said he hadn't renewed his membership for at least forty years. I guess he did a few bit parts before that, but nothing major. I know the secretary, Rose. She told me she wasn't sure, but she thought he'd gone into some other business. I've got his last known address, if you're interested."

"Oh, you sweetheart." Sadie took the slip of paper Glee held out. "Louis Zinfeld?"

"I guess Ty was his screen name," Glee said with a shrug. "I was surprised to see he's living in Denver—or he was a few years ago."

"Denver?" Sadie read the memo carefully, the wheels of her mind turning. "This could be really helpful. Thanks so much."

Glee smiled and patted her shoulder. "No problem."

"So how's it going on the set?" Sadie asked.

Glee sighed. "It could be better."

"What happened?"

"Well, we didn't burn down Mr. Riley's house, so it could have been worse."

Sadie waited, speechless, until Glee went on.

"It was one of the girls, an actress who came out from California with the main players. Fox had told everybody not to smoke in the house, but she lit up in the kitchen. I don't know if she forgot or just figured he wouldn't find out, which was silly. Fox smelled the smoke clear at the other end of the house, where they were setting up for a scene in the family room. He went charging into the kitchen and yelled, 'Put that thing out!' Wendy was so startled, she turned around and threw the cigarette at the sink, because she didn't have an ashtray. Well, it hit the curtain, and kaboom, up it went in flames."

10

———

"OH DEAR," SADIE SAID. "I HOPE THEY WERE ABLE TO PUT OUT the fire right away."

"Yes, one of the boys knocked the curtain down into the sink and doused it with water. But it wasn't a prop—it was the owner's curtain. And they also knocked a little plant off the windowsill into the sink, and the pot broke. Part of my job before tomorrow is to replace said plant pot and curtain with something as close as we can get to match the originals. If Simon is upset, we'll have to pay extra, but that's show biz."

"*Hmm*, Putnam and Sons Hardware, next door, has a lot of gardening supplies, and I think Roscoe has a pretty good variety of flowerpots. Was it a fancy one?"

"No, just run-of-the-mill terra-cotta. It would be great if I can find one that easily, and some potting soil. I think the plant will survive. And that would save me a trip into Denver."

"Oh, you wouldn't have to go that far," Sadie assured her. "Breckenridge has a lot of stores. In fact, you might find curtains there. Of course, if you want an exact match..."

"I thought I'd look online this evening," Glee said. "If there's nothing exactly right, I'll have to get the closest thing I can. Fox was really upset, though, because they'd filmed a whole scene in the kitchen and they can't do retakes unless the curtain matches. He really, really does not want to do that entire scene over. It's a very intense one, and the actors did a great job the first time. There were just one or two spots he wasn't entirely happy with, toward the end, so he had been thinking they might reshoot the last few minutes."

Julie stepped up. "Excuse me, but I couldn't help overhearing what you said. Maybe I can help you find something."

"Yes." Sadie smiled at her assistant. "Julie is very good at decorating and fabrics and all of that."

"Well, I'll accept all the help I can get. The crew is starting to say this film is jinxed."

"Really?" Julie said.

"Well, some of them heard about what happened before." Glee glanced at Sadie. "You know—about the boy who died."

Sadie nodded. "I hope they won't get people stirred up about it."

"We don't need distractions, that's for sure. We need to work hard and get this picture made on time. But kids aren't always very smart, you know? One of the gopher boys even mentioned Fox running over J.B.'s suitcase the day they got here, and Fox heard them laughing about it. He was livid."

"That's not good," Sadie said sympathetically.

Glee shook her head. "You have to think before you speak. Why can't they get that through their heads?"

"Gossip always causes hurt," Julie agreed.

Glee dug into her pocket and pulled out a crumpled sandwich bag. "I rescued a little piece of the curtain that didn't get burnt." She held the bag out to Julie.

Julie took it and peered through the plastic at the scrap of charred cloth. "Yellow gingham. I wonder if the late Mrs. Riley made the curtains herself. Did they have any embroidery or anything like that?"

"I can show you a picture." Glee looked at Sadie. "Can you spare her for a little while? Because if Julie can go over to the B and B with me, I can get one of the techs to show her what they filmed this afternoon, and she can see what the curtains looked like before the fire."

"That's a great idea," Julie said.

"It's fine." Sadie looked around the store. "We only have one or two customers left, and I'll be closing up in twenty minutes. You go ahead, Julie. I'll close up and drop by Roz's house when I leave."

"Great! This will be fun. If they're plain gingham, we can get some at the fabric shop in Breckenridge. I could whip up a couple of panels in no time for you. Oh, and if you know what size the flowerpot was, we can pop in to Roscoe's and buy a new one before he closes."

"Aren't you amazing?" Glee said, staring at Julie with renewed hope.

"I don't know about that, but we might possibly be able to replace the props tonight. Just let me grab my things."

Julie and Glee left in high spirits, and Sadie began her end-of-the-day routine. As soon as her last customers left, she looked again at the address Glee had given her. A phone number was scrawled at the bottom.

She held her breath, waiting for the ringing to be answered. A man's voice came on, mature but strong.

"What can I do for you?"

"Mr. Zinfeld?" Sadie asked.

"Yes, this is Lou Zinfeld."

"Hi. I'm Sadie Speers, in Silver Peak. Uh...did you used to go by the name of Ty Zinfeld?"

After a pause, he said, "That was some time ago."

"Mr. Zinfeld, I was a girl when the first version of *Stranger from a Strange World* was made here in Silver Peak. I wondered if I could talk to you about that."

"That's something I'd rather forget," he said.

"A lot of us would, but please—it would mean a lot to me. My best friend is Mike Tabor's sister. You—you do remember Mike?"

"Yes, and I heard what happened to him. I'm very sorry. But I wasn't in Silver Peak when it happened. I don't see how I can help you."

"My friend needs to know what happened to Mike. Even though you had already left, it might help her to hear how things were between you when you were here."

Lou Zinfeld sighed. "I'll be in Breckenridge tomorrow afternoon on business. Could you and your friend meet me there?"

"Of course," Sadie said. "What time should we come?"

"Well, I've got a three o'clock appointment with a client. Why don't we say four? There's a diner near the main road. We could get some coffee."

"I know where it is," Sadie said. "We'll be there. Thank you so much!"

She locked up and headed for her Tahoe when she spotted her cousin, Laura Finch, walking toward the stairway entrance to her apartment, which was on the third floor of the Antique Mine building.

"Hey," Sadie called. "How are you doing?"

Laura smiled and veered toward her. As usual, she looked professional and put together. She wore black pants and a tailored jacket, with a bright splash of color from an abstract-patterned scarf.

"Doing pretty well, but busy. I've been doing a lot of work for one of my Boston clients this month."

"That's good, I guess," Sadie said. "I haven't seen much of you lately."

"Do you have plans for dinner?" Laura asked.

"Nope. I'm just going to drop by Roz's house to see her latest decorating efforts. Want to come along? We can pull something out of my freezer afterward."

"Sure, but I might have a better offer. I put minestrone in the slow cooker this morning."

"Oh, that sounds wonderful," Sadie said. "Hop in. We'll pay Roz a call and come back to your apartment."

Roz met them at her door and greeted Laura enthusiastically.

"I'm so glad you came."

"Good," Sadie said, "because Julie told me you were in a showing-off mood."

"Wait until you see it." Roz led them into the hallway that led to the bedrooms. "Laura, I don't know what Sadie's told you, but I've done the master bath over. Julie gave me a few pointers, and I love it." She took them to the door of the master bath and flung it open. "Ta-da!"

Sadie and Laura stepped in and looked around.

"*Ooh*, I like the paint color," Sadie said. The cream-colored walls had a rose undertone. "It's delicate and warm, but it doesn't come across as too feminine."

"Roscoe seemed to like it," Roz said.

Sadie's gaze fell on the collage Roz had made from old cro-cheted gloves, doilies, and other bits and pieces of vintage textiles.

"Oh, that came out beautifully!"

"You made that?" Laura asked.

Roz nodded, grinning.

"Absolutely gorgeous," Laura said.

"And there are your tins." Sadie gazed up at the row of old containers that lined the top of the medicine cabinet. On the opposite wall over the towel rack, a knickknack shelf held half a dozen vintage tins and bottles.

"Macassar oil," Laura read off one of the labels. "What's that?"

Roz laughed. "I got that at Sadie's store. She tells me it's what Roscoe would have put in his hair a hundred and fifty years ago."

"Yes, it's why they needed to invent the antimacassar to pro-tect the upholstery in Victorian days," Sadie said.

Laura frowned. "Oh, is that the little doily they put on the back of the chair?"

"Bingo. My great-grandmother used to crochet them by the dozen. There's a box of them in my attic." Sadie turned to Roz. "I think you've done a fantastic job."

"Thanks. Now I just need to convince Roscoe that we need new towels."

The women walked slowly out to the living room.

"I wanted to tell you that I've found Ty Zinfeld," Sadie said. She glanced at Laura. "He was here fifty years ago, during the making of the old movie, and he knew Roz's brother."

"I see," Laura said.

"Anyway," Sadie continued, "he's going in to Breckenridge tomorrow afternoon, Roz, and he's invited us to have coffee with him. I'll come pick you up at three thirty, if you're interested."

"Of course I'm interested," Roz said eagerly. "That reminds me—while I was painting the bathroom and making my collage, I had a lot of time to think, and one of the people I thought about was Joe Pinkham."

Sadie stopped near the front door and faced her. "What about Joe? He was caught…" She stopped.

"That's right," Roz said. "Mike turned him in for cheating on an exam."

"You mentioned that last week, but to be honest, I hadn't thought about it in years."

"It was their senior year," Roz said. "Joe was kicked off the baseball team because of it."

Sadie huffed out a breath. "It's all coming back. He carried quite a grudge, didn't he?"

"He sure did. Some kids even heard him threatening Mike."

Sadie's mind reeled, and she didn't like where it was going. "That was near the end of the school year, wasn't it?"

"It was in April," Roz said. "The team still had a lot of games left."

"And Mike died in July, right?"

Roz nodded.

Sadie stood for a moment in thought. "Joe couldn't have had anything to do with Mike's death. I mean, something would have come out at the time. He didn't stick around that summer, did he?"

"I don't remember."

"Was your dad aware of the tension between Mike and Joe?"

"Oh yeah. I'm sure he and Mom both were. But I don't know what happened to Joe. Do you know where he is now?"

"No." Sadie brushed her hair back from her forehead. "Let's sleep on that, and we can talk more about it tomorrow on the drive to Breckenridge, okay?"

"Yeah."

Sadie gave Roz a quick hug. "Sorry to leave you on such a downer. I really love the 'new' bathroom. You did a great job."

"I love it too," said Laura, who had been quiet during their exchange about Joe Pinkham.

"Thanks." Roz had tears in her eyes, but she smiled as she showed them out.

"That was intense," Laura said when they were back in Sadie's Tahoe.

"Yes," Sadie agreed. "Roz's brother died fifty years ago, during the filming of *Stranger from a Strange World,* and all this activity for the remake has stirred up memories for her."

"Wow, that's rough," Laura said.

"Yeah. I hope I can help ease her mind, but I'm not sure digging up all these details about the past is the best way to do that." It was only a short drive back to the store on Main Street. Sadie pulled in at the curb.

"If there's anything I can do to help, let me know," Laura said.

"Thanks. Now, let's go have some of that minestrone."

After an hour spent in her cousin's cozy kitchen, Sadie went home to Hank. She sat down with a cup of tea and her phone directory. Could the decades-old cheating scandal possibly have anything to do with the note she'd received, warning her not to continue investigating? Was somebody trying to keep those events from coming to light once more?

She thought about it for a while and picked up her phone to call Janet Parks's older sister, Linda Baker.

"Sure, I have the yearbook from 1965," Linda said, in answer to Sadie's request. "That was my junior year. I've got all four of my annuals."

"Would it be too much trouble for you to give me a list of the seniors that year?" Sadie asked. She knew the high school classes had been fairly small back then. If Linda could find the book easily, it shouldn't take long.

"Sure," she said. "I know Andrea Grinnell and Chuck Wayne were in that class. Let me go find the yearbook, and I'll call you back."

"Thanks," Sadie said and hung up. She opened a notebook and wrote down the two names Linda had mentioned. She was pretty sure Andrea Grinnell had married and moved away from Silver Peak, but Chuck Wayne still lived on the outskirts of town. He had a business in Breckenridge.

While she waited, she jotted down Joe Pinkham's name and a couple of others she thought were in the same class. Her phone rang sooner than she had expected, and she answered it eagerly.

"Got it," Linda said. "I blew the dust off. Now, you want all the seniors' names?"

"If it's not too much trouble," Sadie said.

"Not a bit. There were…let's see, about two dozen. Of course, my Hal was in that class."

"Oh, that's right." Sadie wrote Hal Baker's name on her list. "He wasn't on the baseball team, was he?"

"No, he had to help his dad too much on the farm, so he didn't do many after-school sports." Linda read the list slowly for Sadie. Each name brought back memories of her school days. Between her own recollections and Linda's they agreed that at least four members of the class of 1965 had passed away. Several had moved out of Silver Peak, but about a third of them still lived locally.

When Linda had finished, Sadie said, "Now, if you don't mind, could you find the picture of that year's baseball team and read me the names, whether they were seniors or not?"

"Sure." Sadie could hear Linda turning the pages of the annual. "Here it is. Man, they look so young!"

"I'm sure." Sadie carefully copied all the names not already on her list. "Thank you so much, Linda. This is a big help."

"May I ask what you wanted it for?" Linda asked.

Sadie hesitated. "Well, you know Mike Tabor died that year?"

"Sure. We were all pretty shaken up by it."

"Yeah. I'm trying to find out a little more about it for Roz. This whole thing with the movie crew in town has brought up memories, you know?"

"I see." Linda let out a sigh. "That was so sad. Mike was a really nice boy. And his dad was just shattered. I remember the funeral, and Mr. Tabor sitting there with tears streaming down his face."

Sadie's throat tightened. "Me too. I confess I've tried not to think too much about that time over the years."

"I hope Roz doesn't let all this hoopla get to her," Linda said.

"I think she'll be okay." After they hung up, Sadie studied the list. Joe Pinkham had been both a senior and a baseball player. Linda had read his name twice. The team photo for the yearbook must have been taken before Joe was expelled from the team, Sadie reflected.

Luke Conroy was another senior who played on the team. Sadie hadn't seen him for a while, but she had known him since childhood. He was Dr. Tom Conroy's younger brother. While Tom went into medicine, Luke had been drawn to teaching. Doc had mentioned recently to Sadie that his brother had retired from his position as dean of a small private college in Boulder. A little searching online turned up a telephone number. It wasn't too late in the evening, Sadie decided, and she called it.

"Sadie Speers! What a surprise," Luke said when she had identified herself. "How are things in Silver Peak?"

She chuckled. "Don't know if you've heard, but we've got a lot of excitement here."

"Tom told me. A new sci-fi flick, huh? Just like the old days."

"That's right. People either love it or hate it. The businesses they're patronizing, like the restaurants and the B and B, are flourishing. Then there are those who've lost business when the movie crew blocked Main Street off for a couple of days."

Luke chuckled. "Boy, I remember that spaceship they rigged up. That was something, wasn't it? Are they doing that again?"

"I think it will mostly be added later with computer effects," Sadie said. "Luke, I wanted to ask you about something else that happened in 1965."

"What's that?"

"You were on the baseball team, right? With Joe Pinkham and Chuck Wayne and all those guys?"

"Yeah, I was. We thought we had a chance at the championships that year, but then Joe got tossed off the team. He was our shortstop, and we needed him."

"So you didn't make it to the play-offs?" Sadie asked.

"Nope."

"I guess you guys were all disappointed."

"Sure," Luke said. "It was our senior year, and our last chance. But still..."

"What?" Sadie asked softly.

"Oh, just thinking about what happened. I don't blame Mike Tabor for ratting on Joe. But a lot of guys were angry at Mike, you know."

"I thought maybe."

"Oh yeah." Luke sighed. "A lot of kids thought Mike was a Goody Two-shoes."

"They thought he shouldn't have turned in his teammate?"

"That about says it. But, hey, Joe had been coasting all through high school. He knew he had to pull his grades up if he wanted to keep playing ball. School policy, you know?"

"Oh, I know," Sadie said. "They still have rules like that."

"That's right, you taught at Silver Peak, didn't you?"

"I sure did. Many years."

"Then you know exactly what I'm talking about."

"You sound as though you think Mike did the right thing."

"I do," Luke said. "At the time, I wasn't happy about it. The timing was bad, you know? But Mike had to follow his conscience. He was a great guy. And then he went and fell off a cliff. What a waste!"

11

After her conversation with Luke, Sadie hesitated to call more of the aging baseball players. Talking to him had brought on a wave of emotion she hadn't expected, and her nerves were raw. No wonder Roz had been on edge lately. But Luke had suggested that if she wanted a different opinion, she could call Chuck Wayne. He was in her local phone directory, so she topped off her cup of tea and keyed in the number.

When Chuck's wife had called him to the phone, Sadie got right to the point.

"Joe Pinkham? What do you want to poke around about that for?" Chuck asked.

"I'm just curious," Sadie said. "What ever happened to him? He moved away not long after graduation, right?"

"Yeah, but he's passed now."

"You mean, he died?"

"That's right. Heart attack, they say. It happened a couple of years ago."

"I'm sorry to hear that. You kept up with him?" Sadie asked.

"Not really. I only saw him once after we graduated. That was before he got in trouble."

"What kind of trouble?"

Chuck hesitated. "He went East, you know. Got into the stock market."

"He was a broker?"

"Yeah. He called me once and asked if I wanted to invest in some start-up company's stock. I just laughed and told him I didn't have any extra money to blow."

"So he got in trouble for his activity in the stock market?" Sadie asked slowly.

"No, it was something that happened later. Joe was a mess. He was married two or three times. Couldn't keep things together."

"What do you mean?"

"Well, I always wondered if he was into drugs," Chuck replied. "I'm not saying he was, but he sure was doing something wrong. Lost his trading license, and had at least two broken marriages. Then I heard he got arrested."

"But not for insider trading or something like that?"

"I'm not clear on what it was about. Something to do with his family, I think."

"Okay. Thanks, Chuck," Sadie said. "I appreciate your frankness."

"Joe and I were friends in school," Chuck said. "But later, it was like I didn't even know him. He left Colorado, and he had this whole life I couldn't relate to, you know?"

"I'm sorry he went that way." Sadie paused, not sure whether to make the connection to Mike or not. "Chuck, what do you think started Joe down the wrong path?"

"Maybe the drugs, if there were any. Or maybe it started before he left Silver Peak. He was very angry after they told him he couldn't play baseball, you know."

"Yes," Sadie said cautiously. "Can you tell me about that?"

"Joe had an athletic scholarship to UC Denver. But his grades weren't terrific, and he was in danger of losing it. They pulled it after the cheating scandal. Big bummer."

"I remember when that happened," Sadie said. "I was only in eighth grade, but it was a big deal for the whole town."

"Yeah. Joe got a bad deal, if you ask me."

"I guess he was really upset."

"He couldn't leave town fast enough after graduation. Broke up with his girlfriend. He told me once that if he had a chance, he'd kill Mike Tabor. He's the chump who turned Joe in."

Sadie swallowed hard. "But he left immediately after he graduated, and Mike… "

"Oh, he didn't do anything to Tabor. But I almost wouldn't blame him if he had. I know you're friends with his sister, but Tabor was a rat."

"That's…pretty strong," Sadie managed.

"We lost the chance to win the state championship because of him. The whole school suffered, not to mention the team and all the fans. Couldn't he have waited till after the game?"

"I guess not. But Mike was only telling the truth. And it wasn't his fault if Joe got into drugs afterward. Joe wrecked his own life."

"Yeah, right." Chuck didn't sound sincere.

"Well, thanks for talking to me," Sadie said.

She hung up feeling drained. Was this really worth it? At moments like this, she wished she hadn't told Roz she would look into Mike's death.

———

"He wouldn't tell you what Joe did to get himself arrested?" Roz asked.

"Either Chuck didn't know, or he didn't want to say." Sadie pulled up at a stop sign. They were nearly to Breckenridge, where they would meet Louis Zinfeld at the diner. "Does it matter?"

"I don't know," Roz said. "Maybe. What if he was a violent criminal?"

"He was out of town when Mike died."

"So far as we know."

Sadie shot her a sidelong glance. "Well, I'm pretty sure Joe didn't have anything to do with this. How about we stop thinking about him and see what we can find out from Mr. Zinfeld?"

"You're right." Roz let out a deep breath.

Sadie spotted the diner and pulled into a parking spot. Only half a dozen patrons were inside the long, narrow eatery. A gray-haired man with a beard and glasses rose when she and Roz entered and walked toward them.

"Sadie?"

"Louis?" She smiled and shook his hand. "This is Roz Putnam."

"Lou Zinfeld." He shook Roz's hand. "Glad to meet you both. I've got a booth."

They sat down with him and ordered. Lou already had a mug of black coffee before him.

"So you want to talk about the movie," he said.

Sadie nodded. "If you don't mind."

"That was a long time ago."

"Yes, it was," Roz said, "but it was my brother who replaced you when you left Silver Peak, and I'd really like to hear from you how things were between you."

Lou nodded slowly as the waitress set coffee and a dish of creamers on the table. "Mike was a good kid. We got along fine."

Roz picked up a cream container and peeled it open. "I heard that before you left, you and Mike had some words."

"What? Really?" Lou looked truly baffled.

Sadie cleared her throat. "As you said, it was a long time ago. A friend of ours had an interest in Mike at the time. She said that when you were... when Mr. Monahan let you go..."

"Yeah, when he fired me," Lou said with a wry smile.

"Well, yes. This friend said that when you were fired, and then you heard Mike was replacing you, that you..."

"You said something nasty to him," Roz put in, as though her brother were still there to defend.

"Really?" Lou picked up his mug and took a sip. "I'm sorry. I don't remember that. I do remember being upset that I was canned. The job meant a lot to me, and I blew it."

"You and Mike had gotten along before that," Sadie said gently.

"Yeah, we did. I liked him. He was smart. Eager."

"Can you tell us what happened with Mr. Monahan?" Sadie asked.

Lou shrugged. "It happened really fast. J.B. was already put out with me because of something that happened a couple of days earlier. He'd asked me to move his car for him, and I forgot to put on the parking brake."

"Oops," Roz said and took a quick gulp of her coffee.

"Oops is right," Lou said. "The car rolled downhill and smashed into a tree."

"I guess that would do it," Sadie said.

"Sure. But he didn't fire me then, and I was so grateful that he'd given me another chance."

"He said you were late to work a couple of times," Sadie hazarded.

"Really?" Lou frowned. "I wonder if Blaze told him that to get me in trouble, because Blaze didn't like me. Or maybe I was late. Better yet, maybe J.B. didn't want to tell you why he really fired me. Because when Blaze Foster got angry at me, it was over, like that." Lou snapped his fingers. "I hardly knew what hit me."

"Why was Blaze angry?" Roz asked.

"It was something stupid. I'd moved his jacket, I think. It was chilly up there on the mountain, and everyone bundled up between takes. We were getting ready for a scene, and I saw this jacket sitting there and I picked it up to move it out of the way, and Blaze tore into me. Verbally, that is. Cussed me up and down. And J.B. came over. He told Blaze to calm down, then he looked at me and said, 'Pack your stuff, Ty. I can't work this way.' It took me a second to figure out he'd fired me."

"Wow," Sadie said. She and Roz just sat there for a moment, gazing at him.

Lou smiled slowly. "It's all right, ladies. Blaze hadn't liked me from the start. A couple of times he'd accused me of upstaging him. I don't know if J.B. felt he had to appease the star by firing me or what, but anyway, it turned out to be one of the best things that ever happened to me."

"Are you just saying that?" Roz asked.

"Nope. I had a chance to take a job with my uncle. He'd offered it to me before, but I was sure my acting career was going to take off, so I'd turned him down. After J.B. fired me, I went to him and begged, and he found a place for me."

"What kind of business was it?" Sadie asked.

"A toy company. He made sleds and toboggans. Over the years, we expanded, and now Zinfeld makes some of the best snowboards you can buy. My uncle left me the company, and it's taken good care of me. I sold it five years ago and retired."

"You retired?" Sadie asked. "But you said you had a meeting with a client today."

Lou laughed. "That's right. I may be getting old, but I still have a lot of good ideas. Right now I'm into buying and selling mountain property. I met with someone who would like to start a Nordic skiing retreat."

"That sounds interesting," Roz said. "So you really think you were fired because you moved the star's jacket?"

Lou's face scrunched up for a moment. "Oh, there were other things. I was fifteen years younger than Blaze, and the girls seemed to like me."

Sadie could well believe that. Lou had a charming personality, and he was still a handsome man. "Blaze didn't like that?" she asked.

"Well, you know how some big stars can be. They need to be the center of attention. Gina Tarino was the leading lady." He smiled. "She was really something."

"That must have been a thrill, working alongside her," Roz said.

"Oh yeah. And she seemed to show me a few favors. Like offering me part of her french fries. Little things like that. And one day we were filming out at the ranch, and she asked me if she could ride back to town with me. I don't think Blaze liked that. So the jacket may have been the last straw."

Roz nodded. "You could be right. Can you tell me any more about Mike? How was he the last time you saw him?"

Lou sat back and thought for a moment, gazing toward the window. "He was excited. And I truly managed to feel glad for him. Yeah, at first I didn't like it, and I may have said something. I mean, Mike was a rank amateur. He had no credentials, and I had worked really hard to get that part. But we had become friends before the whole thing happened, and I didn't want to leave it that way."

"So you did say something mean to him," Roz said, leaning forward.

"Okay, I did. I'm sorry now, and I was sorry then. Mike was a good kid. It bothered me at first that he benefitted from my getting fired, but I apologized to him before I left."

Roz didn't look convinced.

"It's true," Lou said. "I was packing up my stuff, and Mike came by to talk to me. We parted on good terms. I gave him my home address, and we promised to keep in touch." His eyes clouded. "And then I heard on the news a couple of days later that Mike had died."

They sat in silence for a moment, and then Lou went on. "They said he'd fallen from that cliff, where we were going to shoot the spaceship scene. I wondered if it had to do with those markers that were supposed to keep us from going too near the edge. They were really close to the brink, and it was a little scary."

"That's what I'd like to know," Roz said quietly. "Was it truly an accident? Was the film company negligent? Or was it something more?"

"That I can't help you with, but I can give you this." Lou reached in his pocket and pulled out a postcard with a mountain scene. "I got this the day after I heard. It was kind of a shock."

He handed it to Roz, and she looked down at the message written on the flip side. Sadie could see the four-cent stamp in the corner. She wanted to lean closer and read over Roz's shoulder, but she made herself sit still. After a long moment, Roz looked up at her.

"It's from Mike. It's his handwriting." Roz's voice caught.

"What's it say?" Sadie asked.

Roz passed it to her and dove into her purse for a tissue.

Sadie read the short message and felt tears prick her eyes.

Dear Ty,

You were right. Things went better today. I still wish things had gone differently and you were here doing the job, but this may turn out to be my big break. Best of luck in your new venture!

Mike

Roz wiped her eyes. "I guess you guys did make up."

Lou nodded. "I'm glad, but it was still so senseless. I'm not sure why I kept the postcard all these years. Probably because it arrived the way it did, when I'd just heard about his fall. I dug it out after Sadie called and told me you'd like to talk about Mike and the movie." He looked Roz squarely in the eyes. "Your brother was talented and smart. If he'd lived, maybe he'd have become a great actor. Maybe not. But whatever he did, I'm sure he would have succeeded. And he was a good friend to have on your side."

Roz cleared her throat. "Thank you."

Lou nodded and then smiled. "More coffee? I've got to drive back to Denver, and I might just have a muffin for the road. Will you ladies let me treat you?"

———————

On the way home, Roz took out the postcard and looked at it again.

"It's nice that Lou let you keep that," Sadie said.

Roz nodded. "It caught me by surprise, seeing Mike's handwriting again."

"Lou was right—he was a good friend. He didn't have to write to Lou after he'd left. Mike could have just forgotten about him in the excitement of his new position."

"This shows that he truly cared about Lou." Roz flicked a tear from her eyelashes. "I know he would rather have gotten the new part some other way." She turned on the seat to face Sadie. "Maybe I've had some nebulous idea that it was Ty's fault. I mean Lou's."

"That Mike died?" Sadie asked, frowning.

"Yeah. If he hadn't messed up and gotten fired, Mike would have just been an extra, so he wouldn't have been in that scene on the cliff, and he wouldn't have fallen."

"I guess you could think of it that way. But it's a string of circumstances, not a direct cause. Surely you can't blame Lou."

"No, not consciously. And now that I know they were actually friends, I do feel better. But I still think the movie company was irresponsible."

"That may be," Sadie said. "At least we know Lou was a long ways from here when it all happened."

Roz gazed down at the postcard's glossy picture, an autumn view of Quandary Peak. "I'm glad he's happy with the way his life went. I do wonder about Joe Pinkham, though. It sounds like things didn't turn out so well for him."

"According to what Chuck Wayne told me."

"Yeah. Do you think there's more to it, where Joe is concerned? He was awfully resentful of Mike."

"I don't know." Sadie turned onto Roz's road. "It probably weighed on Mike those last few months, having turned in a classmate. When he did it, Mike might not have realized how deeply it would affect Joe."

"But he did the right thing."

"Oh yes, I'm not arguing that point. But whistle-blowers pay a price." Sadie pulled into the Putnams' driveway. "Maybe I can find some more information about Joe. Something concrete."

"Yeah, I'd like to know if his life turned out as sordidly as Chuck made it sound. I know Mike wouldn't like that."

"If it did, it wasn't his fault."

Roz nodded. "I know that. But I think you're right—Mike carried some guilt, whether justified or not."

"I think J. B. Monahan did too," Sadie said. "Whatever happened that day, he was in charge. I know that would knock the stuffing out of me."

"Yeah. It's a lot to live with." Roz opened her door and swung her legs out of the Tahoe. "Thanks, Sadie. I'll see you."

Julie had closed the store, so Sadie drove on by and went home. She gave Julie a call while she let Hank race around the yard.

"Hey, I wondered how it went with the curtains?"

Julie laughed. "Glee phoned me this afternoon, right after you left. Fox couldn't believe it when she told him we'd made them last night, based on the pictures she showed me and that one scrap of fabric. She said he insisted I submit an invoice for my time, and the producer will make sure I get paid for it. I tried to say no, but Glee told me I should accept it with grace. Sadie, they're paying me a hundred dollars, and the material cost less than twenty."

"That's great," Sadie said. "And Glee is right. You gave up your whole evening to help her with that. You deserve every penny."

After fixing supper for herself and Hank, Sadie got her pocket notebook from her purse and went over various notes she'd jotted about both the UFO sighting and Mike Tabor's death.

Since she had obtained a little information on Joe Pinkham's life from Chuck Wayne, Sadie was able to make a productive online search for more details. She found evidence of his having been an active stockbroker with a firm in New Jersey for several years, but then she turned up a news report stating that Joseph Pinkham had been arrested for manslaughter.

Startled, Sadie went over the short article carefully to be sure she was reading about the same person. Pinkham had been involved in a hit-and-run accident that left two people dead. Later investigations showed that he had been intoxicated at the time.

Sadie checked the dates of the events. Joe would have been close to retirement age when the crash took place. He had been imprisoned to serve his sentence for two counts of manslaughter. Sadie would not have recognized Joe from the photo provided by the news photographer. However, she was able to positively connect him to the stock brokerage. She sat back with her stomach churning. Joe Pinkham had died of a heart attack after two years in prison. She wasn't prepared for the sadness that washed over her.

A call from Edwin at half past eight cheered her up a little.

"I'm taking Sam to watch the filming at Milo's tomorrow. Want to join us?"

"It sounds like fun," Sadie said.

"Well, I know I'll find it interesting, but I don't know how long Sam will stay still. I figure he can have a return visit to Sunflower if he gets restless."

"Oh, did he get to ride yesterday?"

"He sure did," Edwin said. "He loved it. We stayed out about an hour. And Noelle bonded with Scout. She said she almost wished they lived where they could keep a couple of horses."

"Did she really?" The idea tickled Sadie.

"Well, she reneged pretty quickly when Carl asked if she wanted to move out into the country. But I took it as a good sign. She's remarked several times on how much fun the ride was."

"I'm glad," Sadie said. "Why don't you pick me up at the store when you and Sam are ready to go to the ranch?"

They left it at that, and Sadie felt much more lighthearted as she went about her bedtime routine. The past was in the past, she reminded herself. She was very grateful for the present and the prospect of a bright future.

12

Sam's chatter on the way to the ranch kept Sadie occupied. As she pointed out animals, barns, and other things Sam never saw in Atlanta, he got more excited by the minute.

"Am I going to ride the horse again, Miss Sadie?"

"I'm not sure," she replied, with a glance at Edwin. "You had fun the other day, didn't you?"

"Uh-huh. My dad rode with me, and for a while my grandpa rode with me."

"Which horse did you like best?" Sadie asked.

"Sunflower. She's white all over. Do you know Sunflower?"

"Yes, I do. She's a good horse."

Sam nodded. "I love Sunflower. But Mr. Henderson said I can't ride Bronco."

"Not many people can ride him." Bronco was Theo's three-year-old gelding, and he could be a handful at times.

When they arrived at Milo's, several vehicles were parked in his yard. Sadie was surprised to see Derek walking toward the barn carrying a small metal toolbox.

"Hi, Derek," Sadie called.

He paused and greeted them, then fixed his gaze on Sam. "And who is this young man?"

"He's my grandson," Edwin replied. "Sam, this is Mr. Todd. He's in charge of all the special effects for the movie—things that make weird noises and look scary."

Derek laughed. "For this movie, that's about the size of it."

"Are you working in the barn?" Sadie asked.

"Yeah, Milo said I could use his empty haymow for a workshop. It's under cover, and it gives me a place to spread out my tools."

"That's good," Sadie said, smiling. "We thought we'd hike up the mountain to where they're filming this morning."

"You might want to drive," Derek said. "They took the actors up in vehicles, and some of the crew were complaining about the hike. It's not that far, but I suppose the altitude is getting to them."

"That happens if you're not used to it," Edwin said.

"What do you think?" Sadie asked. "You and I would be fine, but Sam isn't used to this either."

"Good point. Maybe we should drive, at least partway."

Sadie nodded and waved a hand in farewell to Derek. "Maybe we'll see you later. We told Sam he could see the horses again."

They drove up to the area being used as a set. Filming was under way, so Edwin parked a couple of hundred yards down the trail, and they walked the rest of the way. For several minutes, they watched the activity. Edwin boosted Sam onto his shoulders.

The actors seemed terrified as they stared out over the valley below, beckoned, pointed, and screamed. Finally they began to run away from the edge of the bluff.

"Cut!" Fox Monahan rose from his folding chair. "Let's do that again, but this time make me believe it, people."

"What are they yelling at?" Sam asked, frowning.

"The spaceship," Edwin said.

"What spaceship?" Sam's brow wrinkled and he swiveled his head, looking all around from his perch on Edwin's shoulders.

"They're pretending," Sadie said, holding back a laugh. "That man we met down at the barn—Mr. Todd—he'll add the spaceship into the picture later with a computer."

Sam frowned down at her. "They can do that?"

"Sure they can," Edwin said. "It's sort of like...well, like if you drew a picture of my house and then later you decided to go back and draw me in too, sitting on the front porch."

"Okay," Sam said doubtfully.

"Places," Fox yelled.

"We have to be quiet now," Edwin said.

They watched another take of the panic scene. The actors seemed disorganized. None of them appeared to focus on the same imaginary spot in the sky over the cliff. When it was over, Fox was again dissatisfied and began barking orders.

Sam patted Edwin's head. "Grandpa, can we go see the horses now?"

"Sure." Edwin swung him down to earth, and Sam reached for Sadie's hand.

"I hope I get to ride Sunflower again."

"We'll see how things are going, down at the barn," Sadie told him. They walked back to the car, and Edwin drove down to the barnyard. When they strolled over to the corral fence, Scout nickered and came over to nuzzle Sadie's hand.

"This is Scout," she said.

"My mommy rode Scout," Sam said proudly.

"Here comes Sunflower." Edwin boosted Sam up onto the rail fence and pointed at the white mare. Sunflower ambled over slowly and whickered low in her throat. Sam giggled and tried to imitate the sound.

Sadie looked around. Milo's pickup was parked near the barn, but he was nowhere in sight. "Why don't I go see if Milo's in the barn," she said. "Maybe we could throw a saddle on Sunflower for a few minutes."

She left Edwin and Sam dividing their attention between Scout, Sunflower, and Sara's Daisy, who came to the fence to see what all the fuss was about.

Sadie stepped into the barn and let her eyes adjust to the dim light. All of the stall doors were open, so she knew all the horses were outside in the corral or the bigger pasture. A sound of hammering came from the far end of the barn. She walked the length of the alley between the stalls, toward the open space where Milo stored hay for the winter. It would be nearly empty now, but soon it would be time for farmers and ranchers to cut their first hay crop of the season and start refilling their haymows.

Before she reached the doorway, the hammering stopped and Derek Todd came out. He stopped short when he saw her, blinking behind his glasses.

"Oh, hi, Sadie."

"Hi. Is Milo around?"

"I think he's in the house," Derek said.

"Thanks." He didn't seem to want to move. Sadie said, "So what are you working on?"

"Just stuff for the movie. How was the filming going up there?"

Sadie wrinkled her nose. "I'm not an expert, but it didn't seem to be going very well. The actors all seemed to be looking for the spaceship, not at it. I don't know—it will probably be fine after you add in your part with the special effects, but it seemed like Fox wasn't too happy."

"Aha." Derek nodded. "That's one good thing about using a mock-up when you're filming, even if you go in and touch it up later. At least then everyone knows exactly where to look."

"I know you said it's cheaper not to use one," Sadie said, "and I imagine it's less complicated, with the timing and everything. And I suppose it might be safer too."

"Cheaper," Derek said. "That's what it always comes down to. The bottom line."

"I suppose they have a strict budget."

"Yes." Derek glanced over his shoulder toward his makeshift workshop. "It would be so much more realistic, though."

Sadie shrugged. "I don't know. I'm not an expert on that."

Derek's phone chirped, and he pulled it out of his pocket. "Excuse me."

Sadie nodded and turned to walk back through the barn. As she went, she heard Derek say, "Uh, no, don't deliver it to the ranch. It's better if you don't come out here today. I'll meet you in town. Yeah, there's a big parking lot at the church on Water Street. It should be empty today."

She frowned. Why would Derek ask someone to make a delivery at Campfire Chapel? And why didn't he want the driver to come to Milo's ranch, where he had his workshop?

She walked to the house and knocked. Milo came to the kitchen door with a mug of coffee in his hand.

"Hi, Sadie. Join me?"

"No thanks," she said. "Edwin and Sam are outside. We wondered if we could give Sam a little ride on Sunflower."

"Sure. You want to take Scout and Opie out too?"

"No, I don't think so. We've been up to watch the movie crew, and I need to get back to the store soon. But maybe I can throw a saddle on Sunflower and lead Sam around the corral a few times."

"Whatever you want. The blacksmith's coming soon, but he doesn't need to work on Sunflower."

Sadie went out and told Edwin the plan. He got Sunflower's saddle from the tack room, and soon Sam was astride.

"Can we go up the trail, Grandpa?" the little boy asked as Edwin led the horse up the driveway.

"I guess this seems tame now," Edwin said. "I think we'd better take it easy today. Miss Sadie needs to go to work."

"Why don't you go to work?" Sam asked him.

Edwin laughed. "Some days I do, Sam. But mostly I'm retired now. That means I don't have to go to work every day anymore. I'll probably check in at the town office this afternoon, but I don't expect there'll be anything too strenuous waiting for me."

"What's that mean?" Sam frowned.

Sadie chuckled. "It means he works, but not too hard."

"Oh."

Edwin shook his head. "I don't know about that. Sometimes town business gives me headaches. But mostly it's not bad."

"Mommy gets headaches too," Sam said.

"Sometimes. But she was doing just fine this morning. Hang on now." Edwin jogged a few steps, coaxing Sunflower to move faster.

Half an hour later, they dropped Sadie off in front of the Antique Mine. She waved and headed for the door. It opened just as she reached it, and Roz came out.

"Oh, good, you're here," Roz said. "I thought I'd missed you."

"I was with Edwin and his grandson. What's up?"

"Oh, it's the *Chatterbox*. I guess I could have just called you, but I thought I'd drop by."

"What does it say now?" Sadie asked.

"It's silly, I suppose. The latest post suggests that this film they're making is jinxed. But it draws a connection to the old one." Roz's jaw clenched. "It mentions Mike's accident."

"Oh no." Sadie drew her into a hug. "I'm sorry. I'd hoped that wouldn't happen."

Roz sniffed. "*The Chatterbox* isn't usually hurtful."

"And you think it is, this time?"

"I don't know." Roz pulled away and swiped at a tear. "It probably wasn't intentional, but it made me feel horrible when I read it."

If the mood had been lighter, Sadie would have simply said, *Well, quit reading it.* But she knew that wasn't what Roz needed right now.

"Come back inside," she said. "Let me check in with Julie. If she doesn't need me, we can get some coffee and sit down."

Julie waved to Sadie as she entered. A couple of customers had her attention in the china section, but only two other people were browsing at the moment.

"Doesn't look too busy," Sadie said to Roz. "Let me pull it up and read it."

"Go ahead." Roz walked away and leaned over the glass case of vintage jewelry while Sadie went to the computer. It only took a minute to find the entry Roz was talking about.

Is the Stranger from a Strange World *movie still jinxed? Fifty years ago, Silver Peak lost one of its residents during filming. Now we hear rumors of a small fire in Simon Riley's house during production, and a mishap concerning the director's luggage. What will happen next? Sure hope it's nothing serious and no one gets hurt! Just watch your back, folks. Those aliens may be waiting to pull another stunt.*

Sadie clenched her teeth and read it again. It could have been a lot worse, she decided. Mike wasn't mentioned by name. *The Chatterbox* didn't always seem to care about the readers' feelings. But if she was being honest, under other circumstances, she might have laughed when she read it.

Roz came over and rested her elbows on the counter. "What do you think?"

"I think it's a typical *Chatterbox* entry," Sadie said.

"I suppose. I shouldn't let it upset me. He always tries to mention something controversial," Roz said.

"You think the *Chatterbox* writer is a man?"

"I don't know."

"You said 'he,'" Sadie pointed out.

Roz shrugged. "I don't know, and honestly, I don't care. But if I knew who it was, I'd make them stop. That is not funny. It can only embarrass people or upset them."

Sadie cocked her head to one side and studied Roz's face. "Honey, you know the *Chatterbox* isn't vindictive. Not really. It's just a quirky little part of this town. If they wanted to upset people, they could have said a lot more. They didn't name any names. It wouldn't have been too hard to learn the name of the girl who was smoking and started the fire in Simon Riley's kitchen."

Roz's eyes widened. "You knew about that?"

"Glee told me. The script girl."

"Oh yeah, Julie was telling me about her. She'd helped her find some items for the set."

Sadie nodded. "Those were replacement items that they wrecked at the Riley house when the kitchen curtains caught fire."

"Wow. Julie didn't tell me that." Roz caught her breath and leaned closer across the counter. "You don't think Julie could be the *Chatterbox*, do you?"

Sadie laughed. "When would she have time?"

"Okay. But she did know about the fire."

"Trust me, a lot of people knew about it," Sadie said. "And I'm pretty sure Julie wouldn't have mentioned those things. She's more discreet than that."

"Well, okay, I admit I feel a little better, but what do I say if someone brings it up? About the jinx, I mean."

"You don't believe in jinxes."

"No, I don't," Roz said slowly. "But I'd like to be able to tell them the real reason my brother died."

Sadie squeezed her hand. "I know. And I'm still looking into things. But I don't know that I'll be able to do anything this weekend. Tomorrow night I'm having dinner with Edwin's family and the Monahans, and I promised to bring two pies."

"It's okay," Roz said. "You've already helped a lot."

"Thanks. I don't know if there's much more to learn, but there are still a couple of things we can check out."

———————

Sadie realized with dismay on Saturday evening that she was a little nervous about the dinner at Edwin's house. She wished she had been able to spend more time with Noelle to get to know her better. And then there was J.B. to consider. She hoped she wouldn't need to constantly choose her words in order to avoid upsetting him.

Her two apple pies looked good, and that was a relief. She'd spent the previous evening making them from scratch. She set out for Edwin's house with the slightest trepidation. Fox Monahan's rental car was in the driveway when she arrived, so she hauled in a deep breath and picked up her pie carriers.

Edwin greeted her at the door and took her pies from her. Through the living room doorway, she saw that Noelle, Carl, Fox, and J.B. were already deep in conversation. Noelle looked stunning in a royal blue dress and a gold necklace and dangling earrings.

"Where's Sam?" Sadie asked Edwin.

He frowned. "In the kitchen, eating his dinner. Noelle insisted on feeding him now, and then he'll go to bed."

"He doesn't usually go to bed this early, does he?"

"No."

Sadie gazed at him and saw dissatisfaction in Edwin's eyes. "May I go in and see him after I greet your other guests?"

"I don't see why not."

Sadie went into the living room, leaving Edwin to deal with the pies.

"Hello, Mr. Monahan." She took J.B.'s hand.

"Sadie, good to see you again."

Fox came over, smiling. "Glad you could come."

"Thank you. I hope all's going well with the production."

"Not bad," Fox said. "The lead actress is in a bit of a snit about her wardrobe, but I've got people working on it. Overall, things are coming along nicely, and we're on schedule."

Sadie chatted with them for a few more minutes and then excused herself.

In the kitchen, Edwin sat at the round table with Sam, who was eating his dessert.

"I gave him a small piece of pie," Edwin said. "Hope that's all right."

"It's fine with me," Sadie told him. "Hi, Sam." She smiled and sat down next to him.

"Hi." Sam licked his spoon. "Your pie is good, Miss Sadie."

"Thanks." She noticed a small toy tractor in the middle of the table and reached for it. Some of the paint was chipped away, but the die-cast toy was in pretty good shape. "What's this?"

"It's a John Deere Model B," Edwin said.

She eyed him in surprise. "Is it Sam's?"

"No," Sam said. "It's Grandpa's."

Edwin smiled sheepishly. "I got some of my old toys out of the attic for him to play with. The spacemen were getting a little boring."

"There's a whole farm set," Sam said eagerly. "The rest is up in my room."

"Wow. That could be quite valuable." Sadie looked at Edwin. "Don't tell me you still have the original box it came in."

"No, but I do have the sheet metal barn."

"Do you want to see it?" Sam asked, wriggling around in the chair.

The kitchen door swung open, and Noelle hurried in. She walked quickly to the stove and pulled open the oven door.

"Looks like the lasagna's ready, Dad. We'd better sit down. I'll put things on the table, and Carl can tuck Sam in."

Sadie stood. "Let me help, Noelle."

"Thanks. You could get out the salad for me." Noelle glanced pointedly at Edwin as she grabbed an apron from a hook near the range.

"Okay," he said, standing. "Good night, Sam. You'll have to show the rest of the farm set to Miss Sadie another time."

"Tomorrow?"

He sounded so bleak that Sadie patted his shoulder. "Maybe so, Sam. I might be able to pop over and see it tomorrow afternoon. I'd love to."

"Sure," Edwin said. "We'll show her the whole set, all the sheep and the rooster, and everything."

Sam seemed content with that.

"Finish up your pie," Noelle told him. "Come on! It's bedtime."

Sadie went to the refrigerator and opened it. "Oh, Noelle, your salad is a work of art."

She helped Noelle get the food to the dining room while Edwin fetched Carl to put his son to bed and then chatted with J.B. and Fox Monahan.

"Your town is so charming," Fox said when they had progressed to the main course.

"Even nicer than it was in 1965," J.B. said. "Edwin, I believe Silver Peak has added quite a few new businesses."

"Indeed we have," Edwin said.

"Why, I remember our having to drive in to Breckenridge to get a decent dinner," J.B. went on. "The bed-and-breakfast took care of us in the morning, but you only had a diner and one or two restaurants. Now we have our choice of cuisine."

"Dad and I ate at Los Pollitos last night," Fox said, smiling. "It was very good."

"Oh, we tried that the other night," Carl said. "I loved it."

Sadie smiled. "Ramon is a very good chef."

"Have you tried Sophia's?" Edwin asked. "Of course, we're giving you Italian tonight, but that's another great place to eat. It's new since I moved away from Silver Peak. A very nice addition to the town's lineup."

"We'll try it," Fox said.

J.B. looked down the table at Sadie. "Did you have Glee check on that actor you asked me about?"

"Ty Zinfeld? Yes," Sadie replied with a smile. "As a matter of fact, my friend Roz and I met him in Breckenridge on Thursday. We had a nice visit."

"Is he still in show biz?" J.B. asked.

"No, he's not. He doesn't use the name Ty anymore either. His real name is Louis Zinfeld. After he left here, he worked in his uncle's toy company for many years and then inherited it. He's retired now."

"That doesn't sound so bad," Fox said. "You see, Dad? Everything works out in the end."

"Yes," J.B. said doubtfully. "I'm glad he found his niche. I still feel bad about the other young man, though. The one we brought in to replace him."

Silence hung over the table for a moment, then Edwin asked, "Do you mean Mike Tabor?"

J.B. nodded. "Such a tragedy."

"And that's all it was, Dad," Fox said quickly. "It was not your fault."

13

"WHAT ARE YOU TALKING ABOUT?" NOELLE ASKED, LOOKING from Fox to his father and then to Edwin.

Edwin cleared his throat. "There was an accident during the production of the first film fifty years ago. One of our Silver Peak boys was killed."

Sadie's heart clenched. Had she made a mistake in approaching J.B. about Louis Zinfeld?

"How awful." Noelle reached for her water glass.

"I wish I hadn't been in such an all-fired hurry," J.B. muttered.

"Dad, cut it out." Fox frowned at him. "I've told you a thousand times, but you don't listen. That was an accident. Nobody blames you. Nobody but yourself, I should say."

"I'm sure you're right," Edwin said. Sadie caught his eye, and he gave her a sympathetic smile.

J.B. shook his head. "After all these years, I keep thinking about it. Can't forget it. It's my recurring nightmare. One minute Gina Tarino is delivering her line. All eyes are on her. Then someone let out a yelp. I turn around, and...the boy's gone. Right over the edge of the cliff. I couldn't believe it. I literally couldn't believe it at first, until half a dozen of the crew insisted it was true.

We didn't have cell phones then. We drove down to the ranch house, the head cameraman, Glee, and I. The rancher let me use his phone to call the police."

The old man sat staring at the flowers in the centerpiece, his eyes unfocused.

Fox's lips twitched. After a moment, he said, "That's one reason I wanted you to come back here with me."

"Hoping to exorcise the demons?" J.B. smiled faintly.

"That and getting your honest input on the project. I respect your work, Dad. I want to make sure this film is credible. I'd like to see it make an impact, the way the first one did. It's more than a sci-fi flick. I really believe that." Fox looked around at the others. "That movie resonated with its audience."

"Yes, it did," Sadie said. She looked at J.B. "Mr. Monahan, what bothers you the most about Mike Tabor's death? Is it that you felt responsible for the actors and the crew?"

"Of course. And the poor chap was so young! We'd just hired him to take Zinfeld's place. He was thankful and eager to please. I'm sure he saw it as the biggest thing that had ever happened to him. And then..." He sighed. "Maybe you shouldn't film up there again, Fox."

"Too late, Dad. We've done half the mountain footage already. Besides, we've made sure the marks for the actors are plenty far back from the edge this time."

"People still talk about it, though. They say it wasn't safe and that I pushed the limits by filming up there." J.B. picked up his water glass. "At least the weather looks good. No soft ground this time."

"You think the weather had something to do with the tragedy?" Carl asked.

Fox shrugged. "No one really knows for sure. It's rugged terrain up there. But I've heard some of the old-timers say the weather was bad during the location filming."

"That's right," J.B. said. "We had to wait for days until it stopped raining so we could drive up there with all of our equipment. Did all our indoor shots first. I even rewrote one scene so that we could do it in the rain and make it fit into the story. I was debating postponing filming the rest, but we couldn't really afford that. Finally the weather broke."

"Sounds like quite an ordeal," Noelle said, a bit too brightly.

"Well, if we hadn't been in that exact spot, the boy probably wouldn't have died," J.B. said. "That's what I've had to live with for the last fifty years. I'll never forget his father's face. He was one of the policemen who came out when I called. And his son was playing the part of a cop."

"That's all in the past," Fox said, looking briefly at Sadie and Edwin, as if asking for help.

"Yes," Edwin said. "This time will go better. In fact, the bits I've seen look very interesting. I'm sure it's going to come out well."

"It came out well the last time," Sadie said. "In spite of the tragedy, you stuck with the job and finished the film."

"Yes, Dad, that's to your credit." Fox nodded at Sadie.

"Well, people are talking about this one now," J.B. said mournfully. "The little things. The fire..."

"That was nothing," Fox said. "I spoke with Mr. Riley on the phone, and he's not even upset. I assured him we've replaced the few items that were damaged, and that he can keep our damage deposit if he's not satisfied with the condition of the house when he gets home."

"I know. And we haven't had to replace anyone yet on this one," J.B. said. He looked bleakly at Sadie. "I put the Tabor boy in Zinfeld's place, but then I had to find a replacement for him after the accident, you know."

Sadie nodded. "That must have been stressful."

"You have no idea. No one here wanted to take the part. I had to call several agents in LA until we found a fellow the right age. I was determined to use someone with a little experience after all that had happened. Well, we got it done in the end, didn't we?"

"You sure did," Edwin said. "Noelle, I think we're ready for dessert."

Sadie jumped up. "Let me help you, Noelle."

"Thanks." Noelle seemed all too eager to retreat to the kitchen. "It's getting a little maudlin in there," she whispered to Sadie once they were through the door.

"Would you like me to cut the pies?" Sadie asked.

"That would be great. I'll put on a fresh pot of coffee and get out the ice cream. Dad has to have ice cream with his pie."

"Oh, I know," Sadie said. "Did you get any chocolate chip?"

Noelle looked at her blankly. "No. I got vanilla."

"That's fine." Sadie opened the silverware drawer and took out a knife and a wedge-shaped pie lifter. "For some reason, your father seems to like chocolate chip ice cream with apple pie. Don't ask me why."

"I don't remember him eating it that way before." Noelle still stood in the middle of the floor, looking puzzled.

"It's no big deal." Sadie took six dessert plates from the cupboard.

"Right." Noelle sounded unconvinced, but she walked to the counter and began to refill the coffeemaker. "I'll admit, I was hoping Dad would invite Jason Singer to come over. I really want to meet him."

"That shouldn't be too hard," Sadie said.

"I did get to watch him filming a scene the other day." Noelle smiled. "He's one of my favorite actors. I'm glad he decided to do this film."

"Ask Mr. Monahan to introduce you," Sadie suggested.

"Oh no, I couldn't. Could I?"

"Why not? You just fed him a fabulous dinner," Sadie said. "I think that was the best lasagna I've ever eaten."

"Really?" Noelle's face brightened. "Thank you. I made the sauce myself, you know. I think that makes the difference. It takes a while, but it's worth it."

"Definitely," Sadie said.

The Monahans seemed to enjoy the evening. As they lingered over their coffee, Sadie said to Fox, who sat next to her, "Noelle was saying how much it would mean to her to meet your stars. She's a huge fan of Jason Singer, especially."

"Oh, that's easy," Fox said, smiling at Noelle. "Come by the set on Monday. I'll make sure you're introduced when we have a break."

"That's very kind of you," Noelle said.

Carl grinned. "May I tag along?"

Noelle chuckled. "You just want to meet Sandra Vitelli."

"I wouldn't say no if I got the chance."

Fox laughed. "Come around and see us after lunch. I think we'll be back on Jefferson Avenue then, shooting more exterior scenes."

"Great," Carl said. "We'll be there."

Edwin told them about plans to screen the original version of *Stranger from a Strange Land* at the opera house.

"The committee would like to do it while your crew is still here," he told Fox. "I realize they've all probably seen it, but…"

"It would be fun," Fox said. "I, for one, never get tired of watching it. When I was a kid, it was my favorite of Dad's films. Eventually I came to appreciate his more serious work, but there's something about this one that grabs the imagination."

"It would be fun to have the entire cast and crew see it together," J.B. said. "We've got—what? Two more weeks of work here?"

"If all goes well," Fox said.

"I'll see if they can schedule it by then," Edwin said.

"I'll speak to Jane about refreshments," Sadie put in. "I think she's in charge of concessions at the opera house this summer. Maybe she could order in some retro snacks. Baby Ruth bars and Necco wafers, that sort of thing."

"Great idea," Carl said. "It almost makes me wish we were staying that long."

Noelle shook her head. "No chance of that. We'll both have to be back to work by then."

Carl groaned. "Don't remind me."

"When do you leave?" Sadie asked.

"A week from today." Noelle looked at her father. "We'll have to take Sam out to ride Sunflower again. He's really going to miss that."

———

Sadie's Monday morning routine began as usual, with her arriving early at the Antique Mine and going over the mail and her receipts for the past week while she sipped a cup of coffee from Arbuckle's. Julie arrived at nine and helped her put out new stock and rearrange a few of the displays.

"I'm expecting a busload of senior citizens this morning," Sadie told her, "and who knows how many other people."

"The Breckenridge paper ran a story in their Sunday edition about the movie," Julie said. "Between that and Troy's coverage of the filming, we'll probably see even more tourists in town this week."

"I wouldn't be surprised," Sadie said. "I'm afraid I've caved to the trend and bought several classic space toys from the 1960s and 1970s. The express driver should bring them today or tomorrow, and we'll want to get them right out on the shelves."

She opened the cash register and cracked open a new roll of quarters for change. "There's an auction later this week that may have some mining tools and items from an old hotel that would interest me too. If I can manage it, I want to go to that."

"Great," Julie said. "Old mining stuff always sells well here."

As they moved the stock about, Sadie told Julie about her Sunday afternoon with Sam and Edwin. The three of them had set up Edwin's miniature farm on the back porch and played for two hours together.

"I think he loves his grandfather's old toys as much as he does his spaceships and alien figures."

"I think that's great," Julie said.

"It may be partly because he lives in Atlanta and doesn't get to be around animals much," Sadie mused. "He got to meet my Hank, and they had the best time. He loves the horses at Milo's too. They're going to take him over there again sometime today for another ride."

A knock on the door surprised them both. They still had a half hour until opening time. As Sadie turned toward it, Julie said, "That's Edwin."

Sadie hurried to let him in. "Good morning!"

"Hi." Edwin glanced down the aisle. "Hi, Julie."

"What's up?" Sadie asked.

"Oh, nothing much, except J.B. stopped by my office this morning before he went to the set. He said the producer called him from LA and said some money has been taken from the funds for production without being accounted for. He accused Fox of spending off-budget without asking permission."

Sadie frowned. "I'm not sure how serious that is. Why did J.B. come to you?"

"I think he just wanted to vent to someone neutral. And to give me a heads-up that Hamilton Dobey will arrive in Silver Peak today. The B and B is full, so I called Wade Marley. He doesn't have any openings either."

Julie, who had come nearer and listened unabashedly, said with a wink, "I guess Mr. Dobey will have to drive all the way to Breckenridge for a hotel room. What a *horrible* inconvenience..."

Sadie smiled. "What did J.B. expect you to do?"

"Nothing," Edwin said. "I asked him if they needed extra security at the filming locations today, and he didn't think so. But I don't suppose it would be a bad idea to ask Mac to swing by where they're shooting after Mr. Dobey makes his entrance. We don't want any trouble."

"And it would send the producer a message that the local constabulary is on top of things. Did he report the loss of the money?"

"I don't think so," Edwin said. "Seems they're not really sure it was stolen. I gathered it's like a petty cash fund for unexpected expenses. The person who took it may have just forgotten to sign for it."

"Where are they filming today?" Julie asked.

"They're going back out to Milo's this morning. Not up on the bluff, but some shots around the homestead and on the trails. J.B. said they hope to be back on Jefferson Avenue this afternoon."

"I thought they were done with the Riley house," Sadie said.

"They are, with the inside scenes. But they're doing some outdoor stuff. Remember, Fox told Noelle they'd be over there this afternoon? They'll be closing off two blocks of the street."

"At least it's not Main Street again," Sadie said.

"Well, they're going to do some restaurant footage later in the week," Edwin said with a shrug.

"Maybe they won't block off the street then."

Julie's face lit up. "Are they going to use Flap Jack's like they did in the old movie and change the sign?"

"I think so. And they were talking about shooting one scene at the opera house. Fox really likes the architecture there."

Julie sighed. "I can't help it. I really love this, even though it's a pain some days."

Edwin smiled at Sadie. "Would you like to go to the set this afternoon if they're back in town?"

"I would love it!"

The bus full of seniors on their outing arrived an hour after opening. The shoppers peppered Sadie and Julie with questions about the movie cast members and were thrilled to hear that Sadie had dined with the director and his father on Saturday night.

"Oh, I just love J. B. Monahan's movies," one elderly woman said. "I'd rather have his autograph than that young man who's starring in this one."

Julie laughed. "I hope nobody tells Jason Singer you said that."

Two more women squeezed in beside their friend. "Jason Singer! Is he really here in Silver Peak?" one of them asked.

"He sure is," Sadie said. "You might even be able to see him at work later today."

Sales were modest for the tour group, although Sadie was glad to see a few small pieces go out the door. She wished the retro posters had arrived, but perhaps the next batch of customers could see them.

Julie took a long lunch break, giving her time to go by the shooting location. When she returned, she pounced on Sadie.

"They did it—they put up a fake sign on Flap Jack's! It's now Annie's, just like in the old movie. Glee Rossignol told me they're doing a diner scene there this afternoon."

"What about the Jefferson Avenue stuff?" Sadie asked.

"Either later today or tomorrow morning. Oh, and I saw Edwin. He and Noelle will come by for you at two thirty if you want to go with them and watch."

"Are a lot of the tourists watching?"

Julie nodded. "Yes, but I heard the bus driver telling them they'd have to leave in twenty minutes, so they should be gone soon." She chuckled. "Those folks were tickled pink to see a real movie being filmed."

"I'm surprised Fox let them all hover around."

"Well, they cleared the area when they actually started shooting, but most of the people got a glimpse of Jason Singer and some of the other actors. And a lot of local people are out there too."

"Is Fox using any locals for extras?" Sadie asked.

"A few for the diner, I think. I heard they hired half a dozen people to just sit there in the background and eat while they film."

"They're probably doing it for free," Sadie said. "I think they get locals to do background stuff like that for nothing."

Julie smiled. "Well, they must be paying Jack a lot to close his whole restaurant for the afternoon."

"Yes. I hope it's a blessing for him," Sadie said.

By the time Edwin and Noelle arrived, Sadie had caught Julie up on the sales she had made over the last two hours.

"You look lovely, Noelle," she said, surveying Noelle's pale blue pants and long vest over a creamy shirt.

"Thank you. Seems like I change clothes every five minutes here."

"Well, you couldn't go horseback riding in those," Edwin said.

"Oh, you rode this morning?" Sadie asked.

Noelle nodded. "Just a short ride, really, but Sam was tuckered out afterward. Carl's staying with him while he has a little nap. I think we'll keep it low-key for the rest of the day."

"This mountain air agrees with Sam," Edwin said.

"He does love it. We all do, Dad, but don't get any ideas. We're not leaving Atlanta."

Edwin sighed. "It was worth a try."

"I thought Carl was keen on meeting Miss Vitelli," Sadie said.

Noelle laughed. "I tease him about that, but I don't think it's a big deal to him. He saw her from afar the other day, and he didn't seem at all put out that Sam was ready for a nap. He suggested staying home with him, so I didn't argue."

Sadie went with them to join the spectators outside Flap Jack's. The inside scene was apparently finished, and the hero, played by Jason Singer, was walking to his car when accosted by a man dressed rather oddly. Sadie wondered about the stranger's outfit—flip-flops, plaid shirt, and what appeared to be tuxedo pants hiked up to show his ankles.

Glee spotted Sadie and tiptoed over to stand beside her.

"What's with his getup?" Sadie asked.

"He's one of the aliens, and he grabbed some clothes out of people's cars, so he would blend in better than he would in his Martian outfit."

Sadie almost burst out laughing.

"The trousers are a little short, don't you think?" Edwin asked with a twinkle in his eyes.

An encounter followed in which the alien somehow disabled the hero and left him lying on the pavement beside his vintage car.

After Fox yelled, "Cut," Glee explained, "In the next scene, the hero comes to and reports the assault. Of course, at this point in the story, no one else believes real aliens are taking over the community."

Sadie smiled. "Poor guy."

"Exactly. But they'll find out pretty soon that he's not crazy."

"Do they film the scenes in order?" Noelle asked.

"No, they skip around, depending on a lot of things—which location is available, what the weather's doing, stuff like that," Glee explained.

"Let's do that again," Fox called out to the cast. "Denny, you've got to move a little faster. Jason, I want to see more fear when you face him."

The actors went through four more takes before Fox was satisfied with the short scene. Sadie noticed a man of about fifty, well-groomed and a bit stiff in his posture, sitting in a folding chair near J.B. She pegged him for the producer and drew Glee aside.

"If you don't mind my asking, how are things between Fox and Mr. Dobey?"

"The producer?" Glee waved a hand through the air. "He arrived all riled up and lit into Fox. Fox seemed nervous beforehand, knowing he was going to come here looking for someone to blame, but he gave Mr. Dobey as good as he got."

"Really?"

Glee nodded and leaned in closer. "Just between you, me, and the lamppost, Dobey practically accused Fox of embezzling almost three thousand dollars. But Fox said he didn't take a penny out of that fund and that Dobey could look elsewhere and let him do his job."

"Whoa. What did Mr. Dobey do?" Sadie asked as Edwin came to her side.

"He fumed around for a while, and then he got back in his car and had the driver take him over to the Mexican restaurant. I'm thinking he'd missed his lunch. But he's back now, sitting over there near J.B. I don't think it's over. Fox is shook up."

"He seems fine," Edwin said.

"He's chewing gum, and he hesitates before every order he gives." Glee shook her head. "I probably shouldn't tell you this, but, Sadie, you were so kind to me after the fire. I've known Fox all his life. He's upset, and that makes the actors nervous. Of course, Sandra's not helping."

"Oh? What's the problem there?" Noelle asked.

"She hates the dress she's supposed to wear in the Jefferson Avenue scene, but Fox told her they need to film it today and there's no time to overhaul her wardrobe."

"That seems like a petty thing," Sadie said.

Glee gritted her teeth. "Not to Sandra Vitelli."

Sadie patted her arm. "I'm sure it will work out."

"Oh yes, it usually does." Glee laughed. "Don't ask me why, but I love this life."

Fox's assistant blew a whistle and called out, "All right, people, those who are in scene twenty-six-B, reassemble on Jefferson Avenue in thirty minutes. Let's move."

J. B. Monahan approached them and greeted Sadie, Noelle, and Edwin. He took out a white handkerchief and blotted his brow. "I don't know, Edwin, I think I'm getting too old for this."

"Everything all right?" Edwin asked.

"You heard, I guess. I warned Fox that working with Ham Dobey is like working with a mad bull. He takes a notion into his head and he won't let go of it. Right now he's accusing my son of stealing. Fox wouldn't do that." J.B. looked at Glee. "Fox is on edge, sweetheart. Could you take him something cold to drink?"

"Of course, J.B.," Glee said. "And would you like something?"

"Later."

"Who has access to that fund he's talking about?" Edwin asked as Glee hurried away.

"Lots of people. Well, not me—not for this picture. But Fox and his assistant do, and the key grip, the head cameraman, the head of wardrobe—basically anyone who's in charge of a production department."

"So any one of a number of people could have taken the money he's talking about," Noelle ventured.

"Yes, and they're allowed to, if they need something for the project. But they're supposed to write down their name and how much they took and what it was for. Then they have to bring receipts in to document that's what they spent it on." J.B. looked toward his son. "I'd better go talk to Fox. He needs to stay on schedule. Maybe I can buck him up a little during the break." J.B. left them and walked slowly over to where Fox appeared to be arguing with his assistant. Hamilton Dobey had left his chair and was disappearing into Flap Jack's.

"I should make a quick stop at my office. Do you ladies want to walk over to Jefferson Avenue, and I'll meet you there?" Edwin asked.

"Sure," Noelle said. "When we get over there, I might pop in to your house and see if Sam's sleeping."

They turned away and started across the pavement. Bob Willis, the cameraman Sadie had met the previous week, was slouched against his camera dolly with his cell phone to his ear.

"Don't worry," he said into the phone as Sadie passed him. "We'll get the money. Just chill."

Sadie glanced at Noelle, who was beside her, but Noelle appeared not to have heard Bob's words, or to think them inconsequential. Sadie made a mental note to discuss it with Edwin later.

Two young women who had served as extras in the parking lot scene strode past carrying tote bags.

"I tell you, this picture's jinxed," one of them said. "Next, Dobey will accuse us of stealing that money."

"I'll be glad when the film's finished," her companion replied.

Dismayed, Sadie stepped aside to let them pass on the sidewalk and looked back toward the parking area, which was emptying fast.

J. B. Monahan was standing by with a helpless air while the lead actress, Sandra, let loose at Fox. From fifty yards away, Sadie could hear her angry words.

"I'm telling you, I've had it, Fox! I'm done!"

14

Fox Monahan glared at his leading actress. "Over a dress? Come on, Sandra. You have a contract."

Noelle stopped and stared back at the pair. She arched her eyebrows at Sadie, but all Sadie could do was shrug.

"It's not just this ugly dress," Sandra continued. "It's every costume they've handed me for this picture. It's supposed to be contemporary, but everything looks like it came out of a thrift shop ten years ago."

"I'm sorry," Fox said. "If we had time…"

"Just give me one day to go shopping in Denver," Sandra said.

Fox hesitated. "I'd love to, but we absolutely cannot go over budget."

"Well, if you hadn't messed with the petty cash, there'd be plenty in there."

Fox straightened his shoulders, glowered at her for a moment, then turned his back and walked away.

J.B. stepped toward Sandra and held out a placating hand. "Now, Sandra, that was uncalled for. Fox didn't have anything to do with that missing money."

"Hamilton Dobey thinks so."

Sadie was glad Mr. Dobey had left the set. She felt as though she should move along and not listen any further, but Noelle and at least a dozen other people seemed rooted to the ground.

"Trust me on this," J.B. said calmly, "Fox would not sabotage his own project."

Sandra's face twitched, and she folded her arms over her chest.

"Sweetheart, you don't want to quit," J.B. went on. "Think about it. You'd be breaking your contract. Everyone in the business would hear about it. It's not good for your image. And we're more than half done with this project. Stick it out."

Sadie leaned toward Noelle. "We probably ought to go."

"Oh. Right." Noelle turned and fell into step beside her. "Sorry. It was just so dramatic. Do you think she'll finish the movie?"

"Mr. Monahan the elder can be very persuasive. He also has influence with agents and casting directors. I'm sure he can make it worth Sandra's while to stay."

"Threaten her with being frozen out of future business?"

"I was thinking more of his pulling a few strings in her favor if she stays on."

"*Hmm.*" Noelle glanced back and then smiled. "They're walking toward the restaurant together. Sadie, I have to say, this vacation has been very interesting."

———

Sadie went to the cemetery occasionally, especially in the early summer, to tend the plants on T.R.'s grave. On Tuesday morning, Roz went with her, taking along a rosebush to plant near her parents' headstone and a smaller plant for Mike's grave.

They each worked alone for a while, a couple of rows apart in the quiet graveyard. When Sadie finished, she brushed off the knees of her jeans and stood gazing at her husband's stone for a few moments, then picked up her trowel and an empty plant pot. She carried them over to where Roz worked.

"That looks nice," she said, smiling at the newly planted rosebush, which was just beginning to bud out.

"Thanks. The one I had here before winter-killed." Roz stood and took off her gardening gloves. "I had hopes when I checked on Memorial Day that it would pull through, but it didn't."

"One of the hazards in this climate," Sadie said. She read the inscriptions on the Tabors' monuments and smiled. "I remember your dad clear as day. He always looked a little tired, but he always had time for us."

"I don't know how he kept such a good temperament, with the job he had," Roz said. "It's not easy being a cop."

"No. But up here we didn't get much violent crime."

"True. I suppose that made it a little easier than it would have been in, say, Denver. I'm glad he was able to stay here in Silver Peak."

"It's a good place to grow up," Sadie said. She helped Roz gather her tools and debris, and they walked back to the Tahoe together.

As Sadie shut the back door on their things, Roz said, "You know, I've got all of Dad's notebooks in a box in the attic."

"Notebooks?"

"You know, the little ones policemen carry to write down their daily activities."

"Are they interesting?"

"I don't know." Roz frowned. "When he died, I was too depressed to read through them. I put them in the attic and let it lapse. I guess I always figured I'd let Raleigh and Randy go through them someday and see if they wanted to keep them."

They both got into the vehicle and buckled up. Sadie maneuvered down the grassy lane to the main road. "Do they go all the way back to 1965?"

"I guess so. Hadn't really thought about it." Roz eyed her keenly. "You're thinking about when Mike died."

"Yes. I wonder if he wrote anything in there about it."

Roz was quiet for a moment, then she stirred. "It's possible. Dad wasn't the investigating officer, of course. When they told him the victim was his son, he had to call in someone else."

"Do you know who took the case?"

"Someone from the sheriff's office, I suppose. They'd be the closest. Or maybe a state trooper."

"I feel so bad for your parents every time I think about it," Sadie said. "When it happened, I was more focused on you and how you felt, but that must have been so hard. For all of you."

Roz nodded and pulled a tissue from her pocket. "I don't suppose you'd like to take a look at the notebooks?"

Sadie mulled that over for a minute. "I guess I could, if you want me to. I'm not doing anything this evening."

"It might say who headed the investigation."

"All right," Sadie said. She drove to the Putnams' house and went inside with Roz. While the teakettle heated, they made a foray into the attic.

Roz oriented herself quickly among the stored bric-a-brac. As Sadie had expected, the attic was neatly organized, and every carton was labeled. Soon they were headed back down to the kitchen with a box of Daniel Tabor's old pocket notebooks. Roz dusted off the carton and set it on the table.

"You open it while I pour the tea," Sadie suggested.

It took a few minutes to locate the notebooks they needed. Sadie put aside three that covered from February to November 1965.

"If there's anything to learn, it should be in there," Roz said, setting the box on the floor. "I'll take this back upstairs later. Let's relax for a minute."

Sadie purposely turned the conversation to lighter topics while they enjoyed their tea with muffins Roz had made that morning. By the time they had finished, they were caught up on Silver Peak news and family goings-on.

That evening after she closed the store, Sadie stopped by Edwin's house. Noelle came to the door.

"Hi!" Sadie said. "I just wanted to tell you about an estate sale being held on Thursday next week. I plan to go and scout for things for my store. I thought you might enjoy it, if you're still here. There's quite a collection of vintage jewelry listed in the catalog." She held out the sheets she had printed from the online information.

"That sounds like a lot of fun," Noelle said, "but we're planning to leave Saturday. We need to get back to our jobs."

"Oh, that's right. I'd forgotten."

Noelle smiled ruefully. "We'll sure miss Dad, and you and all the other friends we've made here. Can you come in for a few minutes?"

"Sure." Sadie entered the living room, where Sam had his action figures spread out on the floor, coffee table, and sofa.

"Sam, give Miss Sadie a place to sit," Noelle told him.

As Noelle browsed the printouts, Sadie joined in Sam's play.

"Who's this red fellow?" she asked, picking up a plastic figure.

"He's a Martian."

"I see. Is he a bad guy?"

Sam nodded solemnly. "We like the ones from Sirius."

"Isn't Sirius a star?" Sadie asked.

"Uh-huh."

Sadie decided it was best not to point out that it would be difficult for beings to live on a star. She watched Sam manipulate a toy spaceship. The blue craft was about six inches long. He made what he considered an appropriate engine noise as he lifted it slowly up over the edge of the coffee table. She stared at the toy, imagining lights flashing on strategic points, so intently that she was barely aware of Edwin entering the room.

"Are you ready...? Oh, hi, Sadie," Edwin said.

She looked up with a wry smile. "Hi. Come look at this."

"What?" He stepped nearer.

"Sam, please do that again," Sadie said. "Just like you did before."

Sam made the spaceship rise from behind the table and hover over the edge, just above the astronauts and aliens on the surface.

"Does that remind you of anything?" Sadie asked.

"I get you," Edwin said. "It does, but it's nonsensical. We didn't see a..." He smiled. "Or did we?"

"I'm thinking maybe we did." Sadie rose and took in Edwin's clothing and light jacket. "You're going out, so I'll be on my way."

"We're just going over to Sophia's for dinner. Why don't you join us?" Edwin said.

"Thank you, but I've got a little homework to do for Roz tonight. I just dropped in to bring an estate sale catalog for Noelle, though it looks like they're leaving before it happens." Sadie turned to Noelle, who was still perusing the list of merchandise to be sold.

"They have some very interesting pieces," Noelle said. "I don't suppose you'd be willing to bid for me on a couple of items and ship them if you get them?"

"I'd be happy to. There's a lot more on the Web site, and photos of the jewelry. Take a look at it later. If you want to place any bids, give me a call."

"I'll do that," Noelle said, standing. "Thank you, Sadie."

Edwin walked with her to the door. Sadie looked up at him.

"Do you think we saw a spaceship?"

"Do you?"

"Maybe you and I should have a talk with Derek Todd," Sadie suggested.

Edwin frowned. "We don't have much to go on. He thinks a mock-up would be better than CGI. But we have no evidence at all that what we saw was one of his contraptions."

At home, Sadie walked Hank and ate a light supper, then settled down on the sofa with Mr. Tabor's notebooks. The handwriting was small and tightly written, but she soon got used to it and was able to decipher most of the entries. Some were obvious abbreviations and police jargon, and she made a mental note to ask Mac Slattery about a few of them, but she was able to get the gist of most notations.

Roz was right—Silver Peak was a quiet town. Unusual events were rare. Mr. Tabor had responded to infrequent road accidents, an occasional domestic dispute, and complaints of theft.

One rancher asked for his help in keeping the coyotes away from his young stock. Other calls included the unattended death of an elderly resident and traffic duty while the fire department put out a fire at an old mine's stamp mill. The investigation for that incident turned out to be quite interesting, as Mr. Tabor wrote "possible arson?" at the bottom of the page. Over the next week, he recorded making arrangements with the fire marshal to inspect the scene and protecting the site until that was finished. The notebook didn't say how it turned out, but Sadie was interested enough that she thought she might look it up later in the newspaper archives.

She realized that officers used these notes later, when they went to write their official reports of incidents to which they had responded, or when they had to testify in court. She stopped reading after an hour, knowing she still had a ways to go before she reached the time of Mike's death. She wanted to keep reading, but if she intended to leave the store for a while tomorrow with Edwin, she'd better make sure she had everything in shape for Julie. That meant a quick trip back to the Antique Mine, and she also needed to decide which items she was interested in buying at the estate sale on Thursday. With a sigh, she stuck a slip of paper into the notebook to mark her place and laid it aside.

———

A phone call from Edwin the next morning altered Sadie's plans slightly.

"Noelle made a list of things she'd like you to bid on for her," he said. "I've got to stop by the office, but I can bring it by the store after."

"Why don't I meet you where the crew is shooting?" Sadie asked.

"Sure. I can be there in half an hour."

The store was quiet when the time came, and Sadie left Julie dusting the merchandise. She walked down the sidewalk until she arrived at the town hall. A camera crew was setting up to shoot in the town square. She wandered over and watched them position the cameras and check their settings. Bob, the camera-man she had met earlier, looked at his watch.

"They might not be here for another fifteen minutes," he said to the gaffer, who was running an electrical line across the street to an outlet beside the steps of the town hall. "I'm going to make a phone call."

Sadie sighed and looked toward the town hall. She and Edwin probably wouldn't get to watch the filming this morning, but that was all right. She didn't mean to overhear Bob's conversation, but she couldn't help it.

"Stop worrying about the money," the cameraman said tersely, with the phone to his ear. "Get off my back. I'll get it."

Sadie moved away, wishing she hadn't heard what he said. Bob sounded worried and upset. Could he possibly be talking about the missing money the producer was so concerned about?

Bob began to pace back and forth on the grass. His voice rose as he talked into his phone. "No, no, we can't do that. We'd get in deeper and deeper."

Sadie caught her breath. Bob seemed like a nice man. In fact, he sounded like someone trying to prevent an embezzlement, not someone who had participated in one.

"Just stop worrying." Bob raised his chin, and his gaze locked on Sadie's for a moment. "I'll talk to you later," he said into the phone and closed it abruptly. He nodded at Sadie.

"Hi," she said uncertainly. "I'm sorry, I wasn't trying to..."

"It's okay," Bob said with a wan smile. "You get kids, you get money problems, you know what I'm saying?"

"Oh yes," Sadie replied. "Money's always tight when you have a family." She looked toward the big wheeled camera platform he had set up. "I've been wondering about the camera equipment you're using here. It seems to me that what the crew had in 1965 was a lot different."

"It would have been," he said. "Well, some things are the same."

"I thought cameras were smaller now," Sadie said.

"Some are. But the dollies and booms are more sophisticated. We can do a lot more with the modern stuff—move it more efficiently and get into more positions for special shots." He smiled. "One thing that's changed a lot is the sound equipment."

"Oh?"

Bob nodded. "The microphones are much more sensitive now—that is, they can pick up sounds better and from farther away. And the mic booms and lighting stands they used back then would have been bulkier."

"So when they filmed those night scenes, with the spacecraft...," Sadie began.

Bob nodded. "Exactly. They had to haul a ton of stuff up that mountainside. J.B. was telling me yesterday how hard it was to set up a location shot back then, compared to now. Not that it's easy now, you understand."

"I think I do," Sadie said. The door to the town hall opened, and Edwin emerged. She waved. "There's my date," she said with a chuckle.

Bob wiggled his eyebrows. "*Ooh*, the mayor."

"Yeah. He's a good friend." She smiled at Bob. "Thanks for the information about all the equipment." The little he had told her had made her more curious. She wondered whether the library would have any material about filmmaking in the 1960s. It might, she reflected, given Silver Peak's history.

She hurried to meet Edwin.

"Hi. Sorry I'm late," he called.

"No problem." Sadie fell into step with him. "Sounds like they're a little behind schedule with the shoot this morning."

"That's okay. At least we can talk, which we can't do while the cameras are rolling." Edwin took Noelle's list out of his jacket pocket and handed it to Sadie. "Here you go. Noelle said to call her if you have any questions."

"Thanks, I will." Sadie told Edwin about her conversation with Bob and what she had overheard.

"Do you think he had something to do with the missing money?" Edwin asked.

"I don't know. I don't want to think so. Everyone has money troubles these days."

When she arrived back at the Antique Mine, she was surprised to find Roz there, leaning on the counter and chatting with Julie.

"Hi," Sadie said. "What's up?"

"Nothing much," Roz said, straightening. "I found Mike's old yearbook, and I thought you might want to take a look at it."

"Thanks." Sadie reached for it and ran her fingers over the embossed cover. "Wow, this brings back memories."

"Have you looked at Dad's notebooks?" Roz asked.

"Some, but I didn't get up to July yet." Sadie glanced around the store. "Is it shaping up to be a slow day, Jules?"

"Afraid so. All I sold while you were gone was one bone-china teacup."

"Better than nothing," Sadie said. "Do you need a break?"

"No, I'm fine," Julie assured her.

Sadie nodded. "Roz, do you want to get some coffee while we look at this?"

"Sure. I'll buy."

They walked into Arbuckle's together. Only a few customers were inside. They chose a booth near the window and sat down.

Sadie paged through the book while they drank their coffee. Although that year's seniors were four years older than she and Roz had been at the time, they knew virtually every student in the small high school. The freshman class of 1965 was only a year ahead of them, and the memories flowed freely as they put together what had become of many of those young people.

"There's Joe Pinkham." Roz pointed to the senior portrait of a young man with sandy hair and sober blue eyes.

"Oh yeah." Sadie studied Joe's face. She hadn't told Roz about the manslaughter charge. It was just too sad and sordid.

"There's another picture later on," Roz said. "Well, the base-ball team, of course, but there's one of him and his girlfriend in the candid section."

Sadie could have lingered over each picture, but she didn't want to leave Julie alone at the store all day, so she flipped to the last part of the book and found the photo Roz had mentioned.

"She was pretty. What was her name?"

"Marilyn, I think."

"That's right." Sadie found a small portrait of Marilyn Smith in the junior class section. "I don't think I've seen her since she graduated."

"No, she moved away. She was really angry at Mike for turning Joe in that spring."

"My memory's fuzzy on that," Sadie admitted. "Chuck Wayne told me Joe broke up with her, I think. Do you know where she lives now?"

Roz shook her head. "No idea. But I don't think she married Joe. For some reason, I've got it in my head that she married somebody else."

"Someone from around here?"

"I can't remember."

Sadie reached for her coffee cup. "Maybe I can find out more about her tonight, although Smith has got to be the most difficult name to trace, because there are so many of them. And I'll try to read some more in your dad's notebooks."

Tracing Marilyn Smith proved as hard as she had predicted. Sadie gave up after half an hour, deciding the Internet was not the best resource for this particular search. Instead, she would ask around and see what local people remembered about Marilyn. Their memories might be fallible, but maybe she could turn up a reliable lead.

Hank came over and nudged her hand.

"I suppose you want to go out," Sadie said. "I don't know why I'm even bothering with Marilyn Smith." But she did know. Marilyn had been close to Joe, who had been furious with Mike fifty years ago, and she wanted to put all the pieces of the puzzle in place for Roz.

After a foray outside with Hank, she sat down to do some more reading. Perusing Mr. Tabor's notes was tedious, but Sadie had an idea that might make it easier for future readers. She got out an old voice-activated tape recorder that she hadn't used in years. If she read the entries out loud, she or Roz could transcribe them more easily than they could while trying to decipher the script in the little notebooks.

At last she came to an entry that concerned the filmmaking. The crew had apparently been in town for a few days. "Mr. Monahan asked me to do a few security checks on their film equipment tonight," Daniel Tabor had noted. Of itself it was innocent, but Sadie's stomach clenched. She knew she was close to the time of trauma.

"Accident on the mountain," was the terse entry on the day of Mike's death. Sadie couldn't prevent the let-down feeling that engulfed her. Was that all Mr. Tabor had to say about it? She sat back and closed her eyes, imagining the officer rushing to the scene at the call of a fatal mishap and arriving to find his own son was the victim. What would he have done next?

She opened her eyes. He would have called in someone else to deal with the technicalities, of course. And then he would have gone to be with his family. Or perhaps he had stayed to make sure Mike's body was properly cared for until the medical examiner arrived.

What a terrible day for a loving father!

She almost put the notebook aside, but she knew she couldn't sleep if she left it there. Instead, she turned the page. There were no entries for several days. Of course. Mr. Tabor had taken some time off from work. This notebook was a record of what he did on duty.

The notes resumed nearly a week later, with commonplace entries about routine calls. Perhaps that was all he had put about his son's death in his record of work.

Sadie turned a few more pages, scanning the entries. About two weeks later, something caught her eye. The movie crew had packed up and left town. The next day, Mr. Tabor had noted, "Ray says they filed the official report on the seventeenth." The seventeenth was the day Mike had died.

After checking the time, Sadie phoned Roz.

"Did you find something?" her friend asked eagerly.

"Maybe. Your dad didn't write much about what happened. But who is Ray?"

"Oh, that would be Ray Fanning. He was a deputy sheriff. He and Dad worked together a lot, and they were pretty good friends. What about him?"

"Your father made a note a couple of weeks after Mike died that Ray told him the official police report had been filed."

"Anything else?"

"That's it so far," Sadie said. "I'll let you know if there's more."

"Thanks. I'd sure like to see that police report."

"I doubt that's possible, but you never know."

Sadie kept on reading, dictating each entry on to the tape. If nothing else, she could give it to Roz's boys. A few minutes later, she stopped reading and turned off the recorder. She knew she had found the most important entry in the notebook.

"Saw the report today," Mr. Tabor had written. "It was hard to read it, but I needed to. The investigators conclude the death of Michael Tabor was an accident. We must accept it as such, though a terrible one. Film footage supplied by the movie director seems to verify this."

Film footage, Sadie mused. J. B. Monahan had given the police some film footage from the day Mike died. Of course, there were no security cameras or anything like that out on the mountain, but it sounded as though the movie crew had been filming at the moment Mike fell.

It made sense, but why had they never heard about this footage before? She supposed it had not been made public. Back then, deaths and other shocking events were not shown on the television news. Nowadays, if a similar incident happened, she supposed that film clips would be broadcast and then put on the Internet for anyone to see. Life was much gentler back then.

And yet, she longed to see that film. If anything could set Roz's mind at ease, it would be film of her brother's fall. That would prove it was an accident, even if Mr. Tabor's notes and the official police report did not.

Hank came to her knee and whined.

"What, you want to go out again?" Sadie looked at her watch and realized she had been working for almost three hours. "Okay, boy, and then I'm going to bed." She got up and stretched. "Let me get my jacket."

She stepped outside a moment later with Hank, into the crisp night air. Hank bounded off across the lawn, putting the crickets to silence. The clear sky above was studded with brilliant stars. No low-hanging clouds obstructed her view.

Remembering the odd lights she and Edwin had seen reflected off clouds the night of the play, she turned and gazed toward Milo's property. She caught her breath, barely able to believe her eyes. At about the same spot they had seen them before, blinking lights shone over the mountainside.

15

SADIE WHIPPED OUT HER PHONE AND PUNCHED IN MILO'S number. She waited through six frustrating rings until the recorded voice mail message came on, then closed the connection and called Edwin.

"Sadie?" came his voice, dependable as ever.

"Yeah, it's me. I see the lights again. I tried to call Milo, but he didn't answer."

"I doubt I can see it from here," Edwin said.

She caught excitement in his voice and heard him moving. She watched the sky over the ranch as she spoke. The object from which the lights shone hadn't moved much. It seemed to float or glide above the mountainside.

"No, I can't see it," Edwin said. "I'm outside, but my view is blocked. No glow in the sky, other than the stars and streetlights."

"No clouds," Sadie noted. "Oh!"

"What is it?"

Her heart pounded. "This might sound loony, but a beam of light came out of it. Like it's shining down onto the ground."

"Beaming up a horse?"

Sadie laughed. "Stop it! I can't…" She broke off as the shaft of light disappeared. "The beam is gone. Now the whole thing is sinking."

"Sinking?"

"Yeah. Like it did before. It's got to be going down behind the mountainside, Edwin."

"Same place as before?"

"I think so, but it's too far away for me to be sure. It could be beyond Milo's place." The aircraft—or whatever it was—slowly lowered beyond the horizon and she sighed.

"Want me to call Mac?" Edwin asked.

"It's gone."

"Maybe he could drive out there quickly enough to see if anyone's out in the pasture."

"Worth a try, I guess. I could drive over there, for that matter."

"Not by yourself," Edwin said quickly. "You stay put. I'll call the sheriff."

Sadie waited impatiently, pacing her yard for ten minutes. No more lights appeared in the sky. She called Hank to her and went inside, where she made herself a cup of hot chocolate. Edwin called back as she took the cup from the microwave.

"Hey, Mac's driving out there," he said. "I tried Milo, and I caught him on his cell phone."

"Where was he?" Sadie demanded.

"He'd been to a stock auction halfway to Denver. He said they ran late tonight, and he was just leaving the building. He'd had his phone off during the sale."

"Great," Sadie said sarcastically. "I'm probably the only terrestrial being who saw it tonight."

"Do you want me to come over?"

"No, I'll be fine."

"Hang in there," Edwin said. "Mac told me he would call you after he's had a look at that far pasture of Milo's."

She had finished drinking her hot chocolate and gone upstairs to prepare for bed before her phone rang again.

"Sadie? It's Mac."

"Did you find anything?"

"Yes and no. There's nobody out there now, but there might have been. The gate was left open."

"Milo left it closed when I was with him," Sadie said, "but I don't think he had any stock out there."

"Well, I closed it," Mac said. "I'll go over the ground with him in the morning, but I think somebody may have driven out there tonight."

"Okay," Sadie said. "I guess that's all you can do. Thanks, Mac."

———

Before she left home on Thursday morning, Sadie called Rita Dodd and made arrangements to meet her for lunch. She had hoped to stop by Roz's house, but was running a little late, so she sent her friend a text, asking her to drop by the store if she could.

She and Julie had a busy morning, with a busload of tourists arriving soon after they opened. The visitors had been told they could observe the filming of an outdoor scene after lunch, so many of them browsed the antique shop and flocked to the various eateries downtown during the wait.

The ranks were thinning when Roz arrived about eleven thirty. Sadie signaled to Julie to take her position at the cash register and bustled Roz into the back room.

"Looks like you're busy," Roz said. "I can come back later."

"That's okay. I wanted to tell you what I found in your dad's notes." Sadie took out the notebook she'd been reading from the night before and showed Roz the entry about the police report and film footage.

"Wow." Roz frowned at the words. "I had no idea there was film. Dad never told me the details. I'm not sure even Mom knew that."

"He didn't want to upset you," Sadie said.

"You're probably right. You told me parents didn't tell kids the really hard stuff back then. They wanted to shield us."

"That's exactly right."

Roz shook her head. "But it had the opposite effect. It made me think worse things than actually happened." She sighed. "It may seem unreasonable, but I need to know everything. I wish I could see the evidence Dad saw."

"We won't give up just yet," Sadie said. "I'll see if I can find out anything about the film or the police report. There's a chance those are still around."

"Do you think so?" Roz's eyes lit.

"I really don't know, but I'll ask."

Roz hugged her. "Thanks. You truly are the best friend ever."

Sadie smiled. She was glad to see that Roz was coming to terms with Mike's death. "I'm having lunch with Rita, so I can pick her brain about Joe Pinkham and Marilyn Smith. I don't think there's any connection to what happened to Mike, but it's another loose end. Want to join us?"

"Sure. I'll just pop in to the hardware store and tell Roscoe where I'll be."

They met Rita at the Depot and ordered spaghetti.

"So you wanted to talk about Joe Pinkham," Rita said.

"Yeah, if you don't mind." Sadie added a generous amount of Parmesan cheese to her spaghetti.

Rita shrugged. "I don't mind, but why the interest in him?"

"We're just trying to sort out everything that happened the year Mike died," Roz said.

"Oh, got it. So what do you want to know?"

"I found out from Chuck Wayne that Joe passed away a few years ago," Sadie said. "Several guys from their baseball team told me Joe really had it in for Mike after the cheating incident. I guess Joe's girlfriend, Marilyn, was very upset too."

"Oh yeah. She was downright vindictive," Rita said. "I heard her say once that if she had a chance, she would kill Mike."

Roz stared at her. "How come I never heard any of this stuff?"

Rita shrugged. "Who would say that in front of his sister? But I was pretty obsessed with Mike at the time, and I paid close attention to anything involving him. That Marilyn was a piece of work."

"What happened to her?" Sadie said. "She and Joe broke up, I heard."

"Yeah, I think so. He broke it off before he left town. Married someone else."

"And Marilyn?" Sadie asked. "Do you know if she's still living?"

"Last I knew." Rita carefully wound several strands of spaghetti around her fork. "When Mike died, I tried to make something of the nasty things Marilyn had said, but I couldn't find a connection between her and the movie. I don't think she was out there the day he died, but I could be wrong." She took a bite and closed her eyes. "*Mmm*. This is the best spaghetti ever!"

After she got back to the store and let Julie go for lunch, Sadie opened the day's mail. A couple in their forties, dressed in casual but upscale clothing, came through the door as she perused an invoice.

"Hello," Sadie said.

"Hi." The dark-haired woman gave her a shy smile.

"Are you looking for anything special?" Sadie asked.

"Not really," the man replied. "We're combining pleasure with a business trip, and we both love antiques."

Sadie's smile broadened. "You're welcome to poke around, but satisfy my curiosity first, will you? I'm trying to place that accent."

He chuckled. "We're from Marble Cove, Maine."

"Well! Welcome to Colorado."

"Thanks." The couple approached the counter, and the handsome man extended his hand. "I'm Jeff Mackenzie, and this is my wife, Beverly. We hoped to find a room for the night in Silver Peak, but it seems everything's full to capacity."

Sadie shook hands with them. "I'm so sorry. It's because of the movie crew. Did you hear about it?"

"The woman at the B and B told us about them remaking an old film," Beverly said. "It's rather exciting, isn't it?"

"Yes, it is. It's good for the town too. And the son of the original director from fifty years ago is shooting the remake."

Jeff nodded eagerly. "We heard J. B. Monahan is here with his son. Is that true?"

"It sure is." Sadie grinned. "You might catch a glimpse of him if you hang around."

"I'd love to meet him."

"My husband's a professional photographer," Beverly said, patting Jeff's arm. "Of course, he does mostly stills for magazines, but I think he's fascinated by the movie-making process too."

"I'm always ready to learn something new," Jeff said.

Sadie looked at the clock. "If you're really interested, stick around for twenty minutes or so. When my helper comes back from lunch, I think I know where you'd be able to find J.B., or at least I could track him down pretty quickly."

"That would be great," Jeff said. "We'll just look around for a while."

"I'll be right here if you have any questions," Sadie said.

Jeff and Beverly ambled down the main aisle, and Sadie went back to the mail. One of her frequent customers came in, and she waited on her. As the woman left, Jeff came to the counter carrying an odd metal object.

"This isn't priced," he said apologetically.

Sadie frowned at it. The item was a bit like a small, metal coat tree, with a clamp on an adjustable arm. "I have no idea what it's worth. I don't even know what it is," Sadie confessed. "Was it in that pile of mystery objects way at the back?"

Jeff laughed and turned the item around in his hands. "I'm pretty sure it's a camera lighting stand. It's quite old."

"I never would have guessed that." Sadie frowned. "Hey, wait a minute. How old do you think it is?"

He shrugged. "Fifty or sixty years, I guess. Post–World War II."

Sadie came out from behind the counter. "Do you think it could possibly be from 1965?"

"Maybe. The era is right."

Sadie nodded slowly. Could this be a holdover from the earlier film? She supposed she could ask Mr. Monahan. People who lived in Silver Peak had brought her all kinds of stuff over the years. Or she might have gotten that in a box lot from a sale. She wished she could remember where it came from.

"I'd like to take it with us when we go to the movie set, if you don't mind," she said. "And you can have it for ten dollars, if you think it's worth that."

"It could be worth a lot more than that. I was thinking more in the fifty-to-a-hundred-dollar range."

Sadie waved a hand in the air. "If you hadn't walked in and picked it up, that thing could have sat there for another fifty years."

"Okay," Jeff said. He looked over his shoulder. "I think Beverly found something she wants too."

"You can leave this here if you want," Sadie said. "I'm sure no one else is going to fight you for it."

He strolled off to rejoin his wife, and Sadie reached for her phone. She'd been meaning to call Mac, and now was as good a time as any.

"Sheriff Slattery," came his crisp greeting.

"Hi, Mac. It's Sadie. Anything new?"

"No. I'm planning to go out to Milo's soon, but I've been busy this morning."

"I wondered if you knew anything about some old film footage from the time when Roz Putnam's brother died," Sadie said.

"That was fifty years ago, right?"

"Yes. We spoke about it."

"Sadie, I was barely a child. What do you expect me to know about that?"

"I've been reading Officer Tabor's duty notebooks from that year. He was Roz and Mike's father, you know."

"Yes, I've heard lots of stories about Dan Tabor. All favorable, I must say."

Sadie smiled. "He was a good cop. Anyway, in his notes, a few weeks after the accident, he said he saw the police report and some film footage from the day his son died. I wondered if those are still available."

"*Hmm.* The report should be on file. I can check, I suppose. A lot of stuff that old isn't computerized."

"Anything you can do would be appreciated," Sadie said.

"Well, don't expect film clips. I doubt they filed that. I'll ask, but don't get your hopes up."

"Thanks, Mac." She hung up. The question of where she got the stand wouldn't stop nipping at her mind, and after a while, Sadie opened her computer files and searched through some of her oldest inventories for the store.

At last she found the entry. "Metal stand, Judith Marley sale $2."

She looked up from the book and racked her brain.

"A yard sale," she said softly. "I bought that from Judith at a yard sale."

Jeff and Beverly Mackenzie were approaching with their arms full of items.

"I found some treasures," Beverly said with a guilty smile. She set a coffee tin, a set of Depression-era paper dolls, and a shaving mug on the counter, and Jeff added a set of four bone-china dishes and a small German vase.

"That stand," Sadie said, and Jeff's eyes widened. "I found a notation of how I got it. I bought it about two years ago at a yard sale here in town. The person who sold it was Judith Marley. She's in her seventies now, but I think she was an extra in *Stranger from a Strange World*. I saw her in a crowd scene when I watched the film a couple of weeks ago."

"So it *could* be something the film crew left behind way back then," Jeff said eagerly.

"I'm going to ask her," Sadie said.

"Careful now," Beverly said with a smile. "If you start finding provenance on an item, it could jack the price up."

Sadie laughed. "Jeff and I have already agreed on our price. But leave me your phone number. I'll let you know if I learn any more about it." She rang up their purchases, and Jeff put them in his car and then reentered the store.

When Julie returned a few minutes later, Sadie introduced the Mackenzies. "We're not too busy today. Would you mind if I went over to the movie set to introduce them to J.B.?"

"That's fine," Julie said. "They're still out in the square, in front of the town hall. I heard someone say they thought they'd be done with that scene before now, but they got delayed out at Milo's this morning."

"Perfect." Sadie beckoned to Jeff and Beverly. "This way, folks. You're about to meet a Hollywood legend."

Jeff retrieved the lighting stand from his car and carried it as they went down the sidewalk. They arrived at the site just as Fox declared a wrap on the scene in the square. He told the actors and crew to get lunch and then reassemble at the opera house in an hour.

"This is great," Sadie assured the Mackenzies. "We can catch J.B. before he leaves the set." She led her guests forward and was able to introduce them to both Monahans.

"Hello, sir." Jeff set down the lighting stand and shook J.B.'s hand. "I'm a huge fan of your work." He glanced at Fox. "Well, both of you, but I admit the classics get to me. *The Oregon Escort* is one of my all-time favorites."

"Thank you," J.B. said. "What is it you do?"

"I'm a nature photographer. I've been shooting some artwork for a couple of magazines, but my wife and I are returning to Maine on Monday."

J.B. nodded. "You do mostly still work, then."

"Yes, sir. No experience in cinematography. Oh, but I found this relic at Sadie's store. She thought it might be a holdover from when you were shooting another film here in the sixties." He stepped back and gestured toward the stand.

"Oh my. That's an old-timer," J.B. said.

Fox studied the item. "The era's right. Do you think it's one of yours, Dad?"

J.B. frowned. "Could be, I suppose."

————

Sadie drove to Judith Marley's house on Adams Street after the store closed. She sat in the driveway for a minute, gazing at the small redbrick home, with its neatly trimmed lawn and thriving flower beds. When she rang the doorbell, Judith answered. As always, she was stylishly dressed, as though expecting company.

"Hello, Sadie. What a nice surprise. Won't you come in?"

"Thank you," Sadie said. "I hope I didn't interrupt your supper."

"No, I was working on my quilt, and I hadn't even thought about the time."

Sadie followed her into the living room and sat down on one of the high-backed love seats.

"Would you like some tea?" Judith asked.

"No, thanks. I won't stay long. I wanted to ask you about an item I bought from you a couple of years ago, at your yard sale."

"Oh?" Judith's brow furrowed. "I did sell quite a few things back then. I was thinking just the other day that I should do it again. The clutter mounts up, you know."

Sadie chuckled. "It does indeed. The item I'm curious about is an old lighting stand."

"A lamp?" Judith asked.

"No, it seems to be one used to hold the lights for photography. Filmmaking, actually."

"Oh, that."

Was it Sadie's imagination, or had Judith's expression darkened?

"I hadn't sold it," Sadie went on, "but a gentlemen who is a professional photographer from the Northeast came into the store today, and he spotted it. He said it's fifty or sixty years old, and I wondered if it might possibly have been left behind when J. B. Monahan's film crew left here in 1965."

"I . . . suppose it might be."

"You were an extra in the film, weren't you?" Sadie asked.

Judith looked away. "Yes. I was young and starry-eyed, I suppose. I signed on for a lark."

Sadie smiled. "Was it fun?"

"To a point, yes." Judith's lips pursed.

"Until the accident?" Sadie asked gently.

Judith nodded. "It was horrible."

"Were you out there that day, when Mike fell?"

"Yes, though I wasn't looking at the precise moment when it happened. A lot of people were up there. Maybe twenty or thirty, counting all the camera crew and a handful of extras. Mr. Monahan..."

"What about him?" Sadie asked.

"He was thunderstruck. Acted at first as though he couldn't believe anything had happened. But girls were screaming—myself included—and the young fellows were getting dangerously close to the edge to peer over to search for Mike and see what happened to him. When it finally registered with Mr. Monahan, he ordered everyone away from the edge and went to his car. He had one of the cameramen drive him down the mountain and around to the base of the bluff. Of course, there was nothing they could do. Mike was already dead."

"What happened next?" Sadie asked. "Did you go down there?"

"No. Some of the fellows did. We were all told not to leave the set, though. The head cameraman sort of took charge of those of us up at the top. We were there for a couple of hours, just sitting in the grass, talking about how terrible it was. Someone brought us sandwiches and Coca-Cola, I remember. It seemed so odd, like a nightmare picnic. Mr. Monahan waited down below until a police officer came. I heard later that it was Mr. Tabor." Tears spilled out of Judith's eyes. "I felt so helpless."

"I'm sorry," Sadie said. "Sorry that it happened, of course, but sorry you were there too, and that you had to stay there at the scene of the tragedy."

Judith produced a handkerchief and wiped her eyes. "Another policeman came finally, and talked to all of us. Those who had seen Mike fall had to stay longer, but the rest of us were allowed to leave."

"Who was the policeman?" Sadie asked.

"I think it was a deputy sheriff, but I saw state troopers too, as I left the ranch. The Hendersons didn't own it then. It was another family, and the owner was out in front of the house when we came down, talking to the police."

"So how did you end up with the lighting stand, if I may ask?"

Judith's gaze flickered away, then returned to meet Sadie's. "The last day of the shooting, the police came and gave some things to Mr. Monahan. Things they had taken away for evidence. That was one of them."

"You mean, it had something to do with Mike's death?" Sadie asked.

"I guess so. As I told you, I didn't see it directly—I was off to one side, waiting for my cue, and I was chatting with another one of the extras. But those who saw it said Mike had tripped over that thing. J. B. Monahan wanted nothing to do with it. I heard him tell one of the boys on the crew to throw it away."

Sadie thought about that.

"Later, I saw it sticking out of a trash can near the town hall," Judith said. "Call it a morbid fascination, if you will, but...I took it."

"A souvenir?" Sadie asked.

"I'm not sure. It was an impulse decision. The whole incident had scarred me, as I'm sure it did all the young people. That implement was part of it. I hated to see it thrown in the garbage like that, but I had no idea what to do with it. So I put it in the attic. It sat there for many years. I remembered that day vividly, but you know, I almost never discussed it with anyone. It was something we all knew had happened, but no one wanted to talk about it. Then, when I was cleaning things out for the sale, I saw that old light stand, and I decided it was time to let it go."

"I sold it to the photographer today," Sadie said. "He saw it as a relic of his profession in another era. But I also showed it to J. B. Monahan first."

"Oh dear." Judith's face paled. "Was he terribly upset?"

"I don't think so, but it may have jolted him for a moment."

"Please, you won't tell anyone that I was the one who salvaged it, will you?"

Sadie leaned forward and patted Judith's hand. "You can rest easy on that. Nobody in Silver Peak will ever know." *Not even Roz*, she told herself. No good could come of it. She already regretted showing it to Mr. Monahan, but that couldn't be undone. Overall, it was time the piece was forgotten.

16

MARILYN SMITH WAS NOT AN EASY WOMAN TO TRACK DOWN, BUT a few strategic phone calls netted Sadie an address about thirty miles away, and on Friday afternoon she drove out there. She pulled into the long lane that led to a ranch house nestled in the foothills. A few plump cattle grazed in the pasture beside her, and near the house two horses stood in a smaller enclosure.

Marilyn came to the door wearing jeans and a plaid shirt over a dark tank top. For a woman in her midsixties, she looked very fit and healthy. When Sadie had introduced herself, Marilyn invited her in. They sat down in the modern kitchen with glasses of iced tea.

"I think I remember you," Marilyn said. "You were a couple of years behind me."

"Three, I think. And I was an only child, so I didn't have any siblings your age."

"Your folks were ranchers, right?"

Sadie smiled. "Yes. I still live on part of what was their property."

Marilyn nodded. "So what brings you out here?"

"I wanted to ask you about Joe Pinkham."

Marilyn blinked and lifted her glass. She took a sip of her tea and set it down. "Wow. That's a blast from the past."

"Sorry. His name came up recently, and I've been trying to find out more about him. What happened to him when he left Silver Peak?"

"It's not good, from what I hear. You know he's deceased, right?"

"Yes. I was sorry to hear it. But you two were close in high school."

She nodded. "We dated most of my junior year. Joe was a senior." She let out a big sigh. "I hope I don't offend you if I say I feel I was blessed not to have married him."

"That doesn't offend me at all," Sadie said.

"He had some good points, but he had some bad ones too. A vile temper, when he was angry. He could hold a grudge longer than anyone else I knew."

"And he held one against Mike Tabor," Sadie said.

Marilyn looked up, her eyes wide. "Oh. So that's what you want to talk about."

"If you don't mind. People have told me you were pretty angry with Mike for what he did to Joe."

"Well, yeah. He wrecked my boyfriend's chances of getting a full sports scholarship to the college he wanted. I was ticked. I thought Mike should pay." She sat straighter and eyed Sadie cautiously. "Wait a sec. You don't think that blowup over the cheating had anything to do with Mike's falling off the mountain, do you?"

"No, I'm not saying that. Do you remember when the movie people were in town?"

"No. I didn't get to see any of that. I spent the summer teaching riding at a camp over near Colorado Springs."

"So you weren't in Silver Peak at all?"

Marilyn shook her head. "I only made it home once that summer, and it was before they started the shooting. Everyone was excited about it."

"Did you see Joe then?"

"No. We'd broken up before I left for camp. We lost touch." She sighed. "I was heartbroken at the time, but I don't think what we had was real love. It was more pride on my part. I'd been dating a senior, and he was good-looking. I hated that everyone knew Joe had dumped me. My friends told me I was better off without him, and I came to see that they were right. It took a while, but yeah, that was not the match made in heaven. Far from it. I came home a couple of weeks before school started for my senior year, but the movie crew was gone by then. I'm sorry I can't help you on that."

"It's all right," Sadie said. "Do you remember Chuck Wayne?"

"Sure. He was one of Joe's friends."

"Yeah. He told me Joe went away right after graduation."

"He did. I was angry about that too. Joe gave me no chance to have it out with him. One day he was there, and the next he was gone. He'd gotten a job somewhere for the summer, and he was going to go to another college in the fall, not UC. I'm not sure now where he went to school, but I heard he decided to major in business, and later someone told me he was into stock trading."

"So you're sure he had left before the film crew came to town?" Sadie asked.

"I'm positive."

Sadie drove home feeling that she'd wasted her energy pursuing the Joe Pinkham angle. Still, she could tell Roz that Joe and Marilyn had nothing to do with her brother's accident. The bad blood between Mike and Joe was unfortunate, but she felt they could now lay it to rest.

On Saturday morning, she turned her attention to a different avenue. The film crew had again tied up traffic around the town square, and Sadie gladly escaped to Breckenridge. Retired sheriff Ray Fanning was nowhere near as difficult to locate as Marilyn Smith had been. The seventy-eight-year-old man greeted Sadie cheerfully at the door of his snug log home. He invited her in and introduced her to his wife, Marie.

"Thanks for coming by," he said heartily as they settled in the living room. "Any friend of Dan Tabor's is a friend of mine."

"Thank you," Sadie said. "I'm more a friend of his daughter, Roz, but I did like Mr. Tabor a lot, and he was always nice to me."

"Of course he was," Ray said. "So what did you want to talk about?"

"You know they're making a movie in Silver Peak?" Sadie asked. "A remake of *Stranger from a Strange World*?"

"We did hear that," Marie said, and her husband nodded.

"I thought of Dan's family when I first heard that. How is Rosalind doing?"

"She'll be all right," Sadie said. "Of course, it's made us all remember what happened in 1965."

Ray nodded solemnly. "Poor Dan. I'd never seen him so broken. That was a dark day for him."

"I've been reading through his old duty notebooks at Roz's request," Sadie said. "She wanted to know what her dad really knew about Mike's death. He never talked to her much about it."

"With something like that, it's hard to put it into words."

"Yes, and I'm sure Mr. and Mrs. Tabor tried to shield Roz from the worst of the pain. But now it's impossible for her not to think about it, and she wants to know what's in the official record."

"I see. Well, I should be able find the police report for you. I responded after Dan did, and the state police came after that. I ended up writing up the report for our department, because Dan took himself off the case as soon as I got there, which was the proper thing to do."

Sadie nodded. "Do you still have a copy of the report?"

"No, but I understand the department's filing system. I can make some calls."

"Thank you," Sadie said. "I also found an entry in his notes that mentioned some film footage of Mike's accident. Did you see that?"

Mr. Fanning nodded slowly. "I did, and it was odd. They were all going in and out of the scene, speaking their lines, and all of sudden, Mike tripped. He was over the edge like that." He snapped his fingers. "If I hadn't known he'd died, I'd have thought it was a movie trick, and that it was part of the story. You couldn't see him after he went over the brim, and with that camera angle, you couldn't really tell how high up it was, and what a big drop-off he'd gone over, so it didn't really look as though anything was wrong. But then the other actors started panicking, and the cameraman stopped filming." He sighed. "When I first saw it, I wished we could rewind and stop it from happening. It didn't seem real."

"But it really happened," Sadie said.

"Yes."

"And you're positive the film is authentic?"

"No question. I talked to every person who was there. About half of them saw him take the dive. The rest were distracted or working on something else. The cameraman was the main witness. He said he couldn't believe it at first, but then he realized it was absolutely real."

"How awful for everyone who was there," Marie said.

"Yes," Sadie said. *But worse for those who hurried to Mike's side down below,* she thought. *And much, much worse for his family, especially his father.*

"I felt so empty for Dan," Mr. Fanning said regretfully. "There was nothing I could do to help him. Except take over his duties, of course. Dan had mentored me through my first two years in the department, and we were close. I respected him so much. He was a good cop and a devoted family man."

"He loved his kids," Marie added.

"Oh yes." Tears misted Mr. Fanning's eyes. "He thought a lot of Mike. He was so proud of him for getting that part in the movie too. And Mike was so happy about it. He'd always liked theater and playacting, I guess, and I think he hoped to go on in the acting field."

"Do you know what became of that film footage?" Sadie asked.

"Well, we gave it over to the state police investigators, but they returned it later, after it was ruled an accident. The movie crew was long gone by then. The film should be in storage."

"Where?"

"There's a warehouse on the other side of Breckenridge. They keep old evidence there. Stuff from closed cases, mostly. In a case like that, there really wasn't anyone to return it to, and nobody's asked about it, to my knowledge."

"Were you with Mr. Tabor when he watched it?"

"No. I think he wanted to be alone. I saw it, though, before he did. I wanted to make sure it wasn't too gruesome before he looked at it."

"Do you think you could get that film for me?" Sadie asked.

Mr. Fanning frowned. "Well, I'm not on active duty anymore, you understand. Technically, I don't have access to that stuff. Somebody who's wearing the badge now would have to put in a request for it. Then they'd send somebody over to the warehouse to see if they could locate it."

"I see. Would Mac Slattery qualify? He's our current sheriff."

"Sure, Mac could ask for it. Doesn't mean the clerks would be able to find it, though."

"I think it would be worth a try," Sadie said.

She drove directly from the Fannings' home to the sheriff's office.

"Well, hi," Janet Parks said when she walked through the door.

"I didn't know you worked Saturdays," Sadie said, approaching the receptionist's desk.

Janet made a face. "I don't, but the usual weekend person called in sick. I agreed to do four hours this morning, not a minute more. What can I do for you?"

"I'd hoped to catch the sheriff in."

"He's here," Janet said. "Let me ring him and see if he's available."

"Thanks. It won't take long, I promise."

A short time later, Janet escorted her down the hall to Mac's private office. Mac sat at his desk, typing on his computer keyboard. He looked up when Sadie paused in the doorway.

"Hi, Sadie. Milo and I didn't find anything out at the ranch, if that's what you're here for."

"It's not, but thank you for checking on it." Sadie sat down in a straight chair facing Mac's desk and explained to him about her visit to Ray Fanning's house. "And he thought you might be able to put in a request for me, so that we could view that film," she concluded.

"*We*, meaning you and Roz Putnam?" he asked.

"Well, I suppose so."

Mac frowned. "Are you sure she wants to see it?"

"I think she does. Or she would if she knew it was available."

"It might be better if she didn't. You told me she wants to put this behind her. Watching the film might do the opposite."

Sadie thought about that. "You may be right. Maybe you could view it first and see what you thought. It could bring closure."

"Or make her think about it even more." Mac leaned back in his chair. "I'll see if I can find out if that film still exists. It's the kind of thing that might have gone missing if someone thought it would make a good souvenir. Or it may have deteriorated if it wasn't stored properly."

"Thank you, Mac." Sadie stood. "I won't take any more of your time. But would you mind asking them soon?"

"I'm not sure anyone could access the warehouse this weekend, but I can put things in motion."

It was time for Sadie to head down the street to Edwin's house. Noelle and Carl were preparing to leave, and they had invited her to take an early lunch with them.

When she arrived, Noelle met her at the door.

"Hi, Sadie! Come right in. I'm putting lunch on the table while Carl and Dad get the luggage ready to load."

"Let me help you," Sadie said.

"Great. Dad gave you my list of bids for that estate sale, right?"

"He sure did," Sadie said. "I noticed that retro Egyptian necklace too. I wasn't sure I could sell it here, though. If I can get it for you, I will."

"We go to a big fundraiser every Christmas in Atlanta," Noelle said, her eyes shining. "I have the perfect dress to wear it with." Noelle turned, opened a cupboard door, and scanned the shelves. "*Hmm*. I know Dad's got a carnival glass bowl that would be just the right size for this fruit salad."

"Oh, I think that's in the hutch in the dining room," Sadie said. "It was one of your grandmother's dishes."

"Of course." Noelle stood with her hand on the cupboard door. "You know this house better than I do."

Sadie didn't have a reply. She couldn't tell if Noelle was chagrined or just stating a fact.

"It's true." Noelle came over to stand near her. "I've realized these past couple of weeks what I've missed out on by living so far away from Dad. I didn't want him to move back here. I guess I was afraid the distance between us would be even greater. The emotional distance, I mean."

"You don't have to feel that way," Sadie said. "Edwin loves you very much."

Noelle nodded. "He dotes on Sam too."

"He sure does. This visit has meant so much to him. He's really gotten to know his grandson, and I know he was glad he could do some fun things with you and Carl. Edwin is big on collecting memories."

"We'll have to come to visit him more often. And I've gotten past my jealousy, I think."

"Your jealousy?" Sadie cocked her head to one side.

"I didn't like to think of Dad getting close to someone else. You're not Mom and..." Noelle turned away. "I'm sorry, Sadie. I can see that you're good for Dad, even if you are very different from my mother. I guess the thing that really impressed me was the dedication you've shown in trying to help your friend Roz."

"Really? I didn't know you were even aware of that."

"Yeah," Noelle said. "Dad told me about it, and how you're helping her learn the truth about her brother's death. Most people would just tell her it was a long time ago and she should let it go."

"She was really hurting inside, not knowing for sure if his death was truly an accident, and I think the fact that her parents never talked to her about that hurt even more."

"Yeah. Talking is good. I've tried to really open up to Dad while we've been here. I realized we hadn't talked about anything important for a long time. So thank you for helping me see that. I know you're as good a friend to my father as you are to Roz."

"He's pretty special to me," Sadie admitted.

"Well, I'd say you're just what he needs now. I'm glad he has you."

Sadie took a step closer and touched Noelle's shoulder. "Thank you. And don't think I would ever come between you two. Edwin told me he's thinking of flying to Atlanta this fall for a visit with you and Carl and Sam."

Noelle nodded. "I hope we can make it happen, or maybe we can come out here again for a few days. Meanwhile, you keep doing whatever you're doing as far as he's concerned."

"I think I can manage that."

"Good. Because I'm not sure what it is, but he almost seems younger when you're around him. More carefree, maybe. I was used to Dad being more dignified, more formal." Noelle looked off out the kitchen window as she spoke, and then chuckled. "I guess it comes with being a judge, but he's seemed so different since he moved back here."

"I like to see him relax and enjoy himself," Sadie said.

"Me too. After Mom died, he was really down for a while. I knew it hit him hard. We all miss her, and I don't want him to forget her ever, but . . . well, I think it's good that he's moved past that."

"Thank you." Sadie drew Noelle into her arms, her eyes burning with tears. "Now, let me get that serving dish for you."

A moment later, Edwin, Sam, and Carl entered the dining room as she was placing the last of the water glasses on the table.

"Hey, Sadie," Edwin said with a grin. He came around the table and kissed her cheek. "Long time, no see."

"Oh yeah, I think it's been almost a whole day."

They all laughed.

"Let's sit right down," Noelle said. "We don't want to be late getting to the airport."

"The luggage is all loaded," Carl assured his wife, pulling out a chair for her. "Sam, hop up there between Mommy and Miss Sadie."

"Hello, Sam," Sadie said with a smile as he clambered into his chair. "Are you excited about flying today?"

Sam shook his head vehemently.

"Why not?"

His face scrunched up, and he reached his arms up to her.

"Aw!" Sadie leaned over and hugged him. "I'll miss you too. And I know your grandpa will. But you probably want to see your friends again, don't you? And your grandpa and grammy Carson?"

Sam nodded and sat up in his chair. "Mommy packed all my spacemen."

"Honey, you have other toys to play with on the trip," Noelle said quickly.

"Yeah, like your Etch-a-Sketch and the little tractor set Grandpa gave you," Carl added.

"Well, I hope you come back again soon," Sadie said. "All of you."

Edwin looked around at them and smiled. "On that note, perhaps we should say the blessing and get started. Time does fly."

Half an hour later, Sadie said her final good-byes to the Carsons in the driveway. "Noelle, I hope you return soon."

Noelle gave her a squeeze and stepped back, smiling. "Maybe we can get to a sale together next time."

"I'd like that."

Sadie watched as they all piled into Edwin's car.

"Sure you don't want to go to Denver today?" Edwin asked, standing beside his open door.

Sadie chuckled at his hopeful smile. "Thanks, but I'd better get over to the store. I told Julie she could have the rest of today off."

"All right, then. I'll see you later."

"Maybe we can get together this evening," Sadie suggested. Edwin would surely feel a bit let down when he came home to an empty house.

His expression perked up immediately. "Sure. In fact, one of the actresses is going to sing live at Sophia's tonight. Maybe we should catch it."

"Oh, that must be the girl who burned Simon Riley's curtains. I heard she's a good singer."

"I'll pick you up at seven."

She nodded, and Edwin got into his car grinning. Sadie waved until the car was out of sight and then walked to her Tahoe. His daughter's visit had been a delight for Edwin, and Sadie was glad that she had gotten to know Noelle and her family better.

———————

The weekend flew by as Sadie enjoyed her outing with Edwin and time with Alice and her children. Most of the people connected to the film project left for the weekend, and Main Street seemed oddly quiet.

Alice's ex-husband, Cliff Macomb, joined them on Sunday for church and dinner. After lunch, Sara coaxed her father to go horseback riding with her.

"Come on, Dad. We can ride up to where they're shooting the movie scenes. No one will be up there today, but I can show you."

"You'd better keep away from that area," Alice said. "Mr. Monahan rented it exclusively, and he might not like it if he comes back and finds trampled grass and horse manure where he's going to shoot some more footage."

"Oh, Mom!" Sara scowled. "Okay, so we'll take the rim trail. You haven't ridden in ages, Dad."

"That's the truth," Cliff said. "If I do it now, I'll go to work tomorrow all saddle-sore."

"I'll go if you will, Dad," Theo chimed in.

Cliff couldn't refuse both his children, so the three of them put on jeans and headed off to Milo's ranch.

"I'm glad he went," Alice confessed when Cliff's car had left the driveway. "Cliff hasn't been up here for three weeks, and I think the kids were feeling a little neglected."

Sadie helped her carry dishes from the dining table into the kitchen. "Sara will come out and say so, but Theo might not. But that doesn't mean he doesn't want to spend time with his dad."

Sadie and Alice spent the afternoon chatting and working on Alice's photo scrapbook. When the trio returned a couple of hours later, Sara charged through the door.

"Grandma, we saw a hawk!"

"That's great," Sadie said.

"And somebody was pounding in the barn," Theo added.

"Pounding?" Alice looked at him sharply.

"Milo said it was the special effects director from the movie," Cliff explained. "Theo and I wanted to go in and talk to him, but Milo said we should leave him alone, so we did."

Sadie nodded. "That's Derek. He's set up a workshop out in the haymow part of the barn."

"What does he do out there?" Theo asked.

"He's building props for the film," Sadie said. "He's very protective of his privacy, though." The crew would only be in Silver Peak another week. *What good would Derek's efforts be*, she wondered, *if he never let anyone see the results?*

17

———

The film crew was back to work on Monday, setting the town abuzz once more. Sadie was rested and ready for business. A tour company had phoned to tell her they were taking two busloads of tourists to Silver Peak that day.

"We'll be open at ten, as usual," Sadie told the caller cheerfully.

"Great. Our clients always love your store. Is the movie production right there in town?"

"Some of it is," she replied. "Some of it's at a ranch farther up the mountain. I'm not sure where they're shooting today."

"We'll take the chance. Some of our guests are very eager to get a glimpse of Jason Singer."

"Oh well, he's been around," Sadie said. She hadn't taken much notice of the young leading man, but she did recall seeing him sign autographs between takes one day in the town square, and Noelle had gotten to meet him. The actors and the Monahans had made themselves accessible to the fans, which Sadie suspected was driving more tourists their way.

The next day promised to be just as busy. Alice, whose teaching job gave her a summer hiatus, offered to help out so that Julie could have a day off.

As Sadie checked her cash drawer a few minutes before opening time Tuesday, a knock came at the locked front door of the shop. She looked around, expecting to see Alice. Instead, Mac Slattery was waving at her through the glass. She walked over to let him in.

"Hey!" The bell jingled as she swung the door open.

He stepped inside. "Hi. I heard back from the police about that old report. You can come by my office and read it there if you want. And they're looking for that film footage you asked about."

"Do you think they'll find it?"

"I don't know. Searching a warehouse for something that old... I'd say it's fifty-fifty."

"Okay, thanks," Sadie said. "I'll stop by later to read the report."

When she saw it that afternoon, the contents did not surprise her. Beyond what Daniel Tabor had written in his notes, she found details of the location and position of the body, names of the witnesses, and their statements. Eight people had reported actually seeing the fall. Their accounts agreed on all the basics, though only two mentioned that Mike had tripped over a piece of equipment. The others said he had stumbled, or that he was too close to the edge and the ground crumbled beneath him. One of the other actors said he stood close by and had reached out on instinct to try to stop Mike's fall, but without success. Clipped to the back of the statements was a report done a couple of weeks later by a geologist from the University of Colorado. In it, he stated that heavy rains that spring might have weakened the face of the bluff. He gave his opinion that this could have contributed to the accident.

Sadie certainly would not recommend that Roz see this report, but she was glad that she could go to her friend and tell her that she had read it thoroughly. She was more convinced than ever that Mike's death was no more than a tragic accident.

It was not until Wednesday that Mac called her to announce that the film footage from the day of Mike's death had been found.

"Wow," Sadie said. "Have you watched it?"

"No, but I can if you like."

"That might be good, if you're sure you don't mind," Sadie said.

He called back later in the day to say he had seen the footage. "It's not graphic—in fact, it's very understated. There's no film of the body. Did you want to show it to Roz?"

"Thanks, Mac. I don't think so. I'd like to view it privately. May I come by later?"

———

That evening, Sadie went to the sheriff's office as soon as she and Julie had closed the Antique Mine. Mac had the short film ready for her to preview.

"I had it copied on to a disc to make it easier," he explained. "The film was pretty fragile, and they said at the lab that the more we handled it, the sooner it would fall apart."

"Thanks." Sadie sat down in Mac's desk chair, and he pulled one of the visitor's chairs over and sat beside her. With a couple of keystrokes, he started the video.

The camera panned the view from the top of the bluff on Milo's ranch. The mountain peaks in the distance and the valley below, where beef cattle grazed, would have made a great advertisement for beautiful Silver Peak. Next, the camera focused on the main character in the movie, played by the famous actor Blaze Foster.

"He sure was handsome," Sadie murmured.

Blaze portrayed a very convincing young man who was frightened. He didn't quite believe what he had seen the night before, but now it was up to him to persuade his family and neighbors that their quaint town was being invaded by extraterrestrials.

"I guess you know that feeling, eh?" Mac asked.

Sadie laughed. "I was glad I had a witness that first night."

On the screen, Blaze said, "I'm telling you, they're hiding their spacecraft somewhere up here on the mountain." He pleaded with the townspeople to believe him.

"I don't know, Rex," a wizened rancher said. "You dragged us all the way up here, but there's nothing to see."

The camera pulled back. About a dozen other townspeople could now be seen too. On the extreme right, Sadie noticed Mike and two other young men.

"This must be where he took over Ty's speaking part," she said to Mac.

"Listen!" Mike shouted.

Everyone else turned toward him.

"Can you hear that?"

Sure enough, the sound track contained a low throbbing sound that gradually grew louder. Close-ups of several faces showed the people experiencing curiosity, then apprehension, then fear.

"It's down there!" Mike ran toward the edge of the bluff and tripped over something. He sprawled on his face, his momentum carrying him forward too fast and too far. The rim of the bluff gave way, and Mike was gone. The other actors stared for a moment, and then the lead actress, Gina Tarino, screamed.

The film clip ended and the screen went fuzzy. Everything was quiet for a moment. Mac reached over and closed the program.

"Well?"

Sadie exhaled heavily. "Very intense. I don't think Roz should see it. But thank you. I can go to her now and tell her there's no doubt. That was an accident."

"I'm glad I could help," Mac said.

As Sadie drove to the Putnams' house, the film kept replaying in her mind. One thing was certain: If it had affected her this strongly, it would be even worse for Roz.

Roscoe answered the doorbell.

"Hi, Sadie. Come on in. Roz is in the kitchen."

"Thanks."

Roscoe walked with her to the back of the house. Roz was taking a pan of meat loaf from the oven.

"Well, hello! Join us for supper?"

Sadie smiled. "Well, maybe I will, if you have plenty."

"Tons," Roz said.

Over the table, Sadie told them about seeing the film footage.

"How do you feel about it?" Roz asked.

"A little unsettled. Sad."

Roz nodded.

"Roz, there's no doubt in my mind now that it was an accident." Sadie looked from Roz to Roscoe and back. "We've looked into every aspect we could, and it all confirms what your dad told you."

Roz was quiet for a moment, and then she smiled. "I'm glad. Really glad. It would have been horrid if it had turned out any other way."

"So you're good with this?" Roscoe eyed her carefully. "You're ready to put it aside?"

"Yeah, I am." Roz's smile widened. "I may even go to the showing Friday night. Are you and Edwin going?"

"We sure are. Want to double?"

Roz arched her eyebrows at her husband. "What do you say?"

"Sure." Roscoe sank back in his chair. "What time?"

"Curtain time is at seven," Sadie said.

Roscoe took a memo book and pen from his pocket. He laid the book on the table and wrote in firm block letters, *Friday, 7:00 PM, Opera House.*

Sadie watched him, and her smile faded. "Wait a minute."

"What?" Roscoe looked up at her, puzzled.

"Roscoe, did you leave me that note asking me to stop investigating?"

"Well, yeah, I..." His face flushed. "You mean you didn't know?"

"I had no idea who had left it there. I thought someone was upset that we were looking into Mike's death."

"What are you talking about?" Roz asked.

"I wasn't upset exactly," Roscoe said. "I could see that all the talk about the movie and Mike was making you sad, and I thought it might be best if Sadie quit digging into it. I went over to the store to ask her to do that. She wasn't there, and Julie was busy, so I left a note by the cash register."

"And you didn't sign it," Roz said.

"Oh. Well, I guess not." Roscoe turned to Sadie. "I'm sorry. I didn't mean to cause you any stress. In fact, just the opposite. I thought if we all quit talking about it, everyone would calm down and forget about it. I guess that was silly, with the movie crew being here and all."

"It's all right," Sadie assured him. "I didn't worry about it…much."

"Well, next time I send you a birthday card, I'll make sure I sign it," Roscoe said, and they all laughed.

———

"Excuse me, ma'am."

Sadie paused on the edge of the sidewalk. She'd been about to cross Main Street from the bank to the Antique Mine on Thursday morning when the driver of a large truck with a flatbed trailer called out to her. Parked on the edge of the street, the man held a slip of paper in his hand.

"Can I help you?" Sadie stepped closer and gazed up at him through his open window.

"Maybe. I'm looking for the Henderson ranch."

"Sure."

The driver smiled. "Thanks. I'm looking for a guy named Derek Todd."

Sadie nodded. "You can probably find him out there." Quickly she gave him directions. "It's on the left, and there's a ranch sign over the driveway."

"Thanks." He put the truck in gear. Sadie watched thoughtfully as he drove around the square and then headed out of town. His trailer was empty, so he was obviously not making a delivery.

She was only a short way from Edwin's office. On impulse, she turned and walked to the town hall.

Edwin looked up as she knocked on his open door. "Well, hi!" He smiled and stood.

"Hi." Sadie walked in and plopped down in one of the visitor's chairs facing his desk. "A truck driver pulling an empty trailer just asked me how to find Derek at the Henderson ranch."

Edwin's gray eyebrows arched. "Is that so?"

She nodded. "I'm thinking it might be time to have a talk with Derek."

"What do you think he's up to?" Edwin asked.

"I'm not sure, but what if that thing I saw the other night was his masterpiece?"

"You think he's going to take it out in broad daylight?"

"He's got to sometime, or what's the point? If he brings it out in the light of day, he can't deny it was what we saw hovering that first time, or what I saw last Wednesday night."

"I agree," Edwin said. "Want to ride out there?"

"Sure. I can have Julie open the store."

Edwin glanced at the open calendar book on his desktop. "I don't have anything until eleven."

"I promise to have you back by then."

Sadie retrieved the bolt she had found from the store and then drove with Edwin in her Tahoe, out on the familiar roads. When they reached the ranch, Milo was in the corral, saddling a horse, and the truck sat next to the barn.

"Is Derek here?" Sadie asked as she shut her car door.

"Yeah. Popular guy today." Milo gestured toward the barn. "I think he's moving his big toy out. You know"—Milo eyed her cautiously—"I've been thinking about that. And that glowing thing in the sky…"

"So have we," Edwin said.

All of them walked toward the back of the barn. The truck driver and Derek came out the door to the haymow section together.

"Okay, I'll back her right in there," the driver said.

Derek noticed Sadie and Edwin and stopped walking. "Hello."

"Hi," Sadie called, smiling. "We wanted to watch you move the spaceship."

18

───────

DEREK'S CHIN ROSE A FRACTION OF AN INCH. "WHAT ARE YOU talking about?"

"You know," Edwin said, "if you're moving it out of the barn today, what's the harm in talking about it?"

Derek heaved out a big breath and shook his head. "I want to surprise the boss."

Sadie stepped closer, taking the bolt from her pocket. "We understand, Derek. But what we saw has been driving us bananas. We think it was your mock-up spaceship for the movie."

The truck driver, who had been standing by and listening to the conversation, looked to Derek. "So are we gonna move that thing or not?"

"Yes," Derek said.

Milo had trailed Sadie and Edwin over to the barn. Now he spoke up. "I've been wondering about that too. But Derek didn't want to show me what he was making, and that was one of the conditions I agreed to when I rented out the barn—that I wouldn't poke around and ask questions."

"All right," Derek finally said, throwing his hands in the air. "I'll let you see it, but please don't tell anyone else until I have everything ready. I want to ask Fox to take a look at it today."

"Sounds fair," Edwin said.

Derek sighed. "Come on, then."

They followed him into the barn.

"Wow." Sadie stood still for a moment, gazing at the gleaming machine. "It's huge."

"Twenty-four feet long," Derek said with a touch of pride. He patted the aluminum-covered side of the craft.

"Very impressive," Edwin said. "Was it really this thing we saw? How does it fly?"

Derek seemed to struggle with his reply. "Okay, it was. It wasn't finished—it was just the skeleton with the engine and a few lights. I needed to be sure it would fly before I went to the time and expense of finishing it."

"And it worked," Sadie said, stepping closer.

Derek frowned. "Well, it didn't really hover quite the way I wanted, and it wasn't as responsive as I needed it to be. That told me what I needed to fix before Fox saw it, but it's been really hard to squeeze out the time to work on it."

"But you took it out again last Wednesday night," Sadie said. "I saw the beam."

Derek nodded. "That was new. I figured there was a chance somebody would see it, but I had to test it. I think everything's ready now. I was planning to take it down to the bottom of the cliff and try it. If it's successful, I'll ask Fox to take a look tonight. It's even more impressive after dark, with the lights and all."

"Why didn't you tell him what you were working on?" Sadie asked.

"I figured Fox would be mad and nix the project, because he had already said he wasn't going to use a full-size mock-up. And then I'd be out the money it cost to build this. But I think I've worked out all the bugs. Of course, it's not full size for a real spaceship—it's a half-scale model, but it's big enough to look real. It's not too late for him to use it in the film."

"Wouldn't they have to reshoot a lot of the scenes?" Edwin asked.

"Well… Maybe a couple."

Milo had stepped outside, but now he came back into the barn, sliding his phone into his pocket. "I called Fox Monahan. He's on his way out here."

"Oh no." Derek leaned on the fender of the trailer, as if he needed the support. "I'm not ready. I haven't had a chance to give it my final test run."

"I'm sorry. I guess I missed that. Maybe you can do it while he's here," Milo said.

Derek turned to the truck driver. "Hurry! Let's get this thing outside and off the ground before the boss gets here."

"You took the money from the discretionary fund for this project, didn't you?" Sadie asked.

Derek hesitated. "I was going to pay it back. If Fox didn't approve the mock-up, that is. But I was so sure he would… And then it ended up costing more than I'd expected."

"So now you can't pay it back, even if you wanted to."

Derek's shoulders slumped. "I don't know what I'll do if he won't approve it. But we're so near the end of the filming. If I don't tell him today, it will be too late. Once we leave Silver Peak, there won't be any going back and working with my setup."

Edwin nodded. "You're right. You need to tell him today. And, for what it's worth, I think your spaceship looks great."

"It looks a lot like the one in the 1965 movie," Sadie said, tilting her head to one side.

"I tried to test it when I thought no one would see it." Derek grimaced. "I came before anyone else from the crew was here for that first run, and I heard the town was having a big event at the opera house. I didn't think anyone would be out looking over this way. I had to make sure it could sustain the altitude and hover long enough for filming before I went any further. But I sort of forgot about the time difference between here and California. I thought folks would be at the opera house later than they were."

"If you'd done it an hour earlier, we certainly wouldn't have seen it," Sadie said.

"But I might have." Milo stepped forward. "I didn't go to the opera house that night. I was home, and I was outside some that evening."

While they talked, the truck driver attached the cable from the winch on his truck to an eyebolt Derek had fixed at the front of the spaceship. He began winching the craft onto his trailer.

"You weren't working here in Milo's barn at that time, were you?" Edwin asked Derek.

"No. I wanted to test what I had before making a final decision on whether or not it was worth the money—and the risk—of bringing it here and continuing with the project. I hadn't done any of the cosmetic work. It was really just a framework with a few lights. If I hadn't decided to cover it completely in aluminum sheeting, I probably would have been okay. The producer wouldn't have noticed how much was gone from the fund." Derek sighed. "But I really wanted it to look like the *Gray Hawk*."

"What's that?" Edwin asked.

"The spaceship from the original picture."

"Can you help me tie it down?" the truck driver asked.

Milo and Derek hurried to help him.

Derek stepped back when it was secure on the trailer. "Okay, let's go."

"Let Fox see what it can do," Sadie said, patting his arm. "We'll suggest he doesn't make any decisions until he's seen a test run."

"I'd appreciate it if you did that," Derek said. "I'm afraid all this confusion about the money will prejudice him."

Confusion of Derek's own making, Sadie noted silently. He knew he was at fault, and he had one chance to convince his bosses that his project was worth a part in the film.

The truck driver got in the cab and pulled the trailer from the barn. In Sadie's opinion, the spaceship was even more impressive in the daylight. Its shape and buffed metal surface made it beautiful.

A car came quickly up the driveway, raising a cloud of dust. It parked five yards from the truck. Fox leaped from the passenger side, and Hamilton Dobey, the producer, climbed more slowly from the driver's seat.

"What's going on, Derek?" Fox strode toward them. "What is this thing?"

"What does it look like?" Derek asked.

"Well, it looks like the *Gray Hawk*."

Derek smiled, but his eyes still held anxiety. "Do you like it?"

"Where did it come from?" Fox walked toward the ship on the trailer, eyeing it in wonder.

"I've been working on it."

"It looks great. Even better than the one in *Stranger*. It's too bad..." Fox whirled and stared at Derek. "This is what you wanted to build, back in California, but I told you not to. I told you we'd be using CGI and smaller models."

The producer walked toward them, his face stony. "Is this where the money from the discretionary fund went?"

Derek's eyes shifted, but he squared his shoulders. "Yes, sir."

Fox studied him for a moment. "Why didn't you speak up?"

"I'm sorry. I guess...I was afraid. Scared I'd lose my job. And that you wouldn't let me build this. I know I shouldn't have done it behind your back, Fox, but I thought once you saw it the way I could make it, you'd love it. Only it took longer than I estimated. I had so many other props and extra sets to work on. And then I ran out of money. At first I only borrowed three hundred dollars. I thought no one would miss it before I finished. And then I needed more for the sheet metal. I hoped no one would notice for a week or so." He sighed and dropped his chin. "I was wrong."

"I'll say you were wrong." Hamilton Dobey glared at Derek. "That was a stupid thing to do, not to mention dishonest. You're..."

"Don't." Fox stepped between them.

"You can't want to keep him on after this," Dobey said.

"Think, Hamilton. We're less than a week away from wrapping this film. I need Derek for these last few scenes. He's the only person with the skill to help us get the technical stuff right."

"The others can handle it."

"No," Fox said. "I don't want to get it ninety percent right. I don't want this film to be a laughingstock. I want it to be compelling and believable." He turned slowly and looked at the spaceship. "I think Derek's right. A few shots with this in it could make a big difference. It looks real. It will resonate with the viewers. Those who have seen the old film will identify with it."

Derek's jaw dropped, but he had sense enough to keep quiet.

After a moment, Hamilton huffed out a breath. "Fine, but he'd better replace that money."

"How much total?" Derek almost squeaked.

"Four thousand, seven hundred, and forty dollars."

"I didn't take that much!"

Fox turned to study Derek. "How much did you take?"

"About three grand. I've got receipts for everything. I didn't take one penny more than what I spent on this machine."

"So maybe we should look a little closer at who has access to the petty cash," Fox said with a tight smile at Hamilton. "Meanwhile, I'd like to see what this baby can do."

Derek's face smoothed into a smile. "Yes, sir." He waved to the truck driver. "Let's go." He walked quickly to the truck and called over his shoulder to Fox, "If you want the full effect, drive up to the top of the bluff. We'll have liftoff in twenty minutes or so."

He jumped into the truck cab, and the driver put the engine in gear.

Hamilton Dobey watched them pull out of Milo's yard, scowling. "What if that thing never leaves the ground?"

"Then we can't use it, can we?" Fox didn't seem too worried about the possibility.

"Would you mind if Edwin and Milo and I rode up there to watch too?" Sadie asked.

Fox grinned. "Sure, why not?" He started to walk away, but halted and whirled back toward them. "Don't tell me this is what you two stargazers spotted the weekend before we came here?"

Sadie laughed. "Believe me, it makes a big impression after dark."

Fox nodded slowly. "I'll bet it does."

Sadie and Edwin got into the Tahoe, and Milo jumped in the backseat. Fox and Mr. Dobey followed them as they wound their way up the trail to the head of the bluff. Meanwhile, Derek and the truck driver rolled off toward the lane that would take them to the base of the cliff.

"I suppose this will take some time." Fox glanced at his watch and paced near the edge of the cliff.

"Don't get too close to the rim," Dobey warned him. "The last thing we want is a repeat of 1965."

"I shouldn't have told Derek I'd wait for him to set it up." Fox's face was reddening. His phone rang, and he pulled it out of his pocket. "Yeah, Dad? Yeah, I'm out at the ranch." He listened for a moment. "I know. Sorry, but it'll probably be another thirty minutes before I'm back. Have Phil go ahead and prep for that police scene. Yeah. If I'm not back, he can do a take. Might as well get his feet wet." Fox threw his head back for a moment, listening but tapping his foot. "Yes, I'm sure you could do it, Dad, but we're paying Phil to assist. If he goes ahead with it, he'll at least be earning his pay. If the take's no good, we'll do it over. Just make sure he has Jason properly indignant for that bit."

He ended the conversation a moment later and looked at his watch. "Come on!" He craned his neck to see what was going on below.

"It's a little safer over here, Mr. Monahan," Milo called. He had strolled a few yards away to where the mountainside sloped down more gradually. "I can see the truck from here, and there's no abrupt drop-off."

Fox and Hamilton Dobey strode over to stand beside him.

"Want to take a look over there?" Edwin asked Sadie.

"No, you go ahead. I'd rather pretend the truck doesn't exist and get the full effect when the alien spacecraft bursts on our horizon."

Edwin laughed. "I think you're wise. It will be a much more authentic experience that way. Not that anything about this crazy film is authentic."

"Silver Peak is authentic," Sadie said. "We'll always be able to point out our good, solid buildings, not some false front movie set in Hollywood."

"True. And J.B. told me they're having aerial film shot for the opening credits. Everyone will see how spectacular our scenery is here in Silver Peak."

Sadie smiled. "I do hope they acknowledge our town in the credits. It could send some more tourists up here."

They chatted amiably for a few minutes, until Fox yelled, "There it goes!"

Sadie listened closely and heard a faint humming noise. "Not very loud, is it?"

"No, and we thought when we saw it that first time that it was too quiet for a plane or a helicopter."

"I wonder if it's battery-operated."

Edwin frowned. "Maybe it starts with an engine, but keeps going on a battery, the way some of those hybrid cars do."

The humming became more intense.

"Think we'd have heard that from over at my house?" Sadie asked.

"I doubt it. Not with other background noise—traffic in the distance, animals, a breeze in the trees, that sort of thing."

The suddenness of its appearance beyond the rim of the cliff startled Sadie, and she jumped back a little, though she was at least forty feet away from it.

"Wow! It looks huge."

Edwin chuckled. "Like the rising moon. That's great! I hope Fox likes it."

"If I saw that, and I didn't know about the film, I'd be scared out of my boots," Sadie said, watching the silvery ship rise higher. It hung there for several seconds, then lights on each end began to flash. It rose another ten feet and hovered once more. A bright spotlight shone from its undercarriage. Then the ship began to drift slowly downward.

Sadie let out her pent-up breath as it sank below the rim. "Wow. I'm not sure how it would come across on film, but I absolutely loved that."

"Does it make you believe in men from Mars?" Edwin asked, smiling. "I agree, it's quite a sight."

Fox was walking quickly toward Dobey's car. "Come on, let's get down there. I need to talk to Derek. We could do that one scene over again with the camping family that saw it, and we can use it in the big finale."

Sadie smiled at Edwin. "Sounds like Derek won't have to worry about scraping up that money."

19

GLEE POPPED INTO THE ANTIQUE MINE SHORTLY AFTER NOON THE next day.

"Hi, Sadie. I've only got a minute, but I wanted to make sure I get that old flour sifter I saw in here, if you haven't sold it. We'll be leaving in a few days, and I might not get another chance to come in here."

"I haven't sold it." Sadie walked with her to where the cooking utensils were displayed. "I heard the whole film crew is out on the mountain again today."

"Yes, we just drove into town for lunch. They're doing a scene with Derek's mock-up of the spaceship. That is really cool!"

"I saw it," Sadie said. "I'm so glad Fox changed his mind about it."

"Me too. I think it's going to be a great addition. And they're going to do some filming after dark tonight too, for one scene."

"Oh, good." Sadie picked up the sifter with peeling green paint on the wooden handle. "I believe this is the item you wanted."

"It sure is." Glee held it up and nodded with satisfaction.

"So Derek is forgiven for using the money without telling any-one?" Sadie asked.

"Yes, I think that's all straightened out now."

"Oh? I thought there was more missing than Derek could account for."

Glee smiled and shook her head. "That was a mix-up. The day Hamilton Dobey arrived, there was only three thousand missing from the fund, or so they thought. But the head of wardrobe had made a trip to Denver that day to pick up some new outfits for Sandra. You knew she'd been complaining about her costumes?"

Sadie nodded.

"Well, the wardrobe director decided to see if she could replace some of the clothes and accessories to keep Sandra happy. She hadn't signed for money out of the account yet, but she spent about twelve hundred dollars in the city that day. When Dobey went to check the account, it was missing more than four thousand dollars."

"Derek's three thousand, plus the twelve hundred for wardrobe?"

"That's right," Glee said. "Only the wardrobe director hadn't brought in the receipts yet or accounted for the money she'd used out of the fund."

"So everybody's happy now?" Sadie asked.

"I'm not sure Mr. Dobey is. But then, I'm not sure he's ever happy."

Sadie laughed.

"He's gone back to California," Glee said. "It's sort of a relief. Everyone feels a little less on edge."

Bob Willis, the cameraman, opened the shop door and came inside. "There you are, Glee. Come on! I'm done with lunch, and I'm leaving for the ranch. If you want a ride, hustle it!"

"I just have to pay for this sifter." Glee and Sadie hurried to the counter.

"Bob, is everything going okay for you?" Sadie asked as she made change for Glee.

He smiled. "Yeah. A lot better now than it was a couple of days ago. I don't know if you knew this, but we had some financial problems in the family."

"You hinted at something like that to me," Sadie said, handing Glee her receipt. "Everything better now?"

"Yeah. My son got a new job. He lost his old one last spring, and things were pretty tight. He thought he was going to lose his car because he couldn't make the payments. But then he wouldn't have a car to drive to work, so…" He broke off with a shrug. "Anyway, it's okay now."

"Great," Sadie said.

"Come on, Bob," Glee said, as if offended by his lingering. "I'm in a hurry, you know."

Sadie laughed as the two of them left the store.

———

On Friday evening, Sadie dressed carefully. The gala at the opera house wasn't a premiere, but the showing of the old version of *Stranger from a Strange World* would be significant for Silver Peak. For Roz, it would be her first screening of the film, and she wanted to make it a special night, one that would honor her brother. Sadie had agreed, and so she forsook her jeans and opted for a shimmery blue dress that sparkled when she moved, along with a gold locket and earrings. She even put on lipstick.

When she went downstairs, Hank barked at her, as if he didn't recognize her. Then he gave a little snort and went back to his bed. Sadie laughed.

"Always a critic," she said.

Edwin called for her at 6:40. When Sadie opened the front door to him, his eyes lit.

"You look fantastic."

"Thanks." Sadie looked over his dark three-piece suit and abstract-patterned tie. "You look pretty swell yourself."

He laughed and crooked his elbow. "Shall we?"

Sadie smiled and took his arm. She turned to give Hank a final command to be good and locked the door.

Roz and Roscoe were waiting for them in the parking lot. Roz wore a silver blouse and a long black skirt. A soft pink scarf about her neck brought color to her face. Sadie hugged her.

"You look great."

"Thanks." Roz sounded a little breathless.

"Are you ready for this?"

Roz nodded. "I've waited fifty years to see it. I'm not putting it off any longer."

Together the four went inside and found seats five rows from the front. Although the committee had avoided advertising the event, in hopes of keeping the audience to local residents, more and more people flocked into the building.

"Looks like the whole town turned out," Roscoe observed.

Several people stopped by the end of their row to say hello to all of them, and a few seemed eager to turn the occasion into an opportunity to bend the mayor's ear. J. B. Monahan and his son came in together, and everyone clapped. They waved, smiled, and shook a few hands on their way to their seats. The rest of the cast and crew filtered in. Jason Singer and Sandra Vitelli were thronged by local residents.

"I guess everyone figures this is their last chance to get autographs," Roscoe said.

"It's nice of them to do it," Sadie added. Sandra looked very glamorous in an emerald green evening gown—much fancier than anything she had worn for the film. Jason, Fox, J.B., and several of the other actors had donned tuxedos.

"Am I underdressed?" Edwin whispered.

"I don't think so. It sort of makes the Hollywood crowd stand out, you know?"

He nodded and settled back in contentment.

"It was generous of the Monahans and the cast to stay for this," Roz said.

"I think they're enjoying it." Sadie smiled as she watched Jason sign an autograph with a flourish.

Roscoe nodded. "This is definitely a place where you can be a big fish in a small pond."

Troy Haggarty flitted about the auditorium, snapping flash pictures of the stars, the crew, the Monahans, and many of the local citizens.

At almost the last minute, Alice and her children came in at the back. Sadie waved, but she hadn't saved seats for them, as Alice hadn't been positive they would make it. Alice waved back and followed Theo, who had scouted seats for them near the back.

As Sadie leaned over to tell Edwin her family had arrived, the lights flickered, and the other stragglers made their way quickly to their seats. Luz Vidal walked up onto the stage and stood before the curtain. At the restaurant, she usually wore her hair up, but tonight her silky black locks flowed over the shoulders of her jade-green gown. How she could walk on those four-inch heels, Sadie couldn't fathom, but Luz pulled it off without a hitch.

"Ladies and gentlemen, it gives the Silver Peak Opera House Committee great pleasure to present the 1965 film *Stranger from a Strange World*, shot right here in our town. As chairman of the program committee, I must say this was one show we had no disagreements over. All of us who have come to town since this picture was made want to see it. But perhaps even more exciting is the presence tonight of its director, Mr. J. B. Monahan."

Clapping and cheering broke out, and Luz smiled and nodded toward J.B., who sat in the second row with his son. After a moment, J.B. stood and nodded, then waved as the crowd continued to applaud.

"And, of course," Luz resumed, "his son, Fox Monahan, is also our honored guest. Both have been with us for the past several weeks while Fox has directed the new version of this classic film."

Fox rose as the people once more applauded enthusiastically. When he had sat down, Luz gazed at the father and son. "We as a town would like to thank you for choosing to set your films here, and for all the excitement and economic benefit you've brought to Silver Peak."

After another round of applause, she said, "We also thank each member of the film's cast and crew for your contributions to the project's success. We know most of you will be pulling out in the morning. Sometimes when a bunch of movie people invades a small town, the residents end up feeling steamrollered. Well, we don't feel that way. You've all been very kind and generous, and the inconvenience of blocking off a few streets for short periods of time was well worth it. We'd like to thank you for behaving so well as guests of our town and invite you to come back again anytime."

This brought out a surge of laughter and more applause from the audience.

"Without further ado," Luz said, "let's watch the movie."

She sat down beside Ramon amid more clapping and a few whistles. As the auditorium dimmed and the curtain before the screen rose, Sadie reached over and squeezed Roz's hand. Her friend smiled at her and squeezed back.

"You okay?"

"Just like when we used to go to the movies after school," Roz whispered.

About twenty minutes into the film, when the townspeople began to reach out and share their fears that something very strange was going on, Roz gasped and grabbed Sadie's arm.

"Look! It's him!"

"What?" Sadie stared at the screen.

"He's gone now, but I saw Mike in the crowd, on the right side of the screen."

The people in the movie had gathered in the town square and were piecing together the odd things they had seen—much as Sadie and Edwin had done the night they saw the UFO after the dinner theater.

As the story went on, Sadie watched closely.

"Right there," Roz hissed.

This time, Sadie saw him too. Mike Tabor, looking young and dashing in a police officer's uniform, and a little scared as he panned the sky with the others, staring up past the distinctive facade of the opera house into the blue summer sky.

"It *is* him," Sadie breathed. "Wow, he looks great!"

"Doesn't he?"

"Which one is he?" Roscoe asked.

Edwin leaped to his feet and turned to face the crowd and the projection room operator.

"I'm sorry, folks, but we've just noticed something. If nobody objects, we'd like to run the film back a couple of minutes and watch that part again."

The pictures played over Edwin's face and chest, while behind him, his shadow blocked a large portion of the screen. He waved toward the projection box and called, louder, "Can you stop it for a minute, Danny? Sorry. Thanks!"

The film stopped, and the room went utterly dark for a moment before someone flipped a switch and the emergency lighting on the left side wall gave off a subdued gleam.

"What is it, Mr. Mayor?" Luz asked. J. B. Monahan was also on his feet.

"If I could have that microphone you used at the beginning," Edwin said.

"I'll get it." Jerry Remington, who was a member of the Opera House Committee, hurried to the side of the stage and brought it over. Edwin met him at the center front of the auditorium.

"Thanks. Folks, I'm sorry to interrupt the show," he said, "but something important just happened. Those of us who were around fifty years ago saw something remarkable on the screen. We'd like to see it again." Edwin glanced over at the Monahans.

"I saw it too," J.B. said. "I've watched it a hundred times, and I don't know why I never noticed him before."

"What?" several people called out.

Edwin cleared his throat. "There's something we don't talk much about around here. Fifty years ago, when this movie was made, a young man died. His name was Mike Tabor, and he was a fine young man with a promising future. He was the brother of Roz Putnam, who is here with us tonight. Because of her brother's association with the picture and his untimely death, Roz has never watched this movie before. Tonight she's seeing it for the first time. A few minutes ago, several of us—including Roz—noticed a familiar face in the crowd. We believe that it was Mike, and we'd like to run the film back and watch that scene in the town square again."

J.B. stepped forward and reached for the microphone. "Mr. Marshall is right, folks. We reshot several scenes after Mike Tabor died. I thought our editors made sure that he wasn't in any of the previously filmed footage they used. But somebody slipped up, and Mike is in the movie. Why I never saw it before, I don't know."

"We're all set, Mr. Mayor," Danny called down from the projection box.

Edwin waved to him and took the microphone back. "Thanks for indulging us, all of you. We wanted to dedicate tonight's screening to Mike Tabor, and this has made it extraspecial." He gave the microphone to Jerry and went back to his seat.

The movie started again, at the point when the people began to gather in the town square. Once again, Mike appeared on the right side of the screen with a cluster of other young people.

"There he is," Wade Marley called out, "and my aunt Judith's just to the left of him."

Everyone laughed as the film went on uninterrupted. Sadie glanced over at Roz. Tears rolled freely down her friend's cheeks. Sadie burrowed in her purse, took out a clean tissue, and tucked it into Roz's hand.

When the film ended an hour later, the lights came up. Roz gave her a trembling smile. "It was wonderful to see him again, so natural and carefree."

"Wasn't it?" Sadie said, patting her arm.

"I never met Mike," Roscoe said. "I'd seen pictures of him when he was a kid, but that was special. Getting to see how he moved and all. I'm glad I got to see it."

"I think it touched all of us who did know him," Edwin said. He smiled at Roz.

Luz Vidal had taken her place at the front of the auditorium, and she turned on the microphone. "Folks, I'm sure you enjoyed that as much as I did. Now, Mr. J. B. Monahan has asked to say a few words."

J.B. pushed shakily to his feet, and Fox stood beside him and accepted the microphone from Luz. They faced the crowd, and everyone waited in silence.

"A few minutes ago," Fox said, "Edwin Marshall mentioned that we wanted to dedicate the new film to Mike Tabor. My dad is in agreement with this, and he has suggested adding Mike's name and his lifespan dates to the credits of the new film."

The people clapped at this, and Fox's features relaxed into a regretful smile. His father took the mic from him.

"Friends—and I don't call you that lightly," J.B. said, "the film that we made here fifty years ago was a success, and you as viewers and supporters are just as big a reason for that as are we who worked on it. So thank you for making this film so beloved that my son wanted to do a remake. You know, I thought it was a bad idea at first."

The crowd was pin-drop silent as he spoke.

J.B. gave them a wry smile. "Well, Fox insisted, and I decided not to get in his way. I wasn't planning to be a part of it, but he cajoled me in. I have to say that Fox has stayed true to the artistic direction of the original film. I don't know that I added much to it, but I was happy to consult and to be here with you all again, in this delightful little town. Thank you."

Fox grinned and leaned in to the mic. "Yes, I brought Dad along to make sure we did everything right. Thanks, everybody!"

The audience clapped enthusiastically. As the people began to leave the opera house, Sadie's cousin Laura stopped to speak to Roz.

"I'm so sorry," Laura said as she squeezed Roz's hand. "I wasn't here then, but I know your brother was precious to you."

"Thank you," Roz said, misty-eyed.

A dozen more people paused to speak to her. Several of them remembered Mike and told Roz how deeply his death had affected them.

"And I'm sorry I never told you that before," Wade Marley said gruffly.

"Thanks, Wade." Roz smiled wanly at Roscoe, who had waited patiently.

"Ready to go?" he asked.

"Yes."

"What would you say to getting some ice cream at the Depot?" Edwin asked, looking from Roz to Sadie.

"I think that would be nice," Roz said.

"Sounds lovely," Sadie told him. She was thankful that Edwin had thought of it.

Several others joined them at the Depot, including Milo, Alice, Theo, Sara, and Laura. They all put in orders for their favorite flavors and settled at one of the eatery's larger tables.

"This is nice," Sara said. "And they have pistachio tonight."

"I think they expected a big crowd from the opera house," Alice told her.

Roz smiled at Sadie. "It's kind of like when we'd go to the movies back in high school, and then get milk shakes."

Sara's eyes shone. "That movie was so cool. I can hardly wait to see the new one."

"I thought it was a little campy myself," Theo said. He looked around cautiously, as though expecting to be jumped on by critics.

Milo smiled. "It was, in places. But I think Silver Peak folks are willing to overlook that for sentimental reasons."

"Obviously, other people are too," Roscoe said, "or it wouldn't be so popular, and Fox Monahan wouldn't have decided to do a remake."

They continued to talk as they ate their ice cream. Edwin leaned toward Sadie. "I forgot to mention, I got a letter in the mail from Noelle today."

"Oh?" Sadie paused with her spoon in midair.

"Yeah. She sounded as though they really enjoyed their time here."

"I could tell that," Sadie said.

Edwin smiled. "She also sent a drawing that Sam made. It was of him and me riding horses—with a spaceship flying overhead."

Sadie laughed. "Now, that sounds like Sam."

She looked around the table at her family and friends and savored the wonderful gift of contentment.

About the Author

CAROLE JEFFERSON IS THE PEN NAME FOR A TEAM OF WRITERS WHO have come together to create the series Mysteries of Silver Peak. *Lights and Shadows* was written by Susan Page Davis. Susan is the author of more than fifty novels and novellas in the historical romance, mystery, and suspense genres. She is the mother of six and grandmother of ten. A Maine native, she now lives in western Kentucky with her husband, Jim. Visit her Web site at susanpagedavis.com.

Read on for a sneak peek of another exciting book in Mysteries of Silver Peak!

MYSTERIES
of SILVER PEAK

When Lightning Strikes

SADIE REINED SCOUT PAST THE TEMPTING NEW SPROUTS OF RUSH grass that had pushed their way up alongside the mountain trail near her Silver Peak home. The five-year-old chestnut gelding clearly wanted to linger as they approached the small fishing hole that held so many memories for Sadie. On any other day, she would have enjoyed pausing on this crisp April afternoon to savor the time with her daughter and grandchildren. But nature had other plans.

The weather that, until a moment ago, had been uncharacteristically warm for this scenic part of Colorado, suddenly gusted its chilly breath at the foursome. Fallen leaves scurried along the well worn path before them, as if trying to escape the impending rainstorm that now darkened the sky. Such occurrences were common around here, and usually short-lived, but familiarity didn't leave room for complacency.

Fourteen-year-old Sara's horse danced sideways, and nerves showed on the girl's pretty face. Hank, Sadie's golden retriever, wisely gave distance to the excited equine. Sara was a good rider, but Sadie was also aware of the potential dangers presented by a frightened horse.

"Relax," Sadie reminded her as the bay filly sidestepped into her own horse. "You're channeling your own nervous energy to Daisy."

As if the sky wasn't already dark enough, a heavy gray gloom settled over the area. The storm should be over in a matter of minutes, but it would be foolish to remain out in the elements until it passed.

"Let's go to Dad's old hideaway," Alice called from the back of the line.

"Good idea," Sadie called back over the gusting wind.

A rabbit skittered near the path, and Sara's horse tucked its hind legs as if it might rear up. Theo, thinking quickly, brought his horse alongside Sara's, grabbed the bridle, and quickly looped a thin rope through the ring near the bit. With the hastily fashioned lead in place, Daisy settled slightly, and Theo guided his younger sister's horse off the path and toward the rustic shelter that had been built here many years ago.

"You didn't have to do that," Sara protested with more than a hint of indignation. "I know how to ride a horse."

"You also know how to fall off," the seventeen year old said matter-of-factly.

The group had just about reached the shelter when the clouds ruptured. They all hastily dismounted and, although hitching posts sat on either side of the opening, they brought the animals with them into the bucolic sanctuary.

With its high roof, dirt floor, and open sides, the hideaway looked like a cross between a barn and a picnic shelter. What Sadie was most grateful for at the moment was its roof, which allowed none of the downpour inside. But the pounding of the rain on the tin disconcerted the already antsy Daisy.

"Let's give the horses some treats," Sadie suggested after they secured them to a post near the rear of the shelter.

Hank's ears pricked up at the "treat" word, and Sadie set out the food she'd brought for him while Alice rummaged through her saddlebag for a plastic bag of cut-up carrots and apples.

All but the skittish Daisy greedily took the treats, so Sadie dug into her own stash of goodies. She handed Sara one of the homemade oat bars that she'd made this morning. "Here, try giving her this."

The granola chunks, slightly sweetened with raisins, shredded coconut, and a touch of brown sugar, would have been irresistible under normal circumstances, but Daisy's brown eyes widened at the distant rumble, and she jerked her head away.

"Waste not, want not," Sadie said and passed the bag of untouched granola to the humans in the group. Then, attempting to lighten the mood as the rumbles grew louder, she filled them in on news of a chocolate fest proposed by the Campfire Circle Ministry at their church.

"Why chocolate? I thought they usually did a 5K run to help needy families." Alice reached for another chunk of granola and took a seat on the sturdy picnic bench that commanded a large corner of the shelter.

At forty-one, Sadie's only daughter was not only taller and slimmer than she was—traits inherited from Sadie's now-deceased husband—but Alice had also claimed her father's auburn hair and green eyes.

"It's just a one-time thing to raise money for a local group that aids widows, single mothers, and other women who need a temporary helping hand," Sadie said. "Widows' Mite needs a larger place to store donated items that they pass along to the women. A number of churches in the area are participating, so our group thought it would be nice to do it, too, and go for the chocolate theme."

"Women and chocolate. Ha ha! That's a good one." Theo plunked himself down on the bench and dug through the bag his mother had brought. "Speaking of chocolate, did you bring any with you?"

"Sorry," Alice said, sounding not a bit regretful since the snack bag already contained more healthful options. She glanced around them and added, "Being here sure brings back memories of Dad."

As often happened, whenever the subject of their grandfather came up, Theo and Sara reminisced about the things he'd said or done before he passed away a couple of years ago. Today, they laughed together as they remembered the time T.R. had tried to teach Theo to cast. The worm-covered fishing hook had snagged his favorite Denver Broncos cap and sent it flying into the water.

"He sure loved to fish," Sadie said. His first preference had been to enjoy the sport with her or other members of the family. But he'd also spent lots of time here with Milo's father, Philip Henderson. And, of course, Sadie's best friend's husband, Roscoe Putnam.

Sadie smiled in remembrance. They'd had a lot of good years together, and she still missed him. The rain which had eased up for the past few minutes now resumed again with fervor.

As if sensing Sadie's nostalgia, or perhaps because she missed him, too, Alice rose from the bench and put an arm around her shoulders.

Comforted, Sadie squeezed her daughter in return. It seemed that the only people who truly understood a loss were those who'd known the person themselves. And, although they no longer actively mourned him every day, she knew that T.R.'s presence and influence would remain with them for the rest of their lives.

"Mia says people only have one true love in the world," Sara announced. "She said lightning only strikes once. Does that mean you can never be in love with Edwin?"

"Sara!"

"It's okay," Sadie assured her daughter. Considering her words carefully, she directed her attention to Sara with a smile. "Let's just say that God isn't stingy about letting good people come into our lives."

Or letting them return to our lives, she added silently.

"Were you ever in love with Edwin?"

"We had what I would call a young love in high school." For some reason, the term *puppy love* had always annoyed her, probably because their relationship had gone much deeper than a mere springtime romance. "But college took us in different directions, and it never developed into a more mature love that comes with time and experience."

"I like him. I think you should marry him."

Alice walked over to the front of the shelter and peered out into the tumultuous weather. "It's a little soon for them to be thinking about that. It hasn't been that long since Edwin moved back here to Silver Peak."

The words were spoken without emotion, but as always Sadie sought to tread carefully so that it never seemed to her daughter that she was trying to replace her father with someone else. Or, worse, that she'd carried a torch for her first love while married to T.R.

"Let's just say that we've picked up where we left off." She paused and studied her granddaughter. "Why are you asking so many questions? Is there a boy you like?"

"No, but Theo's got his eye on someone." She pointed a finger at him and chanted, "Ella, Ella, Theo's your fella!"

To his credit, Theo didn't rise to the bait. He just shrugged and gave them a shy smile. "For once, Sara's right about something." He glanced up from where he'd been scratching Hank's belly, which caused the dog's hind leg to quiver. "Unfortunately, someone else beat me to asking her to the prom."

"I'm sorry to hear that." Sadie joined her daughter at the front of the shelter and peered out into the slowing rain. "It should be over pretty soon."

Almost as soon as she'd said it, an eerie, prickling sensation seemed to lift the very hairs on her arms. A streak zagged through the sky, emblazoning it like a neon brand on a gray-hided heifer, and a fraction of a second later, a mega-decibel clap followed.

The horses shifted anxiously at their stations, but it was Sara's horse, Daisy, that yanked loose from her tie-up and bolted from the shelter.

Sara started after the animal, but Sadie stopped her with a hand to her arm. "The storm isn't over yet."

"But…!"

"Daisy knows how to get home," Alice reminded her. "It's not far. She'll find her way."

Sure enough, the little horse was making a beeline down the path, stirrups flapping against her sides as she ran toward neighbor Milo Henderson's ranch, a little over a half mile away, where all of the horses were boarded.

"You can ride the rest of the way back with me," Sadie said. "Scout is strong enough to carry us both."

She had just turned to pack up her belongings when that weird, hair prickling thing happened again. But this time it was much stronger and felt like it might lift the hair right off of her scalp.

A flash filled the sky, pointing to a Ponderosa pine tree a couple hundred yards away. At the same instant, a sharp crack sounded even louder than before and shook the earth beneath them. The open-air shelter suddenly seemed inadequate in the face of the power before them, and Sadie instinctively took a step back.

Fortunately, the remaining horses handled the light show and noise better than Daisy had.

In the next instant, a loud creaking and groaning ensued from the nearby tree that had been struck, followed by a loud rustling *whoosh* and a *whump* as a large branch fell to the ground and made impact across the trail leading home.

"Well, I guess Mia was wrong," Sara said, gently breaking the awe-filled quiet that had followed the spectacular display.

Still reeling from the heavenly theatrics, Sadie wasn't following where her granddaughter was going with that out-of-the-blue statement.

"Wrong about what, dear?"

The girl looked up at her and smiled. "Lightning *can* strike twice."

A Note from the Editors

WE HOPE YOU ENJOYED *MYSTERIES OF SILVER PEAK*, PUBLISHED by the Books and Inspirational Media Division of Guideposts, a nonprofit organization that touches millions of lives every day through products and services that inspire, encourage, help you grow in your faith, and celebrate God's love.

Thank you for making a difference with your purchase of this book, which helps fund our many outreach programs to military personnel, prisons, hospitals, nursing homes, and educational institutions.

We also create many useful and uplifting online resources. Visit Guideposts.org to read true stories of hope and inspiration, access OurPrayer network, sign up for free newsletters, download free e-books, join our Facebook community, and follow our stimulating blogs.

To learn about other Guideposts publications, including the best-selling devotional *Daily Guideposts*, go to Guideposts.org/Shop, call (800) 932-2145, or write to Guideposts, PO Box 5815, Harlan, Iowa 51593.

Sign up for the
Guideposts Fiction Newsletter
and stay up-to-date on the books you love!

You'll get sneak peeks of new releases, recommendations from other Guideposts readers, and special offers just for you . . .
and it's FREE!

Just go to Guideposts.org/Newsletters today to sign up.

Guideposts.

Visit Guideposts.org/Shop
or call (800) 932-2145